The Sister Jane series

Outfoxed

Hotspur

Full Cry

The Hunt Ball

The Hounds and the Fury

The Tell-Tale Horse

Hounded to Death

Fox Tracks

Let Sleeping Dogs Lie

Crazy Like a Fox

Homeward Hound

Scarlet Fever

Out of Hounds

Books by Rita Mae Brown with Sneaky Pie Brown

Wish You Were Here

Rest in Pieces

Murder at Monticello

Pay Dirt

Murder, She Meowed

Murder on the Prowl

Cat on the Scent

Sneaky Pie's Cookbook for Mystery Lovers

Pawing Through the Past

Claws and Effect

Catch as Cat Can

The Tail of the Tip-Off

Whisker of Evil

Cat's Eyewitness

Sour Puss

Puss 'n Cahoots

The Purrfect Murder

Santa Clawed

Cat of the Century

Hiss of Death

The Big Cat Nap

Sneaky Pie for President

The Litter of the Law

Nine Lives to Die

Tail Gate

Tall Tail

A Hiss Before Dying

Probable Claws

Whiskers in the Dark

Furmidable Foes

The Nevada series

A Nose for Justice

Murder Unleashed

Books by Rita Mae Brown

Animal Magnetism: My Life with
Creatures Great and Small

The Hand That Cradles the Rock

Songs to a Handsome Woman

The Plain Brown Rapper

Rubyfruit Jungle

In Her Day

Six of One

Southern Discomfort

Sudden Death

High Hearts

Started from Scratch: A Different
Kind of Writer's Manual

Bingo

Venus Envy

Dolley: A Novel of Dolley Madison
in Love and War

Riding Shotgun

Rita Will: Memoir of a Literary
Rabble-Rouser

Loose Lips

Alma Mater

The Sand Castle

Cakewalk

OUT OF HOUNDS

OUT OF
HOUNDS

A NOVEL

RITA MAE BROWN

ILLUSTRATED BY LEE GILDEA

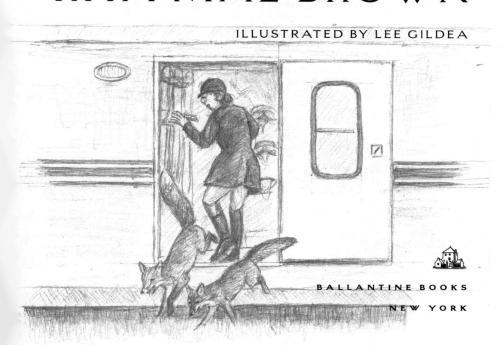

BALLANTINE BOOKS

NEW YORK

Out of Hounds is a work of fiction. Names, characters, places, and incidents
are the products of the author's imagination or are used fictitiously.
Any resemblance to actual events, locales, or persons, living
or dead, is entirely coincidental.

Copyright © 2021 by American Artists, Inc.
Illustrations © 2021 by Lee Gildea, Jr.

All rights reserved.

Published in the United States by Ballantine Books, an imprint of
Random House, a division of Penguin Random House LLC, New York.

BALLANTINE and the HOUSE colophon are registered trademarks
of Penguin Random House LLC.

LIBRARY OF CONGRESS CATALOGING-IN-PUBLICATION DATA
Names: Brown, Rita Mae, author. | Gildea, Lee, Jr., illustrator.
Title: Out of hounds: a novel / Rita Mae Brown; illustrated by Lee Gildea.
Description: First edition. | New York: Ballantine Books, [2021] | Series: Sister Jane; 13 |
Identifiers: LCCN 2020027150 (print) | LCCN 2020027151 (ebook) | ISBN 9780593130063
(hardcover; acid-free paper) | ISBN 9780593130070 (ebook)
Subjects: LCSH: Arnold, Jane (Fictitious character)—Fiction. |
Murder—Investigation—Fiction. | Fox hunting—Fiction. | GSAFD: Mystery fiction.
Classification: LCC PS3552.R698 O96 2020 (print) |
LCC PS3552.R698 (ebook) | DDC 813/.54—dc23
LC record available at https://lccn.loc.gov/2020027150
LC ebook record available at https://lccn.loc.gov/2020027151

Printed in the United States of America on acid-free paper

randomhousebooks.com

2 4 6 8 9 7 5 3 1

First Edition

Dedicated to
Professor Francis McGovern
An extraordinary man and a kind one.

CAST OF CHARACTERS

THE HUMANS

Jane Arnold, MFH, "Sister," runs the Jefferson Hunt. *MFH* stands for "Master of Foxhounds," the individual who runs the hunt, deals with every crisis both on and off the field. She is strong, bold, loves her horses and her hounds. In 1974, her fourteen-year-old son was killed in a tractor accident. That loss deepened her, taught her to cherish every minute. She's had lots of minutes, as she's in her early seventies, but she has no concept of age.

Shaker Crown, the huntsman, suffered a bad accident last season. He is hoping to recover, has seen specialists, but while he can ride he can't risk another fall.

Gray Lorillard isn't cautious in the hunt field, but he is cautious off it, as he was a partner in one of the most prestigious accounting firms in D.C. He knows how the world really works and, although retired, is often asked to solve problems at his former firm. He is smart, handsome, in his early sixties, and is African American.

Crawford Howard is best described by Aunt Daniella, who commented, "There's a great deal to be said about new money and Crawford means to say it all." He started an outlaw pack of hounds when Sister did not ask him to be her joint master. Slowly, he is realizing you can't push people around in this part of the world. Fundamentally, he is a decent and generous man.

Sam Lorillard is Gray's younger brother. He works at Crawford's stables. Crawford hired Sam when no one else would, so Sam is loyal. He blew a full scholarship to Harvard thanks to the bottle. He's good with horses. His brother saved him and he's clean, but so many people feel bad about what might have been. He focuses on the future.

Daniella Laprade is Gray and Sam's aunt. She is an extremely healthy nonagenarian who isn't above shaving a year or two off her age. She may even be older than her stated ninety-four. Her past is dotted with three husbands and numerous affairs, all carried out with discretion.

Wesley Blackford, "Weevil"—he's just tipped over thirty, is divinely handsome, loves hounds. He fills in for the injured Shaker Crown, whom he respects. Weevil has brilliance and the foundation of ballast.

Anne Harris, "Tootie," left Princeton in her freshman year, as she missed foxhunting in Virginia so very much. Her father had a cow, cut her out of his will. She takes classes at the University of Virginia and is now twenty-four and shockingly beautiful. She is African American.

Yvonne Harris, Tootie's mother, is a former model who has fled Chicago and her marriage. She divorced Victor Harris, a hard-driving businessman who built an African American media empire. She built it with him. She is trying to understand Tootie, feels she was not so much a bad mother as an absent one. Her experience has been different from her daughter's, and Tootie's freedoms were won by Yvonne's generation and those prior. Yvonne doesn't understand that Tootie doesn't get this.

Margaret DuCharme, M.D., is Alfred's daughter and she's acted as a go-between for her father and uncle since childhood. Her cousin, Binky's son Arthur, also acts as a go-between and both the cousins are just fed up with it. They are in their early forties, Margaret being more successful than Arthur, but he's happy enough.

Walter Lungrun, M.D., JT-MFH, is a cardiologist who has hunted with Sister since his boyhood. He is the late Raymond Arnold's son, which Sister knows. No one talks about it and Walter's father always acted as though he were Walter's father. It's the way things are done around here. Let sleeping dogs lie.

Betty Franklin is an honorary whipper-in, which means she doesn't get paid. Whippers-in emit a glamorous sheen to other foxhunters and it is a daring task. One must know a great deal and be able to ride hard, jump high, think in a split second. She is Sister's best friend and in her mid-fifties. Everyone loves Betty.

Bobby Franklin especially loves Betty, as he is her husband. He leads Second Flight, those riders who may take modest jumps but not the big ones. He and Betty own a small printing press and nearly lost their shirts when computers started printing out stuff. But people have returned to true printing, fine papers, etc. They're doing okay.

Kasmir Barbhaiya made his money in India in pharmaceuticals. Educated in an English public school, thence on to Oxford, he is highly intelligent and tremendously wealthy. Widowed, he moved to Virginia to be close to an old Oxford classmate and his wife. He owns marvelous horses and rides them well. He thought he would forever be alone but the Fates thought otherwise. Love had found him in the form of Alida Dalzell.

Edward and Tedi Bancroft, in their eighties, are stalwarts of the Jefferson Hunt and dear friends of Sister's. Evangelista, Edward's deceased sister, had an affair with Weevil's grandfather; although hushed up, it caused uproar in the Bancroft family.

Ben Sidell is the county sheriff, who is learning to hunt and loves it. Nonni, his horse, takes good care of him. He learns far more about the county by hunting than if he just stayed in his squad car. He dates Margaret DuCharme, M.D., an unlikely pairing that works.

Cynthia Skiff Cane hunts Crawford's outlaw pack. Crawford has gone through three other huntsmen but Cynthia can handle him. Sam Lorillard helps, too.

Cindy Chandler owns Foxglove Farm, one of the Jefferson fixtures. She's a good friend and a good foxhunter.

Freddie Thomas has run her small accounting business for years and is a CPA in her early forties. She is a good friend of Alida Dalzell. As the IRS grows insanely complex as well as being deeply unfair she has grown to hate her work, but she cares for her clients so she hangs in there. She rarely talks about her profession. She is a good rider, a very sensible person.

Manfredo Sabatini, "Gigi," had made a fortune producing and distributing premier plumbing appliances. He and his wife are completing Showoff Stables and are new to the area.

Elise Sabatini is much younger than Gigi. She rides, he does not but he gives her whatever she wants. She likes people and horses.

Carter Nicewonder has the best of everything. He's middle-aged, a good rider. His business is buying and selling antique jewelry. He has an eye for what will make a woman look good and he has terrific contacts.

Buddy Cadwalder, like Carter, has connections among the rich, old money and new money. *Cadwalder* is a great, old Pennsylvania name, so no door is closed to him. His business is buying valuable antique furniture. He and Carter are friends, working with some of the same people.

Catherine Clay-Neal, one of the directors of the Headley-Whitney Museum in Lexington, Kentucky, rides sidesaddle hunting with Jane Winegardner, MFH, "O.J." Revitalizing the museum with like-minded people has been a labor of love.

Parker Bell probably never did anything out of love but he works hard at Showoff Stables.

Father Mancusco is the new Catholic priest at St. Mary's. An avid foxhunter, he was delighted to be assigned to Virginia where, like so many priests, he has to cover a lot of territory, not only his parish.

Sally Taliaferro, pronounced Tolliver, is the new Episcopal priest at Emmanuel Episcopal in Greenwood, Virginia. She, too, rides and has made friends with Father Mancusco. Both face many of the same problems.

Kathleen Sixt Dunbar inherited the 1780 House, a high-end antiques store, last year. She's becoming part of the community. Her Welsh terrier, Abdul, helps at the store.

THE AMERICAN FOXHOUNDS

Lighter than the English foxhound, with a somewhat slimmer head, they have formidable powers of endurance and remarkable noses.

Cora is the head female. What she says goes.

Asa is the oldest hunting male hound, and he is wise.

Diana is steady, in the prime of her life, and brilliant. There's no other word for her but *brilliant.*

Dasher, Diana's littermate, is often overshadowed by his sister, but he sticks to business and is coming into his own.

Dragon is also a littermate of the above "D" hounds. He is arrogant, can lose his concentration, and tries to lord it over other hounds.

Dreamboat is of the same breeding as Diana, Dasher, and Dragon, but a few years younger.

. . .

Hounds take the first initial of their mother's name. Following are hounds ordered from older to younger. No unentered hounds are included in this list. An unentered hound is not yet on the Master of Foxhounds stud books and not yet hunting with the pack. They are in essence kindergartners. **Trinity, Tinsel, Trident, Ardent, Thimble, Twist, Tootsie, Trooper, Taz, Tattoo, Parker, Pickens, Zane, Zorro, Zandy, Giorgio, Pookah, Pansy, Audrey, Aero, Angle, Aces** are young but entered. The "B" line and the "J" line have been just entered, are just learning the ropes.

THE HORSES

Keepsake, TB/QH, Bay; **Lafayette,** TB, gray; **Rickyroo,** TB, Bay; **Aztec,** TB, Chestnut; **Matador,** TB, Flea-bitten gray. All are Sister's geldings. **Showboat, Hojo, Gunpowder,** and **Kilowatt,** all TBs, are Shaker's horses.

Outlaw, QH, Buckskin, and **Magellan,** TB, Dark Bay (which is really black), are Betty's horses.

Cardinal Wolsey, TB, Flaming Chestnut, is Gray's horse. His red coat gave him his name, for Cardinal Wolsey.

Iota, TB, Bay, is Tootie's horse.

Matchplay and **Midshipman** are young Thoroughbreds of Sister's that are being brought along. It takes good time to make a solid foxhunter. Sister never hurries a horse or a hound in its schooling.

Trocadero is young, smart, being trained by Sam Lorillard.

Old Buster has become a babysitter. Like Trocadero, he is owned by Crawford Howard. Sam uses him for Yvonne Harris.

Pokerface and **Corporal** carry Ronnie Haslip. If a guest is a strong rider, Ronnie will lend Pokerface. They are good horses.

THE FOXES

Reds

Aunt Netty, older, lives at Pattypan Forge. She is overly tidy and likes to give orders.

Uncle Yancy is Aunt Netty's husband but he can't stand her anymore. He lives at the Lorillard farm, has all manner of dens and cubbyholes, as well as a place in the mudroom.

Charlene lives at After All Farm. She comes and goes.

Target is Charlene's mate but he stays at After All. The food supply is steady and he likes the other animals.

Earl has the restored stone stables at Old Paradise all to himself. He has a den in a stall but also makes use of the tack room. He likes the smell of the leather.

Sarge is young. He found a den in big boulders at Old Paradise thanks to help from a doe. It's cozy with straw, old clothing bits, and even a few toys.

James lives behind the mill at Mill Ruins. He is not very social but from time to time will give the hounds a good run.

Ewald is a youngster who was directed to a den in an outbuilding during a hunt. Poor fellow didn't know where he was. The outbuilding at Mill Ruins will be a wonderful home as long as he steers clear of James.

Mr. Nash, young, lives at Close Shave, a farm about six miles from Chapel Cross. Given the housing possibilities and the good food, he is drawn to Old Paradise, which is being restored by Crawford Howard.

Grays

Comet knows everybody and everything. He lives in the old stone foundation part of the rebuilt log-and-frame cottage at Roughneck Farm.

Inky is so dark she's black and she lives in the apple orchard across from the above cottage. She knows the hunt schedule and rarely gives hounds a run. They can just chase someone else.

Georgia moved to the old schoolhouse at Foxglove Farm.

Grenville lives at Mill Ruins, in the back in a big storage shed. This part of the estate is called Shootrough.

Gris lives at Tollbooth Farm in the Chapel Cross area. He's very clever and can slip hounds in the batting of an eye.

Hortensia also lives at Mill Ruins. She's in another outbuilding. All are well constructed and all but the big hay sheds have doors that close, which is wonderful in bad weather.

Vi, young, is the mate of Gris, also young. They live at Tollbooth Farm in pleasant circumstances.

THE BIRDS

Athena, the great horned owl, is two and a half feet tall with a four-foot wingspan. She has many places where she will hole up but her true nest is in Pattypan Forge. It really beats being in a tree hollow. She's gotten spoiled.

Bitsy is eight and a half inches tall with a twenty-inch wingspan. Her considerable lungs make up for her tiny size as she is a screech owl, aptly named. Like Athena, she'll never live in a tree again, because she's living in the rafters of Sister's stable. Mice come in to eat the fallen grain. Bitsy feels like she's living in a supermarket.

St. Just, a foot and a half in height with a surprising wingspan of three feet, is a jet-black crow. He hates foxes but is usually sociable with other birds.

SISTER'S HOUSE PETS

Raleigh, a sleek, highly intelligent Doberman, likes to be with Sister. He gets along with the hounds, walks out with them. He tries to get along with the cat, but she's such a snob.

Rooster is a harrier bequeathed to Sister by a dear friend. He likes riding in the car, walking out with hounds, watching everybody and everything. The cat drives him crazy.

Golliwog, or "Golly," is a long-haired calico. All other creatures are lower life-forms. She knows Sister does her best, but still. Golly is Queen of All She Surveys.

SOME USEFUL TERMS

Away. A fox has gone away when he has left the covert. Hounds are away when they have left the covert on the line of the fox.

Brush. The fox's tail.

Burning scent. Scent so strong or hot that hounds pursue the line without hesitation.

Bye day. A day not regularly on the fixture card.

Cap. The fee nonmembers pay to hunt for that day's sport.

Carry a good head. When hounds run well together to a good scent, a scent spread wide enough for the whole pack to feel it.

Carry a line. When hounds follow the scent. This is also called working a line.

Cast. Hounds spread out in search of scent. They may cast themselves or be cast by the huntsman.

Charlie. A term for a fox. A fox may also be called **Reynard.**

Check. When hounds lose the scent and stop. The field must wait quietly while the hounds search for the scent.

Colors. A distinguishing color, usually worn on the collar but sometimes on the facings of a coat, that identifies a hunt. Colors can be awarded only by the Master and can be worn only in the field.

Coop. A jump resembling a chicken coop.

Couple straps. Two-strap hound collars connected by a swivel link. Some members of staff will carry these on the right rear of the saddle. Since the days of the pharaohs in ancient Egypt, hounds have been brought to the meets coupled. Hounds are always spoken of and counted in couples. Today, hounds walk or are driven to the meets. Rarely, if ever, are they coupled, but a whipper-in still carries couple straps should a hound need assistance.

Covert. A patch of woods or bushes where a fox might hide. Pronounced "cover."

Cry. How one hound tells another what is happening. The sound will differ according to the various stages of the chase. It's also called giving tongue and should occur when a hound is working a line.

Cub hunting. The informal hunting of young foxes in the late summer and early fall, before formal hunting. The main purpose is to enter young hounds into the pack. Until recently only the most knowledgeable members were invited to cub hunt, since they would not interfere with young hounds.

Dog fox. The male fox.

Dog hound. The male hound.

Double. A series of short, sharp notes blown on the horn to alert all that a fox is afoot. The gone away series of notes is a form of doubling the horn.

Draft. To acquire hounds from another hunt is to accept a draft.

Draw. The plan by which a fox is hunted or searched for in a certain area, such as a covert.

Draw over the fox. Hounds go through a covert where the fox is but cannot pick up its scent. The only creature that understands how this is possible is the fox.

Drive. The desire to push the fox, to get up with the line. It's a very desirable trait in hounds, so long as they remain obedient.

Dually. A one-ton pickup truck with double wheels in back.

Dwell. To hunt without getting forward. A hound that dwells is a bit of a putterer.

Enter. Hounds are entered into the pack when they first hunt, usually during cubbing season.

Field. The group of people riding to hounds, exclusive of the Master and hunt staff.

Field Master. The person appointed by the Master to control the field. Often it is the Master him- or herself.

Fixture. A card sent to all dues-paying members, stating when and where the hounds will meet. A fixture card properly received is an invitation to hunt. This means the card would be mailed or handed to a member by the Master.

Flea-bitten. A gray horse with spots or ticking that can be black or chestnut.

Gone away. The call on the horn when the fox leaves the covert.

Gone to ground. A fox that has ducked into its den, or some other refuge, has gone to ground.

Good night. The traditional farewell to the Master after the hunt, regardless of the time of day.

Gyp. The female hound.

Hilltopper. A rider who follows the hunt but does not jump. Hilltoppers are also called the Second Flight. The jumpers are called the First Flight.

Hoick. The huntsman's cheer to the hounds. It is derived from the Latin *hic haec hoc,* which means "here."

Hold hard. To stop immediately.

Huntsman. The person in charge of the hounds, in the field and in the kennel.

Kennelman. A hunt staff member who feeds the hounds and cleans the kennels. In wealthy hunts there may be a number of kennelmen. In hunts with a modest budget, the huntsman or even the Master cleans the kennels and feeds the hounds.

Lark. To jump fences unnecessarily when hounds aren't running. Masters frown on this, since it is often an invitation to an accident.

Lieu in. Norman term for "go in."

Lift. To take the hounds from a lost scent in the hopes of finding a better scent farther on.

Line. The scent trail of the fox.

Livery. The uniform worn by the professional members of the hunt staff. Usually it is scarlet, but blue, yellow, brown, and gray are also used. The recent dominance of scarlet has to do with people buying coats off the rack as opposed to having tailors cut them. (When anything is mass-produced, the choices usually dwindle, and such is the case with livery.)

Mask. The fox's head.

Meet. The site where the day's hunting begins.

MFH. The Master of Foxhounds; the individual in charge of the hunt: hiring, firing, landowner relations, opening territory (in large hunts this is the job of the hunt secretary), developing the pack of hounds, and determining the first cast of each meet. As in any leadership position, the Master is also the lightning rod for criticism. The Master may hunt the hounds, although this is usually done by a professional huntsman, who is also responsible for the hounds in the field and at the kennels. A long relationship between a Master and a huntsman allows the hunt to develop and grow.

Nose. The scenting ability of a hound.

Override. To press hounds too closely.

Overrun. When hounds shoot past the line of a scent. Often the scent has been diverted or foiled by a clever fox.

Ratcatcher. Informal dress worn during cubbing season and bye days.

Stern. A hound's tail.

Stiff-necked fox. One that runs in a straight line.

Strike hounds. Those hounds that, through keenness, nose, and often higher intelligence, find the scent first and press it.

Tail hounds. Those hounds running at the rear of the pack. This is not necessarily because they aren't keen; they may be older hounds.

Tally-ho. The cheer when the fox is viewed. Derived from the Norman *ty a hillaut*, thus coming into the English language in 1066.

Tongue. To vocally pursue a fox.

View halloo (halloa). The cry given by a staff member who sees a fox. Staff may also say tally-ho or, should the fox turn back, tally-back. One reason a different cry may be used by staff, especially in territory where the huntsman can't see the staff, is that the field in their enthusiasm may cheer something other than a fox.

Vixen. The female fox.

Walk. Puppies are walked out in the summer and fall of their first year. It's part of their education and a delight for both puppies and staff.

Whippers-in. Also called whips, these are the staff members who assist the huntsman, who make sure the hounds "do right."

OUT OF HOUNDS

C H A P T E R 1

February 6, 2020 Thursday

Wind carries messages. As Jane Arnold, "Sister," flew across a large pasture sleeping under a light snow, the message hitting her face was a dramatic change in the weather. Jefferson Hunt started the day at ten in the morning under relatively balmy skies for early February. The temperature hung at a decent 42°F.

Clods of earth, the grass brown mixed in with it and a smattering of snow, flew off Keepsake's hooves, her marvelously balanced horse. Hounds screamed up ahead. They'd been running at top speed for twenty minutes.

Sister passed low bushes festooned with stoplight red berries, took a sagging coop at the end of Beveridge Hundred, an estate from the late eighteenth century, and kept flying. These are the runs one dreams about on a torrid July day pitching hay. Tears filled her eyes from the speed. Up ahead she could see the scarlet coat of her young huntsman, Wesley Blackford, "Weevil." In front of him like a football team racing downfield to attack the offense waiting for the kicked-off ball, those tri-color American hounds ran, sang, stretched flat out.

While she kept her pride to herself, she loved those hounds, hounds whose bloodlines she had known for over forty years. Her late husband's uncle had known and bred them for forty years before that.

The wind licked her face with a cold hard tongue. A storm would follow, but when? She couldn't turn back. Nor was she going to twist her head around while galloping to check the northwestern sky. She was heading due south.

Out of the corner of her right eye she saw her dearest friend, Betty Franklin, on the outside of the pack on the right. Betty had the good fortune to be running on a decent farm road. The other whipper-in, Tootie Harris, in her early twenties, no farm road but still pasture, kept apace. The women wore black, the old attire for a lady hunting. As this was America in the twenty-first century they were entitled to scarlet but both passed. Sexism wasn't an issue for either of them and given that men hardly ever get the chance to be the peacocks that women can be, they wore their black or deepest navy, an especially attractive color.

Keepsake's ears, forward, flicked a moment. Sister slowed just a bit, rating him, for she trusted him with her life, as does anyone astride a horse.

She faced another coop, this one newer and no sag. Over they went, hitting the slick earth on the other side. Keepsake, a Thoroughbred/quarter horse cross, was so handy he could turn on a dime and give you a nickel's change. He slid slightly, pulling his hind legs up under him. Sister reminded herself to give him an apple cut to fit a peppermint inside, his favorite treat and one she made for him.

Keepsake's ears flicked again. As they approached the woods, a trail running through the middle of it, out lumbered an unamused black bear—a large, unamused black bear.

"Jesus H. Christ on a raft," Sister cursed under her breath.

The bear, irritated, for the hound music was not music he liked, stopped, stood up on his hind legs.

Keepsake swerved to the left, making a large detour. The bear looked at them and then decided to be the center of attention for the large field, perhaps twenty yards behind Sister, the forward part of First Flight now beheld the bear. Horses spooked, people hit the ground as their horses abandoned them to their fate.

Pleased with himself, the large fellow, at least four hundred pounds, dropped down to all fours to saunter back into the woods.

As master of this hunt and field master, Sister was in charge of the field, forty-four strong today. She might have stopped but she felt cleanup was the obligation of whoever was riding tail. Today it was her joint master, Walter Lungrun, M.D. She would stick close to hounds. The pace was too good.

As times have changed, some First Flight masters will stop when someone bellows, "Rider Down." However most of the older masters did not. It's the way they were taught and the way they were going to ride.

Fortunately, Keepsake, a lovely bay, was nimble and smart. But a true Thoroughbred had speed. Fast as Keepsake was, if Sister had been on one of her pure Thoroughbreds she might have nudged a bit closer, for her huntsman was on Kilowatt, a horse of blazing speed. Kilowatt had washed out on the track but not because he wasn't blindingly fast. He did not feel compelled to run in circles even if they were big circles.

He wasn't running in circles now. That long, effortless stride, that magical reach from the shoulder backed up by a powerful engine in the rear, made Kilowatt look as though he wasn't really going that fast.

He was.

Weevil, breathing hard as much from excitement as the long run, didn't bother to blow his horn. Hounds were on. They knew they were on. He'd blown "Gone Away" when everyone hit. Snaking through the woods he emerged on the far side, passing a huge rock outcropping perhaps a story and a half high. All manner of creatures lived in there but the hounds did not veer toward it. Their hunted fox was moving, moving straight. Weevil felt certain this was a gentleman fox who had visited a lady in hopes of wooing her. Fellows will travel for miles to be in the company of a vixen. The vixens can take them or leave them. Those vixens look them over. No sensible girl wants a lazy bum, regardless of species.

Now Sister rode by the rock outcropping, colder there, a deep chill, the water that seeped between the rocks froze ice blue, beautiful despite the cold.

The tall six-foot woman, in her early seventies, long legs, could stick on a horse. Since she kept moving all her life, never indulged in smoking or much drink, she remained in fantastic shape. Good thing. She needed it now.

She knew to the right of the woods, across the road, rested another old estate, a small Virginia farmhouse called Old Dalby. Like many farms and estates in central Virginia things remained in the family, passing through either the male line or the female line but the name of the estate stayed the same.

Coming out of the woods, she slowed to a trot, for hounds lost the scent on a patch of running cedar, a scent killer known to foxes. They know every trick in the book. People who don't have an acquaintance with them think all those stories about a fox's superior mind are fanciful. Not if you're hunting one.

Grateful for the respite, rider and horse stopped to watch the hounds work. High, driven, frantic to pick up the scent, they cast themselves, pushing, pushing, pushing.

The wind, stronger now that they were in the open, moved, as it usually does in this part of the world, from west to east, most often from the northwest down.

Weevil studied the situation. Sister could have told him what to do but as this was his second year hunting the hounds she would not interfere. Nor would his two whippers-in, standing at a distance on the right and the left. If he wanted help he would have asked.

Weevil did not suffer from false pride.

He looked up, watched treetops swaying back in the woods. Taking a deep breath, he asked Kilowatt to walk thirty yards to his right and forward. The woods somewhat shifted the wind but not too much.

"Get 'em up," he encouraged them.

Aces, a young hound, eagerly followed, as did the others. The other twenty-three couple of hounds, which is to say forty-six hounds, for hounds are always measured in couples and have been since the days of the pharaohs, followed. Cora, a brilliant hound, started feathering, that tail picking up speed like a windshield wiper.

"Got him!" she shouted as she took off.

Within seconds the pack moved off, Weevil behind. Again, the pace was blistering.

The brief wait allowed Sister to check the field. Some had fallen behind. Not all horses were as hunting fit as they might be, and then again, not all horses were fast. A few would finally bring up the rear or fall back to Second Flight, which took small jumps but often used gates, a time-consuming process.

The wind bit now. Glad she wore her white cashmere sweater under her heavy Melton coat, a white stock tie covering the neckline, Sister again moved out.

On and on they rode, the pace faltering then picking up again until hounds reached Bishop's Court, formerly the only Catholic church in Albermarle County in the early eighteenth century before, as the population grew, the economy finally soared after we had paid our war debt and other Catholic churches cropped up. In those days being Catholic was no advantage, as most of the settlers came from the British Isles where, with the exception of Irish ones, if one was Catholic, they often hid it. Henry VIII and the Dissolution saw to that as well as mass deaths from turning out the monks, nuns, hunting down priests like vermin.

Sister saw the quarry, a healthy large male red fox who sped to the church, ducking into a den he'd dug under it. Hounds reached the spot perhaps four minutes after he'd gone to ground.

Weevil hopped off Kilowatt, his legs the tiniest bit shaky, for it was a long, long, hard run, where he blew "Gone to Ground." Patting each hound's head he praised them by name as Kilowatt patiently stood.

Finally Weevil turned to his horse, stroked his head, and kissed his nose. He loved animals and they loved him. Swinging up in the saddle, he smiled at his whippers-in.

The hunt had to turn back, as this was the last fixture before the end of the road, the southern spike from Chapel Cross, each road called by its direction, north, south, east, or west. The road ended before an odd ridge, left by the glacier, prevented further travel by car. The ridge was thick up there and steep. It was also full of game and perhaps a few illegal activities, for the waters ran crystal clear down to creeks below.

Sister rode up to Weevil. "The best."

He grinned. "The breeding season runs are always the best."

"So they are." She turned to indicate the field. "We have about a seven mile walk back and I think we do need to walk. They look tuckered out but happy."

"It was a test." He nodded.

"I wouldn't admit this to too many people but I feel it. This was the longest continuous run of our season. It's been a spotty season." She looked up and west. "And we're about to get more snow. Okay. Let's go."

As the horses, hounds, and people turned to walk along, Sister joined the field, chatting with people as they walked. No need to be silent now. One does not speak in the hunt field, but the hunt was over so, of course, everyone wanted to weigh in on the bear. Death defying.

She smiled, listened, enjoying what she thought of as her people.

Their goal, Tattenhall Station, would take a good forty minutes at this pace but that was fine.

First Flight and Second Flight merged, more fun for all.

Crawling along on the road, driving her big BMW 5 SUV was Yvonne Harris and Aunt Daniella Laprade with, in the backseat, Kathleen Sixt Dunbar, an antiques dealer who had moved here when her husband died last year, leaving her his business. Kathleen, Daniella, and Yvonne became dedicated car followers, and soon good friends. Tootie waved to her mother, Yvonne, as she kept her eye on the hounds, just as happy as the people to return to water and a biscuit. Once at the kennel they would be given a warm mash after such a day. Sister would pour in a bit of whiskey. She claimed it was her secret ingredient for a terrific hound. It was a secret, or not-so-secret, ingredient for many in the field as well, for they drained their flasks. It may not have slaked thirst but one felt warm.

Twenty-five minutes later Sister reached the hill behind Tattenhall Station, which could be viewed in the distance, as welcome a sight as it once was for much of the county, being the old train station for the Norfolk Southern Railway, the line running east and west. Falling into disuse as passenger lines vanished, cars taking over, the Victorian structure held many memories. Norfolk Southern finally sold it to an Indian gentleman, Kasmir Barbhaiya, who restored it to its bric-a-brac glory, as well as the over one thousand acres he purchased around it. Educated at private, called public, school in England, thence on to Oxford, he had a brilliance that resulted in an enormous fortune made in the pharmacy industry in India. Once free of running the business he repaired to central Virginia, for he had fallen in love with the place.

Not only did Sister daily give thanks for this warm, loving man, she especially gave thanks as she looked at the train station, now perhaps seven minutes away. Anything to feel warmth.

Weevil, Betty, and Tootie reached the parking lot before the others, already dismounted, and were loading hounds into their trailer, filled with fresh straw so hounds could bed down. Once hounds were up, the three did not untack their horses except to take off the bridles. Each threw a heavy blanket over their mount, keeping the saddle on to keep the animal's back warm. Most people removed the saddle but Sister believed the saddle and the pad kept the horse warm until you reached home. No point having a cold-backed horse. Also loaded onto the trailer, feed bags hanging inside, they were happy. Good hay can make most any horse happy.

Reaching her trailer, Betty and Tootie's horses already inside, Sister steeled herself. Once her feet hit the ground they would sting like the devil. Swinging her right leg over, she slowly slid down Keepsake's left side. Good boy that he was he didn't mind this slow dismount. Accustomed to Sister's ways he knew he'd soon be toasty in his heavy blanket, eating hay with his buddies.

"Dammit to hell," Sister cursed under her breath.

Father Mancusco, at the next trailer, remarked, "I heard that."

"Father, I apologize. But I will not do the stations of the cross."

"Of course you won't. You're an Episcopalian. These things happen." He teased her good-naturedly. "By the way, I do hope you realize that we were running Catholic fox. Popped right in at Bishop's Court."

"I did." She adored the middle-aged priest, glad he was a hunting man, for he had been transferred to the area within the last six months.

Fewer and fewer men dedicated themselves to the priesthood, so Father Mancusco's taking over of the church in Charlottesville was good for all. Sally Taliaferro, also a new member, had been assigned as the priest at St. Emmanuel's Episcopal church in Greenwood, and the two hunting divines, which was how Sister thought of them, struck up a friendship. Both faced many of the same problems.

"Need a hand?" Weevil offered, his lips about blue.

"Almost done. Honey, go inside and warm up."

"Forget her, Weevil. She's a tough old bird," Betty called as she opened the trailer door.

"Watch your mouth." Sister led Keepsake into the trailer while Betty held the door.

"Hell of a run." The mid-fiftyish Betty beamed.

"Was. It's been an on-again, off-again season for everyone but those hunting coyote."

"Right." Betty closed the door as Sister emerged. "Come on, I can't feel my feet."

"I can't either."

The two hurried into the Tattenhall Station, each step a little stab of pain. Once inside it felt like heaven. Two fireplaces, the original heating system, blazed at either end of the large room, the original waiting room, while an enormous wood-burning stove commanded the center of the room. A fence had been placed around it, as sometimes hunters imbibed too much and might lurch into it. No danger of that with the cavernous fireplaces, simple brick with deep white mantles.

Kasmir and his lady friend, Alida Dalzell, had staff to prepare hot food, hot drinks, put out a full bar. He happily shared his wealth. Kasmir and Alida chattered with animation, as did everyone, concerning the hunt.

Carter Nicewonder, a private jeweler, a Jefferson Hunt member for a year, visited everyone, eagerly describing the estate "new" jewelry he purchased recently. He pulled out of his pocket an antique pin, Artemis's visage thereon. Freddie Thomas, an accountant who often worked with Ronnie Haslip, club treasurer, passed on it but she would think about it.

Kasmir walked over to Carter. "How was your trip?"

"Cold, rainy, wonderful. England will always be England."

"That it will. Any luck?"

"Yes. I bought a few good things. I always enjoy finding old jewelry wherever I go, but as England and America are so close in taste, or once we were, the pieces are lovely. The Saudis buy quite a bit, as many have been educated in England. I don't have as many contacts there but yes, it was good."

"Glad to hear it." Kasmir clapped him on the back. Then he left to circulate.

"Notice how cold it was, piercing cold, by that huge rock outcropping?" Alida mentioned to Margaret DuCharme, M.D., who had hunted today.

"Cut you to the bone but wasn't the blue ice gorgeous? Like Ginger Rogers's dress in 'Cheek to Cheek.' "

"Margaret, that movie was in black and white." Alida, another movie buff, laughed.

"The pictures were of an ice blue dress. What an athlete she was, and she loved horses."

As they chattered on, warming up with hot toddies, Aunt Daniella, ninety-four, although that was fudging, sat in the large wing chair in front of the eastern fireplace. "I was in the car and I got tired. You all must be exhausted and famished."

"Yes, but I am happy to bring you a drink." Weevil doted on the elderly lady, one of the great beauties of her day.

"A double bourbon would be most restorative." She beamed at him and off he went to fetch her the drink.

Kathleen Sixt Dunbar sat next to Aunt Daniella, as the irrepressible African American lady, who could pass for white if she wanted to and she did not, knew everyone and would introduce her to people.

A clap of thunder cut the talk.

Sister walked with Weevil to Aunt Daniella. "It's been years since we had a thundersnow but that sounds ominous. Better get hounds home."

"Yes, Master." He handed Aunt Daniella her drink.

Aunt Dan, in a deep purple cashmere turtleneck, thanked him then said to Sister, "What next?"

"Aunt Dan," Sister said with a smile, "never say that."

CHAPTER 2

February 6, 2020 Thursday   7:00 PM

February is rarely anyone's favorite month. Social events, special fundraisers, are not scheduled, as they are starting in April. The variability of the weather, cold adding to that discomfort, discouraged people from leaving home.

They were bored. If the weather wasn't horrid many would throw on winter clothes to get out.

Kathleen Sixt Dunbar, factoring in the February doldrums, thought a grand reopening for the 1780 might prove successful. Her husband's death meant she inherited the store built in 1780, hence the name.

He had lived in Charlottesville, she had lived in Oklahoma City. They never divorced, remaining friends. His untimely passing brought her to Virginia.

Enough time had passed that she felt she could have a gala opening. One needed to respect manners in these things.

Wisely paying professionals to improve the lighting, to keep an open bar, and to have hors d'oeuvres served, she could follow the hunt without fretting.

Kathleen was determined to enjoy her own party. Another wise decision.

Manfredo Sabatini, his wife at his elbow, stared at a Lionel Edwards on the wall. Edwards worked in the early twentieth century, having been born November 9, 1878, in Bristol, England. Kathleen knew when it came to any equine art, the purchase was usually emotional.

Carter Nicewonder, smartly turned out in a tweed light brown jacket with a light lavender windowpane overlay also admired the painting. His lavender tie completed the outfit; he had an eye for color.

Speaking to the Sabatinis, whom he knew from various fundraisers, Carter remarked, "He was very good. Lived to be eighty-seven. And, as you may know, he remains affordable."

"I know so little about art." Elise Sabatini smiled. "Fortunes today are made with paintings that look like someone did it with their feet."

Carter smiled. "Give it time. Someone will do so and the art dealers, hoping to clean up, will declare this a comment on a peripatetic, rootless society."

"At least I can see the workmanship in Lyne's work." Elise nodded at his comments. "I have a lot to learn."

"You are too modest. Any woman who selects understated, stunning ruby and diamond earrings has a sense of proportion and color. I always think of color as paprika thrown on the roast."

She laughed. "What an interesting description. Actually the compliment goes to my husband. He selected the earrings."

Carter nodded to Manfredo. "Beautiful jewelry for a beautiful woman."

Winding through the crowd, Kathleen introduced herself, as she had missed these two when they had walked in. Given that Elise Sabatini wore a man's thin gold Patek Philippe watch, her husband had funds, the type of watch an indication of some originality.

Women usually don't buy their own watches if married. As for her husband, his jewelry consisted of a complementary thin Patek Philippe watch, a signet ring on his little finger, and a suit obviously bespoke. Kathleen had to size up a customer quickly and nothing announced money for a man faster than a bespoke suit and a thin watch as opposed to a sport watch. But it announced it quietly unless the materials were flashy. Carter was working the room. Kathleen found him amusingly single-minded. She returned her attention to the Sabatinis.

For a Virginian to judge someone with an Italian name was unfortunate, but the old ones often did or asked, quietly to others, "Who are their people?" Times had changed and the idea that someone with an Italian surname would wear a shiny suit, a gold chain around his neck, were gone except for those who studied you head to toe when you weren't looking. Kathleen did so but not in an obvious fashion nor did she believe in stereotypes, but again could someone afford a true Hepplewhite sideboard? The newly rich in sweatpants could but had no idea of the aesthetic value. At least they bought Maseratis and Lamborghinis, which kept the great Italian car makers rolling. Actually Kathleen wouldn't mind a Ferrari herself.

Extending her hand, she said, "Thank you for coming tonight, I'm Kathleen Sixt Dunbar. If you have any questions, I am happy to try to answer. If you have any questions regarding genealogy, do ask Aunt Daniella, the lady in the aqua dress holding court by the fireplace."

Elise smiled, extending her hand. "Elise Sabatini."

"I'm with her. Please call me Gigi, an old nickname." He, too, held out his hand. "We're new to the area, just now getting out, as our construction is almost complete."

"Welcome. Having driven by Showoff Stables . . . a delightful play on showjumping, by the way . . . the show ring, I should say. I can see how much you've accomplished. When I saw your sign I burst out laughing and thought, 'I must meet them.' Beautiful pro-portions, beautiful colors. Everything laid out for the benefit of the horses."

Elise glowed. "Thank you. Gigi and I tormented ourselves over every detail. Well, I tormented him."

She was quite a bit younger than Gigi. He grinned. "She's the rider. I resisted some things but when I saw how practical her ideas would be, I stopped complaining. Always marry a woman smarter than yourself."

Kathleen laughed. "Well said. Come along. Allow me to intro-duce you to Daniella Laprade. She admits to being ninety-four. I don't know, but Aunt Dan looks maybe seventy, if that."

As the couple approached, Aunt Daniella looked from wife to husband and back again. Yes, she had the picture, then she beheld the smile on Kathleen's face, which brightened her own.

After the introductions, Kathleen inclined her head. "Aunt Dan, I leave the Sabatinis in your capable hands. Who better to make them feel at home but you? They have built a gorgeous, gor-geous stable."

As Kathleen walked away she already heard Elise's laughter. God Bless Aunt Dan.

Sister came over. "You've outdone yourself. I thought the store lovely but this makes it almost exotic, warmer, really, and the furni-ture bathed in soft light, fabulous gilded mirrors, make me want to buy every one."

"Please do." Kathleen laughed at her.

Gray walked up. "Honey, did you see the old weather vane?"

"Yes." Sister nodded, focusing on Kathleen. "Wherever did you find that?"

"I called all of Harry's older clients and as luck would have it, one of them was . . . the word now is *downsizing* . . . and she wanted to sell things from the barn, the weather vane, mmm, late 1700s, up to maybe 1820. The simplicity of it makes me lean toward the first part of the nineteenth century, that breakover from Georgian to Federal. Well, we had Federal in the eighteenth but it was very simple, became what we now know, still simple yet with artful touches later. Oh, forgive me, Crawford and Marty just walked in and with Skiff. Amazing how she has lasted as his huntsman."

As she walked away, Gray, usually prudent with money, took Sister by the arm, walking her to the large weather vane, golden, smack in the middle of a large, tremendously expensive Sheraton dining table, the real deal not a knockoff, which while not the real deal is still impressive.

"Beautiful." Sister then added, "What has provoked you to be drawn to a large rooster weather vane?"

"Mother kept chickens. She had a big Plymouth Barred rooster, St. Paul, who followed her everywhere. If she were alive I would buy it for her."

"Let's buy it together. We can move the horse weather vane somewhere else. There are times, Gray, when one should give in to nostalgia, memory, love. We will of course call him St. Paul." She kissed him on the cheek, which she could do without standing on her tiptoes. She was originally six-one but had shrunk to six foot. Gray stood at six-two. They were hard to miss.

Kathleen moved from group to group, chatting, pointing out what may be of interest to them, but all was low-key. Kathleen believed a good piece of furniture or art sold itself.

Crawford studied a painting by Ben Marshall, circa 1897. Like Stubbs, he received commissions to paint successful racehorses, a practice carried down to the modern day by twentieth-century artists like Richard Stone Reeves.

Gigi joined him. Crawford turned to the new fellow. "What do you think?"

"For an antiques shop she has incredible things. When I received the invitation I didn't expect art or those studies for painting by Michael Lyne." He held out his hand. "Gigi Sabatini. Showoff Stables."

"Crawford Howard. Old Paradise, which I'm restoring, and Beasley Hall, which I built. I take it we're both not native Virginians."

"Medford, Massachusetts."

"Jasper, Indiana." Crawford shrugged. "It was a start."

"I've only ever been to French Lick, Indiana. Good golf course."

"Not my game. Haven't the patience. If you're ever interested, I'm happy to show you and your wife Old Paradise. It has quite a history."

"I've just met Aunt Daniella, speaking of quite a history."

Sister joined them. "Sister, this is Gigi Sabatini," Crawford introduced them.

"Pleased to meet you. Your place sits between two of our fixtures. Forgive me, I should explain, I'm the master of Jefferson Hunt and Crawford has a private pack that I call the Kingmaker's Hunt since his hero is Warwick the Kingmaker, the man who helped put Edward IV on the throne during the War of the Roses."

"Ah," replied Gigi, clearly not someone who cared much about anyone's history, much less England's.

"There you are." Elise joined them and introductions were made.

"If you are interested in foxhunting, either of us can help you," Sister offered.

"Thank you. I'm not sure I could do that. I'm a show-ring girl." Elise smiled. "I'm sure it's exciting."

"It can be." Sister smiled. "Your estate rests between two of our fixtures. I'm not asking to hunt it, especially since you all are new to the area. It is our state sport, for what that's worth. I have no control where the fox runs and Welsh Harp and Wolverton, the two fixtures you sit between, are good fixtures. We rarely run your way but should that happen, do I have permission or could I ride on your outskirts to stay with hounds?"

Elise answered for both of them. "We have very expensive show horses boarded there. Is there a way you can go around us that doesn't disturb the horses?"

"Yes, the riders can, but the hounds will follow the fox and the huntsman will follow the hounds. What I can do is tell my huntsman to do his best to turn hounds away. As it happens, we have never run a fox in your direction from Welsh Harp, which is east. But you never know. Perhaps you would like to see a hunt. We can take you in an SUV or truck."

"I would like that. We're pressed for time now, as we are finishing up the indoor arena, finally putting in the dehumidifier. I'll spare you the details." Elise smiled. "When that's finished I will take you up on your offer."

"Sister," Walter called.

"My joint master. By the way, he's the best cardiologist in central Virginia. I hope you don't need him, but put Walter Lungren in your vital people book." She waved to him and left.

Crawford and the Sabatinis broke up while Betty Franklin, seeing Sister chatting with the new people, walked over to do the same.

Crawford asked Kathleen about the drawings of Michael Lyne in front of Kasmir; Alida; Walter; Sister; Buddy Cadwalder, the Philadelphia furniture dealer; Father Mancusco; Reverend Sally Taliaferro; and Freddie Thomas.

"He is terribly underrated, Lyne. If you study the draftsmanship in those sketches for the full painting you can see how talented he was, but when you are working at the same time as Sir Alfred Munnings, well?" She held up her hands.

"You must come to Beasley Hall. I own the painting of his wife, Violet, sidesaddle habit, standing next to Sir Isaac," Crawford invited her.

"I had no idea," Kathleen exclaimed.

Buddy Cadwalder, shrewd enough to cultivate Radnor Hunt outside of Philadelphia and Fair Hills, once the private hunt of Will Dupont and Mr. Stewart's Cheshire Foxhounds, the man knew his business, blurted out, "My God, that's worth millions."

Crawford shrugged this off. "Bought for my wife when she rode sidesaddle."

The Sabatinis and Betty drifted over as Crawford discussed this treasure. As that group broke up into smaller groups, Betty, who had caught the tail end of it, explained Sir Alfred Munnings to the Sabatinis, who did know of him but had no idea such an extraordinary work would be in the community. Betty with tact explained Crawford's fortune began when he built strip malls in Indiana, his subsequent generosity to Custis Hall, the private school, as well as the work archaeologically, architecturally at Old Paradise.

The grand opening was a success. Kathleen kissed Sister on the cheek when she left, thanking her for her help in getting people there but especially for introducing her to Aunt Daniella after Harry had died. Aunt Daniella took Kathleen under her wing, never sparing her salacious gossip regardless of decade.

Yvonne and Sam also attended but there were so many people, so much going on, they didn't get to talk to Sister and Gray.

In Gray's Land Cruiser driving home, St. Paul in Sister's lap, she looked at the rooster. "He is quite the fellow. Just don't read Saint Paul's letter to the Ephesians to me. Why did your mother name her rooster St. Paul?"

"I have no idea. But she would tell us the story of his conversion to Christianity on the road to Damascus. She had favorite Bible stories. Sam listened more closely than I did but Mother was insistent."

"I guess whatever religion one practices your parents have their favorite stories often repeated to keep you in line."

"What were yours?"

Sister laughed. "Christ preaching to the men in the temple. Mother would give me her look and say, 'Don't get any ideas to tell me what to do. You have no halo and if you did remember, when a halo slips it becomes a noose.'"

As they were laughing, Kathleen, tired, thrilled, climbed the stairs to her living quarters, where she was rapturously greeted by her Welsh terrier, Abdul.

"Did you miss me?" He wagged his tail.

She sat down as he crawled into her lap. "Abdul, we made enough for good dog biscuits, greenies, and maybe a knuckle bone or two."

"I should have been downstairs. There could have been a bad person there. I should always be with you. I will protect you."

She listened to his little noises, petting his head, happy but exhausted. "Did you know, Abdul, that there is a famous Munnings's painting in this county?" She paused. "Maybe there is more than one. I haven't been here long enough to know and I haven't asked the right questions. But now that I am finally settled, I should discretely investigate."

"Take me with you," he wisely advised.

CHAPTER 3

February 7, 2020 Friday

Raleigh and Rooster, the Doberman and harrier, barked upon hearing a deep motor outside. Golliwog, the calico longhair, evidenced no interest, lying on her back in her special fleece bed on the counter, no less.

Sister rose, opened the back door, stepping into the cold coatroom just as the door opened. Frigid air enveloped her.

"Sweetie, get back in the kitchen." Gray Lorillard kissed her then propelled her back into the warmth.

"*You're home,*" the Doberman happily declared as Gray reached down to pet him.

Rooster, standing on his hind legs, put his front paws on Gray's jacket.

"Rooster," Sister admonished him, to no effect.

"I'll be right back." Gray placed a small bag of groceries on the counter next to the refrigerator, flipped up his collar, stepped into the coatroom then outside. He ran back in.

"Must be seventeen degrees out there."

"It's been a long, cold week." He took off his heavy jacket, draping it on the back of a kitchen chair. He placed a rectangular box on the table.

"I know you didn't wrap that." She smiled.

"The corners are too neat," he agreed.

"Gray, I don't recall you making corners," she teased him, picking up the package, the paper silver and red stripes.

"Maybe it's a diamond collar for you." Golly raised a long eyebrow as she addressed Raleigh.

"I'd rather have a big bone, meat still on it."

"Good idea," Rooster seconded the thought.

Sliding her fingernail under the paper, Sister carefully opened the package, preserving the paper. "Cashmere!"

She held up a sweater, a soft but thick turtleneck of navy blue with flecks of gold.

"Be perfect with your beautiful self." He kissed her on the cheek. She kissed him on the lips.

Holding the sweater under her chin she felt the richness under her fingers. "This must be four-ply. You know nothing is as warm as cashmere. Thank you, honey. How about you sit down and relax?"

"I'll fix myself a drink first." Which he did then sat down. "I thought I was retired. Sometimes I think I have more work than before. At least this short task is here, not Washington."

"You can handle sensitive issues. Which keeps your old firm and others wanting your services. You don't represent your old firm. They can use you in new ways. Everyone knows how discrete you are and honest."

"That's kind of you to say." He watched her fold the paper, a habit of hers, carefully placing it on top of the cardboard box into which she put the sweater, the box now on the counter, away from food and Golly, who evidenced a suspicious interest.

"Where did you find fresh asparagus in February?" She admired the fat ends as she put goods away in the refrigerator with one hand, flicked on the stove with the other.

"Wegman's."

"Soup is heating up. Made it this morning after checking the hounds and the horses. I told you we put a Catholic fox to ground yesterday, didn't I?"

"Well, you'd better find an Episcopalian one for the Reverend Taliaferro."

They both laughed as Sister brought two large bowls of chicken rice soup with all manner of vegetables in it. Sister had known Gray since he was young, saw him married then divorced. As he lived and worked in D.C., she knew him slightly, whereas she better knew his aunt Daniella and brother, Sam, who blew a scholarship to Harvard thanks to drink. Sam cleaned himself up with Gray's help but never returned to higher education. She also knew Mercer Laprade, Aunt Daniella's son, who died a few years ago.

"The barking dog ordinance. I read the so-called authorities have taken three dogs away from three people," Sister filled him in.

"That ordinance will be a great way for people to get even with one another. Then again, maybe that's the purpose of such things. When you and I and the other hunt clubs attended those open meetings it became clear, to me, anyway, that this is one more way for people to control anyone who doesn't think like they do. You dress it up with pious pronouncements about the public good."

"I don't think it much matters who is in charge but at least if you get country people you have a bit more reality. The hunt club kennels are exempted from punishment for barking. Some of the people running the county realize how much money we generate for businesses. But so many in Northern Virginia, Richmond, new people, think we're deplorables." She shrugged.

"I would give anything if Mrs. Clinton had not said that." Gray meant it.

"Me, too, but having said it, you and I and other rural people are more or less damned. Maybe this is the first shot across the bow." She feared and always would fear people who felt they had the right to tell you how to live. "Imagine what it was like when religion was the stone that was thrown at you? And that wasn't that long ago. Well, the Dissolution was but you know what I mean. Being Catholic was an issue during the Kennedy election. I was young but I sure remember. My mother was appalled that people said the stuff they said."

Feeling better thanks to the hot soup and the good scotch, Gray smiled. "Well, my mother, God rest her soul, used to say, 'People are no better than they should be.' Aunt Daniella certainly lived up to that."

As Aunt Daniella married three men plus enjoyed numerous affairs, she did.

"She looked great, by the way. Well, she always does and she and Yvonne are almost inseparable. Yvonne is finally relaxing, the anger over her now despised ex-husband has dissipated. When she and Victor would visit Tootie at Custis Hall, I could feel their disapproval. Wasn't a lot better when Tootie enrolled at Princeton either, disapproval from afar. Given that she is Tootie's mother I walked carefully around her. But back to this barking thing, let's say someone has had it with Crawford Howard," she posited a suspicion. "Wouldn't this be a way to get even with him?"

Gray smiled. "Well, they'd be risking years in court because he would never give up and he has the money to never give up. The law exists for those who can afford it."

She smiled back. "You're right, you usually are, but we would all be dragged into it. Foxhunters have to stick together."

Leaning back he noticed Golly's claw under the box top. "Golly, don't you dare."

She looked Gray directly in the face, her golden eyes wide. *"Bother."*

"Golly." Sister stood up, took the package away from the gorgeous cat, opened the broom closet, slipping it inside. "Until I can take it upstairs. She has to know everything."

"I think she already does."

"It really is a beautiful sweater."

He finished his scotch, exhaling with pleasure. "Here we are talking about the dog ordinance, how long before a motion is floated to punish cat owners when the cats kill birds? Hear that, Golly?"

"Good Lord."

"I'll scratch their eyes out!" Golly threatened.

Once in the library, Sister's favorite room, they sat with their feet up on hassocks. Gray had his arm around Sister's shoulders. The warmth of each other felt like a glow for each of them. Theirs was a tested love, one that endured and deepened.

"Gray, what if you and Ronnie," she named the club treasurer, "got together with Keswick, Farmington Hunt Club, and the Farmington Beagle Club, along with Waldingfield Beagles, and yes, Crawford, and pulled numbers. It would take time, but put together a package of the economic benefits to those communities hosting hunt clubs. The truck dealers alone would plump up those numbers. The real estate agents. The hay dealers, the food dealers."

He squeezed her shoulder. "Okay. Okay. It will take time but it is a good idea." He sighed. "Crawford will be a handful."

Unknown to either of them, Crawford Howard sat in his living room with the Albemarle Sheriff's Department. Someone had stolen his priceless Munnings painting from his room while he and his wife attended a hospital fundraiser. Whoever did it knew how to disarm an expensive alarm system and knew the Howards owned a stunning piece of art.

C H A P T E R 4

February 8, 2020   Saturday

The painting by Sir Alfred Munnings of his wife, Violet, standing with a dappled gray, Isaac, is so beautiful, so perfect that the vision of it has passed into national consciousness in the British Isles and North America. Even people who are not horsemen would recognize it if they saw it, given that it represents an eternal bond between woman and horse. Violet, painted in 1923, wears a black sidesaddle habit, her hair folded in a bun, hairnet over that, her top hat glistening. Her left hand rests on her hip, her right hand holds Isaac's reins. His head is dipped slightly, a moment of quiet understanding between horse and rider. The size of the stolen painting, fifty inches by forty, meant the thief or thieves must have been prepared. Certainly they wouldn't risk a work of art worth millions to rough handling in transport.

Sister sat with Crawford Howard and his wife, Marty, in their huge den, the empty space where the painting hung underscoring their loss.

Crawford, although restoring Old Paradise across from Tattenhall Station, lived in a grand house, Beasley Hall, that he had built when first moving to Albermarle County ten years ago. The entrance to the place, guarded by two huge bronze boars, each atop a stone pillar to which the wrought-iron gates were affixed, also announced if not his intentions at least his interests. They were replicas of Richard Neville's insignia, the boar. The Duke of Warwick, confidant and adviser to Edward IV, proved brilliant, filled with high courage, high ambition. He was ultimately disenchanted with the young man he helped place on England's throne. He was Warwick the kingmaker but he underestimated Edward's sexual impulsiveness. Elizabeth Woodville, a young widow, was and is considered even today to be one of the most beautiful women to have ever lived. She upset Warwick's applecart, as he had planned a marriage with the daughter of the king of France, politically useful but not as beautiful as Elizabeth.

Crawford felt he, too, carried Warwick's intelligence, ability to see ahead, and high courage. He wasn't afraid to take chances, which set him apart from most Virginians, who are sluggish about risks. He branched out from strip malls, turning everything he touched to gold. But like his hero he often neglected to consider how irrational the human animal can be. Not that he was ever irrational. Just ask him.

Sister was still in hunt gear, for she had driven directly over while Betty and Gray carried the horses back to the farm. Today's hunt had been erratic. You just never know about scent. She pulled off her boots on the big bootjack placed by the front door for just such an occasion.

Marty kept the house to perfection. Sister's stockinged feet glided across the floor.

Facing the two as she sat by the fireplace she gratefully sipped a hot Assam tea. Sister and Marty got along famously. Not so much with Crawford, as he was loath to forgive her for not selecting him joint master years back. Instead she had picked Walter Lungrun, M.D., who by Crawford's standards was a pauper. Walter was Big

Ray's outside child, which Sister suspected even while Ray was alive. Walter's father, the man considered his father, accepted his wife's transgression and raised Walter as his own. It was never discussed. The young man rode as a child. Sister had known him all his life. There was no need to trumpet his genetics. But Walter touched her heart and he was great with people. Crawford barked orders. Not a good idea. Money can buy you everything but respect. He would have been an economic godsend as a joint master, but a disaster in every other fashion.

Sister and Crawford managed a truce over the years, working together on those boards on which they served.

"I spent a fortune on that security system," he fumed.

"You always have the best but criminals study what they do as we study what we do. The smartest can figure things out. Crawford, if people can hack the Pentagon they can get into anything."

Marty put a plate of scones on the coffee table, poured herself tea, and sat down. "That was my fiftieth birthday present. Has any woman ever received anything better?" She smiled at her husband.

"I doubt it." Sister smiled back. "I am so very sorry. You owned and protected a national, I mean international, treasure."

"Sheriff Sidell said it would not appear on the open market. It would be sold privately and the buyer may have instigated the theft." Crawford was calming down, thanks to the praise, which he did deserve.

Sister shook her head slightly. "It's hard to believe. For one thing, sooner or later whoever has it will feel compelled for friends to know about it."

"Oh, I don't doubt that." Crawford put his cup in the saucer. "But if the buyer is, shall I say, a crazy, rich Asian, the lawsuits will drag on for years."

Sister nodded. "One doesn't have to be a crazy, rich Asian; I suspect you are right about ego finally trumping good sense."

Marty crossed her legs. "Did you know the Chinese are building a horse city? They want to attract world-class riders for five-star events. Honey, where is that?"

"Tianjin, near Beijing. I hear they may be having flu problems. No matter. We aren't taking horses there."

"I was reading in my *London Times*." She then added, "China is so big there's bound to be winter bugs. The government says they aren't worried. But they sure are competitive. They want five-star equine events in China."

"Fair Hills won the competition for the second five-star location in our country. Much as I wish Morven Park had secured the win," Sister named a wonderful equine setting in Northern Virginia, "Fair Hills sits right where Pennsylvania, New Jersey, and Delaware plus Maryland itself, come together, or almost come together. Will Dupont created it. Well, the Duponts also saved Montpelier, then Will's sister, Alice, took it over. Same color scheme, dark hunter green with white trim on the old buildings. Stunning, really. Now, if a venue like that had bought the painting, we could understand—not that you would sell it."

"I would never ever sell a Munnings, any Munnings, nor would I sell a Stubbs."

"Yes."

"How was today's hunt? Mousehold Heath? Right?" Marty inquired.

"So-so. A few bursts, but that was it. And Thursday we had our best hunt of the year. You never know."

"About anything," Marty agreed. "Sister, you are an amateur enthusiast of sporting art. Have you any thoughts on what might have happened to our painting?"

"No, but if you will allow me, I will call the Sporting Library and Museum in Middleburg, as well as the Museum of Hounds and Hunting at Morven Park. Given their training and contacts, they might be able to think of something. You know Sheriff Ben Sidell will do a good job, but the art world, the museum world, like any other, contains people who know one another or know about one another."

"What about the Virginia Museum of Fine Arts?" Marty asked.

"I'm sure our sheriff has already called them. As the museum has the Paul Mellon collection of equine art, you know they know the painting's history . . . or provenance, as it is called. And I will call Ben to remind him, if the VMFA doesn't, that Yale's museum has some of Mr. Mellon's collection. He was a Yale man."

"So was Cole Porter." Crawford sighed.

"Honey, the day will come when Indiana University touts you as one of their outstanding graduates." Marty smiled.

"I suppose if I built a new football stadium, they would." He shrugged. "Sister, I have to get that Munnings back."

"I hope you do. I will make those calls." Sister sipped the last of her tea. "Thank you for allowing me in here, as I reek of *eau de cheval.*"

"Best perfume on earth." Marty smiled. "You were kind to come."

"*Violet Munnings with Isaac* is one of the great paintings of the twentieth century. We have never discussed art but I do think Sargent, Whistler, and Munnings to be outstanding. When so-called modern art came along they were overshadowed, but that is shifting. Good work is good work and fashions in art are like hemlines."

"An awful thought, really," Marty chipped in. "Human nature, I expect."

"Ever really think about what humans want no matter the century?" Crawford sat up a bit straighter. "Power over others. Greed. Doing whatever they please without consequences. Think of the Greek gods."

Sister knew they, too, paid consequences, but arguing with Crawford, or offering any form of correction, was never well received. "At least the Greek gods had good taste." She half laughed then added, "And so did your thieves."

Marty thought a moment. "Well, I guess they did."

"Time and the tides. We'll see." Sister rose to leave.

Driving out of the too showy estate, Sister really felt sorry for Crawford. His need to be the center of attention, to run the show, would never change but he had learned what money could and couldn't buy in central Virginia. His labors to restore a historically important home and grounds, Old Paradise, brought him some of the respect he had squandered when first moving to the area. He hired a historian and archaeologists who, using the latest technology, uncovered graves grown over by trees, decades of growth since the second decade of the nineteenth century. Many of the graves contained slaves but some may have been graves of Monacan Indians, the humans who preceded African Americans and Europeans. Irritating as he could be, Crawford did good things, things few could afford to do.

As she turned off the two-lane state road to her farm, she thanked the powers-that-be that her late husband, Ray, left her comfortable but not disgustingly rich. Too much of anything isn't good. Then again, some people have to be king. Crawford was one of them. What was the man like who took that extraordinary painting?

CHAPTER 5

February 10, 2020   Monday

"Good thing Crawford hasn't seen this." Sam Lorillard lifted one eyebrow.

"He'd . . . well, you know." Skiff Kane, Crawford's huntsman, kept the rest of the thought to herself.

Best not to criticize or bite the hand that feeds you.

Sam, older, wasn't one to complain but the sight of Showoff Stables alerted him to the fact that big money had been spent.

"Anyone home?" Skiff walked to the main office.

Sam waited with the empty trailer as Skiff walked back.

Horses, blankets on them, the expensive Irish kind, played in the large paddocks. A lone figure walked up from the farthest paddock, bucket in gloved hand. As he reached the trailer, he hung the bucket on the fence post.

"Hello. You Crawford Howard's people?"

"Yes, Sir." Sam reached out his hand to shake the middle-aged man's hand, as did Skiff.

He did not remove his glove to shake hands, a small breach of manners but it was cold.

"Skiff Kane."

Sam smiled. "I should have introduced the lady. Well, we're here to pick up the blood bay mare. Mr. Howard has already paid, which you probably know."

"Parker Bell." He gave his name. "Boss said all was ready. Follow me. I put her in a stall."

The three walked into the cavernous, light stable, where Parker stopped, a snort inside greeting him.

"A true blood bay," Skiff said admiringly.

Parker nodded. "Don't see many." He walked into the stall, slipped a halter on her, the good leather ones from Fennell's in Lexington, Kentucky, leading her out with a Fennell's lead shank. "She goes by Sugar. Come on, Sugar."

Obediently, the stunning horse followed him out. He removed her light sheet, her indoor rug, to reveal her glistening coat.

"Beautiful shoulder." Sam admired her.

"Good athlete. Long stride. You need to coax her across water but she'll do it if she knows you mean it."

"Well, let's load her up." Sam smiled.

"Mr. Sabatini . . ." He paused. "Be right back, I left her papers in the office. Let me load her up first. She's easy."

Sugar walked up the dropped ramp, beheld a full hay net, went right for it.

Sam stroked her neck then closed the inside divider of the three-horse trailer.

Crawford owned the three-horse trailer, his most practical; a four-horse; and a six-horse. Did he need all those trailers? No, but he had to have them.

Skiff closed the doors when Sam walked out, both lifted the ramp, securing it as Parker returned, handing Sam a fat envelope. "He's sending the rug, too. Outside she used a heavier one."

"We've got plenty. Anything else you think we should know?" Sam talked while Skiff observed everything, including a large plumbing box truck parked at a distance. This was the basis for Gigi Sabatini's fortune. The high-end sinks, showers, tubs, and copper pipes were sold nationally.

One of the advantages of being overlooked as a woman is one could study surroundings and other people.

They shook hands, Sam and Skiff, stepped up into the cab of the dually.

"How's it look? Can't see Parker. Don't want to run over him." Sam checked the side mirrors.

"He's out of the way." Skiff snapped her seatbelt. "Let's hope Sugar's not hotter than a pistol. Loaded easily enough."

"Never know until you throw your leg over," Sam truthfully said.

"Maybe Sugar won't be ridden at all. The boss is determined to breed blood bays." She noticed the brand-new fencing, mentally tallying up the cost.

"If color were that easy to breed there'd be more blood bays, more paints, more blanket Appaloosas." Sam cruised at forty miles per hour.

No need to hurry, especially on the back roads.

"You know the late Aga Khan bred fabulous horses but I don't know if color was important to him." Sam read as much as he could about great former horsemen. "But on the other hand, Tesio, the other great breeder in the first half of the twentieth century, felt that grays were mutations. He wouldn't have one. I can't say as I see a difference. A good horse is the right color."

"When is Yvonne coming over for a lesson?"

"This afternoon. She's almost ready to go out hunting. The rear of Second Flight. I'll ride with her but she has that long leg. She really has stuck with it."

"Be good to have a mother and daughter, Yvonne and Tootie, in the field. It's good when families ride together."

"When I was a kid, we all did. Even Aunt Dan would get up there for the hunt club's annual show. We did the family class, my mom, Aunt Dan, Gray, Mercer, and myself. If Mercer were here he'd know every name on Sugar's papers. What's her registered name, by the way?"

Skiff opened the fat envelope, which wasn't sealed, pulling out Sugar's Jockey Club registration plus her medical papers, shots as well as her last shoeing date. Also enclosed was her feed, the protein content, the fat and sugar content. She was too good a horse to wing it.

"Aspasia's Dynamite." Skiff turned to him. "Greek?"

"Pericles's lover."

"Did you major in history at Harvard?"

"No, but we took basic courses the first two years; in those days you had to do that before you truly majored. The idea was you'd best understand your own culture, along with calculus."

"Gone by the time I was at Radford. Not calculus, but I didn't have to take it. Hate math."

"I learned a lot. If you don't know where you've been you don't know where you're going. It's a sure bet our enemies know their own culture. It's pretty stupid not to learn your own."

"You have Aunt Dan, you'll always know where you're going." She laughed, as did he. "What was her son like?"

"Mercer. Good-looking like Aunt Daniella. Being a bloodstock agent, he had a terrific memory. He could see a horse once and remember everything about the animal. He was gay, which you probably heard, but he was discrete. Gray and I didn't care but we made him come with us to buy clothes. We teased him that gay men were the best dressers. Even when I was at the bottom of the barrel he would find clothes and bring them to me. He believed you only have one chance to make a first impression."

"True."

"Also, Gray and Mercer helped me sober up. I wouldn't be alive without them. His death was a blow. I think," he counted in his head, "he was fifty-nine or close. I don't know. The years go by too fast."

So did the miles, for he pulled into the long drive at Beasley Hall. No sooner did the trailer stop at Crawford's main barn than his old Hummer rolled down the driveway.

Out he popped to watch Sugar unload. He did have sense enough to get out of the way. Sam walked her into the barn, Skiff handed him the papers.

Sam quietly guided Sugar into an empty stall, prepared for her, peanut hulls for bedding and alfalfa/orchard grass hay flakes in the corner.

"How about I give her two days then ride her, if that's all right with you?" Sam asked. "Get her a bit settled."

"Sure." Crawford nodded. "What did you think of the operation?"

"Everything's brand new. Fences newly painted. Brass bolts on the stalls. Brass plates by the door. The wrought iron from Cynthiana, Kentucky. PaveSafe on the floor. Equi-grip in the stalls. He spent a fortune." Skiff smiled.

"Huge barn, good paddocks. Very well laid out. Someone knew what they were doing," Sam added. "Place already full of boarders, and you know, he's hired an Olympic show jumper for a trainer."

Crawford rubbed his chin. "We'll see."

A big Lexus slowly drove down the drive, turning toward the house.

"Nineteenth-century expert from the Virginia Museum of Fine Arts. I know Ben Sidell is a good man, but how many law enforcement officers do you know who understand the art market? Especially for a Munnings? All right. Keep me informed about her."

"Yes, Sir." Sam opened the Hummer door for Crawford.

As the boss drove away Skiff, watching the new horse, said to Sam as he walked back in, "That was one of the most beautiful paintings I have ever seen. I hope he gets it back."

"I do, too. I hope it's not on a private jet flying to wherever."

"Me, too."

"What did you think of Showoff?"

Turning to look at Sam, whom she greatly respected, she remarked, "Aptly named. A lot of wasted money. Who needs cast-iron lampposts lining the drive? That's like Custis Hall." She cited the expensive private girls school over the mountain, founded in 1812 by the founder of Old Paradise. The school grew after the war was won. "Chandeliers? I could make out a chandelier in the office."

"Mmm. Waste, yes, but intelligence, too. Every single paddock had frost-free waterers. The hay was stored in rows with space for air to flow in the hay barn, and that was sort of behind the main stable. So no hay overhead. Makes for more work but also makes for safety. Few can afford that extra hand to move the hay every single day."

She considered this. "You're right. But I only saw Parker Bell."

"To run a place like that, Sabatini has to have a lot of people to drive the tractors, plow the roads, move the hay, keep the fences painted. The man has white fences. Nonstop labor. Washing the windows. Then there's the Olympic trainer who also has to have an assistant. Who will muck the stalls? Sabatini has about a two hundred thousand dollar nut to crack to keep all perfect. Well, let me drop that back because I don't know what he pays the Olympian. He'll have to house him."

"Her."

"Ah." Sam pulled off his gloves, walked into the stall to feel Sugar's pulse. "Should have thought of that."

"Sugar looks fine."

Counting, he stopped and smiled. "She is."

"She really is beautiful, but pretty is as pretty does," Skiff repeated the old horseman's phrase; truer words were never spoken.

"Funny, isn't it? How money impresses most people?"

"Yes, but in your figuring remember Showoff probably gets at least seven hundred fifty dollars a month board, plus money for trailering to shows if the owner doesn't have a trailer. Then the client pays for shoeing, probably directly to the farrier. If there are special foods, he or she will pick that cost up. The annual shots, etc. So there is money coming in for board and whatever else is needed. I expect the trainer is paid directly by the student, horse owner for lessons, plus her base salary, plus her living. So add the cost of electricity and heat to the house, which I expect is the small clapboard house in the rear there just visible."

"Okay, so maybe he has to crack a one hundred and fifty thousand dollar nut. If he has it, why not? Think of the hay dealers, the truck dealers, the workmen, etc. Money is useless sitting still. And if he sells a horse, good."

"I still think it's crazy," Skiff, a New Hampshire girl and tight with the buck, said.

"I wouldn't do it but you only live once. Why do we think a so-called purposeful life is the way? If someone wants to spend their life showing off, what is it to me so long as he doesn't harm anyone? I don't know that I have a purposeful life but I like what I do, I pay my bills, and I get to foxhunt. If I had graduated Harvard, wound up in D.C. like my brother, would I have a better life? No. I'd have more money. My brother now is the happiest I have ever seen him."

She smiled. "He is a kind man."

"Mom taught us manners as well as the usual. Plus we still have Aunt Dan to keep us on the straight and narrow."

"You know, Sam, I wouldn't use *straight and narrow*. Aunt Dan lived large."

They laughed again then Sam thought a moment. "What did you think of Parker Bell?"

"He did his job."

"That doesn't answer the question."

"I'm glad you didn't go to Harvard law school." She then answered, "I didn't like him. I couldn't tell you why."

Sam grunted low, "Me, neither."

CHAPTER 6

February 11, 2020   Tuesday

Shelby County, Kentucky, blessed with good soil, sat east of Louisville by twenty-five miles. Abutting Shelby County was Oldham County. Long Run–Woodford Hunt territory and wonderful territory it was, as long as it could last, for Louisville fast encroached on surrounding counties.

Jane Winegardner, MFH, of old Woodford now merged with Long Run, sat on a hill. As Sister Jane was one of her oldest friends and she was younger than Sister, she was known as O.J., the Other Jane.

At this moment the Other Jane felt her sixty-odd years, for the wind, nine miles per hour, blew from the west to the east. The Ohio River divided Indiana from Kentucky. Even thirty miles away, the touch of water filled that wind. The Ohio was a mile wide between Louisville and Indiana. With the mercury sitting at 38°F one's pores tightened, the skin glowed. Who needed a face-lift?

The hard-riding master chose to flank the hounds today. Much as she loved running and jumping, sometimes as a tune-up, a master ought to sit and watch, moving from good view to good view. In this way she or he could judge how well the pack was working to-gether, how good the communication was between huntsman, staff, and hounds. Since hounds could not carry a cellphone or walkie-talkie, there had to be that invisible thread that marks a person with the horn from a person truly hunting hounds. Fortunately, the huntsman, Spencer Allen, truly hunted hounds.

Many packs, especially those crisscrossed by highways where formerly the roads were dirt, used walkie-talkies. Sister Jane, thanks to the vastness of her territory for an East Coast hunt, refused this prop for her whippers-in and huntsman. If you hunted with Jeffer-son Hunt you hunted as was done in the seventeenth, eighteenth, nineteenth, and most of the twentieth century. You used your five senses.

The great maw of Louisville added to the dangers of hunting. All those paved highways, all the new people, lots and lots of new people, innocent of country ways, demanded constant communica-tion between staff. One couldn't trust a new person to slow if he or she observed hounds hunting. Then, too, there needed to be a road whip equipped with a radar screen that showed the tracking collars of the hounds. This allowed the driver to speed, and he did speed, to the spot where it looked like hounds would cross one of these hateful highways. Also, the road whip could hear the commu-nication between huntsman and his staff. In this manner hounds were saved from accidents. Of course, the quarry could care less and many a clever fox and sharp-witted coyote learned to use the roads.

O.J. had seen a mother coyote teach her young how to cross the highway, to look both ways, to shrink back if needed, to surge across when safe.

One does not hunt dumb animals. The dumb animals are the ones on two feet.

So she sat, fingers tingling despite good gloves, to behold the pack, surging across a wide lower pasture, the coyote well in front, seemingly unstressed. Her keen eye noted which hounds were forward, who was in the middle, who was tailing.

Like any good master or good huntsman, O.J. knew your pack is made in the middle. A brilliant hound is a thrill but it's the good soldiers that keep it right. Then, too, it's easy for a huntsman to draft from the rear, but hell to draft from the front. Yet if your forward hounds are so fast they pull away, you now have two packs, so it must be done. She hated that, of course. Sister Jane could never do it. She'd keep the speedsters in the kennel, pay for their food herself, but eventually breed to a hound a step slower. Sister never wanted to blunt drive. Her deep love for hounds was both a strength and a weakness. She simply could not draft a speedster or a senior citizen. She and O.J. would talk for hours about hounds, hunting, management of territory, shifts in quarry. They could empty a room, so they only spoke of such things when together with staff from other hunts. Foxhunting is a blinding passion like skiing, surfing, you name it. Logic gets in the way of the emotional release, and release it is. You have not a second to consider the cares of the day. If you do you will soon be entertaining others with an involuntary dismount.

O.J. liked what she saw. Yes, a few hounds were now tailing, they were older and would probably be retired this year, but they had not fallen so far behind as to be a big worry. The big worry was that the damned coyote was heading straight for a busy road.

Watching, heart beating a bit faster, she saw the road whip. She could almost hear him banging on the side of the truck to alert the forward hounds not to cross. Sometimes they obeyed and sometimes not. A burning hot scent can't be denied.

At the last minute the large gray fellow cut hard right, dropped into a narrow creekbed, high sides, to run in the water then leap out and head back away from the road. Sure enough the pack, stymied at the creekbed, did slide down but the damage to scent was done.

After about a two-hour stop-and-start run, O.J. hoped her

huntsman, Spencer Allen, would lift. He could cast back, for one often picks up another line, but best to ride back toward the east, away from those roads. Not that there weren't other roads on the return but none quite so heavily traveled.

As she turned her mare, Blossom, the wind picked up a bit, hitting her right between the shoulder blades. Kentucky lacks the heavy forests in this part of the state that cover Virginia.

There were no ravines to dip into. You were exposed to the elements. Maybe this was the trade-off for that impossibly rich lime-stone soil. O.J. thought Mother Nature had a sense of humor.

Much of what a master has to do depends on how the duties are divided up if there is more than one master. O.J. shared managing hunt staff with the other masters. As for the hounds, she loved them, so sitting on a hill, walking to another hill to watch, did not seem troublesome to her. Prudently, she kept her thoughts to herself. Any staff, whether hunting or not, wishes to put their best foot forward when observed. People can and do lie. Not everyone, for which any master is grateful, but as the old adage tells you, one bad apple can spoil the whole bunch. No one wants to carry a difficult person. Cohesion frays. O.J. made sure it wasn't going to get to that point. Her whippers-in were honorary. Long Run formerly had a professional . . . good, too . . . but she had retired to have a baby. Still, O.J. liked how the whippers-in moved forward, negotiated terrain, supported the huntsman.

Once back at the trailers, her longtime friend and former Second Flight field master, Louise Kelly, untacked Blossom.

"Can you feel your fingers?" Louise asked.

"Not very much." O.J. smiled. "My feet stayed warm. I finally did what Sister Jane has been telling me to do. I wore three thin pair of silk socks. My toes are a little cold. If we'd been out there much longer I'd feel it more. What's funny is poor Sister. Nothing really works for her feet. She says the longest she can keep them warm is an hour."

"How was it today?"

O.J. looked around then spoke. "Good. I was glad the huntsman hunted back when he did. Long, hard run. Thank God for Barry. He was at the crossroad just as the coyote was due to cross but, smart fellow, the coyote dropped into the creekbed, ran in the creek. By the time he got out he had fouled his scent for a good hundred yards. The wind took care of the rest. Staff did good. We do need another professional whip but our budget is stretched to the max. Our whippers-in are good but they can't always show up. It's a problem. Sister and I were talking about it. Most hunts are in the same boat."

"Do you need to check in with anyone?"

"No. Everyone is ready to go home." O.J. smiled.

"Okay." Louise loaded up Blossom, closed the door, and the two old friends headed back to the barn.

"Sounds like we both had good days but I usually get good runs at Cindy Chandler's Foxglove Farm." Sister spoke to O.J., it now being about seven o'clock.

"Any word on the stolen painting?"

"No. I talked to the curator at the Sporting Museum, called my friends at the Museum of Hounds and Hunting. All knew the painting but no one had any ideas where it might be now. Sometimes these thefts run in cycles, kind of like the old days when silver would be stolen from houses in the same area by teams. There is an odd twist. When I drove home Saturday a sign on the telephone pole before you turn into my driveway blared 'Stop Hounds Barking.' A crank. Well, yesterday another sign went up. 'Stop Foxhunting: A Cruel Sport.' This appeared on the stone pillars, the gates into Crawford Howard's Beasley Hall. He's livid and believes he's been singled out for abuse by the same people who stole his painting. I don't see how the two can be connected. I told him I had a similar sign here, too. He brushed it off." Sister thought a moment. "I begin to think we live in a time when no one can enjoy themselves without others passing judgment, dressed up in terms of great moral offense."

"True," O.J. replied. "Then again, think how even in Ancient Rome, moral judgment was used to attack others. Maybe it's human nature. If you haven't the brains or the resources to succeed, you rip apart others who have."

"So why do people run for president? It's a blood sport."

"I have no idea." O.J. shook her head. "I wouldn't even run for the lowest elected position in Lexington."

Sister laughed. "Are there any low elected positions?"

"Well, there's head of the police department. And he takes nonstop abuse. One shooting. The police should have had a crystal ball, seen into it, and stopped the violence. It really is crazy, but back to the painting, it seems to me the only way it could leave the country is in a private plane with security paid off and customs in the other country paid off, or it could be smuggled in. If the thief or thieves aren't the best at what they do, something or someone will make a mistake."

"We can hope. Yet it could still be in our country. No one has a clue." Sister listened to the old wall clock tick in the kitchen. "As you know I have had my struggles with Crawford, whose ego is inextinguishable, like JFK's flame, but I don't wish this on him. In his defense, he is generous in good causes. His biggest mistake is bullying and bragging. He could have looked at that gorgeous Munnings daily. He didn't need to brag about it. Too many people knew. It's even crossed my mind that this is a revengeful act."

"Sister, you and I come from secure backgrounds. We knew who we were and who our people were. We never had a reason to publicly promote ourselves. We see it as vulgar."

"It is," Sister said with unusual vehemence.

"Millions would disagree as they hustle to rise. Look at this another way. You and I don't mind a man putting his hand on our shoulder even if we don't know him well. We don't mind a man opening a door for us. We expect it as a courtesy. Many women, some even our age, would experience this as a form of diminishment. They would feel belittled."

A long pause followed this. "Okay. I get your point. But the underlying emotion is fear. Fear you won't make the grade. Fear someone is subtracting from your worth. Fear, fear, fear, and it's sold daily like cars and underarm deodorant."

O.J. laughed. "You know, you'd never be allowed to teach."

"Funny you say that. I really liked teaching geology at the college level. It's wonderful to watch someone grasp concepts, to become excited." A long intake of breath followed. "Do you ever feel like this isn't your country anymore?"

"All the time," came the sad answer. "I love that young people are passionate about the environment. They are sensitive about other people's backgrounds and feelings. But I know they don't understand country life and they don't really care. They will buy Brussel sprouts for way too much money at one of these so-called organic food stores but they don't know how to grow them."

Such a long pause followed this that O.J. said, "Are you there?"

"Am. You got me thinking. That Munnings painting. Could this have provoked some anger? You know, like she is promoting woman oppression?"

"What?"

"Sidesaddle. Men expected women, until really the 1920s and 1930s when we rebelled, to ride sidesaddle. Could it be a reminder of oppression, of the patriarchy? Hence the theft."

"Well, Sister, you'd think the radical who stole it would be making her case. Or his case? I can't believe a man would do that."

"What about a woman who started life as a man? If anyone has clarity of vision about the crap women still live with, it seems to me it would be a transgender woman."

"I don't doubt that but I would think she has better things to do than steal a Munnings. This is about money. Has to be."

"O.J., you're probably right. You usually are. Do you think we will live to see the end of foxhunting?"

"We might live to see the end of the First Amendment."

Sister gasped. "Dear God, don't say that."

After they concluded their talk, which ended on a happier note about the difference between fox scent and coyote scent, coyote being stronger, Sister sat in the library absentmindedly stroking Golly.

Rooster grumbled. *"Why is she always petting that damned cat?"*

"Golly is on the sofa. We're on the floor." Raleigh rolled over.

"Yeah." Rooster put his head on his paws while Golly looked down from her perch, such a satisfying position.

Gray stayed with his brother at the old Lorillard home place two days a week, so Sister was alone. She never minded being alone, but then with two dogs and a cat, she never was.

Tempted though she was to call him, she refrained. The two brothers were slowly restoring the clapboard house, lovely proportions, simple lines, dark navy shutters, almost black. They needed their time together but O.J.'s comment about the First Amendment bothered her. She believed in the U.S. Constitution just as she believed in the Ten Commandments.

"Thou Shalt Not Steal," she whispered out loud.

C H A P T E R 7

N orth central New Jersey could face a blizzard, a rainy day, or an odd warmish day in the middle of February. Many residents considered February the longest month of the year, but they did not hunt with Essex Fox Hounds, whose members had burned a high number of calories this Lincoln's birthday.

The field walked back to the trailers after a bracing day flying across the open fields and negotiating what wasn't open. Their pack of mostly American hounds stuck to the line. The low clouds helped scent and the temperature hung above freezing. This kind of day yields deceptive footing, for patches can still be hard as a rock, a deep frost, while others have softened.

Out for the day on a borrowed horse rode Buddy Cadwalder. Essex wasn't that far from Newtown Square, Pennsylvania, where he lived. He and his late wife loved the history, the closeness to the Brandywine Battlefield, Andrew Wyeth territory, the painter who captured the area.

Since Sophia died two years ago he became increasingly lonely.

He wouldn't admit it but he hunted around the many hunts in that area, New Jersey, Maryland, also quite close.

He had hoped he might find companionship with a hunting lady. So far he had not but he had sold furniture. Some good came out of it.

This part of New Jersey still has farms, estates with cultivated land. Most people in this section of a much misunderstood state are well off. The taxes are outrageous. Property owners needed to be rich to pay them.

One of whom came home, handed over her horse to her groom, walked into her gorgeous home, and didn't notice immediately the painting by Munnings of an American, Mrs. Prince, was missing from the parlor. When she noticed she blinked. No, she was not imagining that blank spot. The evocative work, entitled *The Ride to the Chateau,* Mrs. Prince riding sidesaddle wearing a top hat with a wider ribbon than most, was missing. Munnings liked Americans. For one thing we paid straight up. But he did like us and he very much liked Mrs. Prince, who evidenced no sense of time, often late.

The painting of Mrs. Prince, relaxed, showed a woman of middle years, good-looking, walking along, a background not manicured but country. Frederick Prince was master of the Pau Hunt, no longer in existence. They were enormously wealthy.

Geneva Mansfield came to own the work through her mother's family. The Mansfields had money but not pots and pots of it. When her grandfather bought the painting it was affordable. The surprise was the Prince family letting it go after the subject passed away.

When the police arrived she had composed herself. No one could figure out how the thief could walk out with this work; the frame alone was heavy. The stable girl, mucking stalls, did not hear or see any vehicles. No one else but her was on the small farm at the time.

Given that this was the second priceless Munnings stolen in five days, it made the news.

Sister watched with Gray.

"There must be a new, huge market for Munnings," Gray, feet up on the hassock, fire warming them, remarked.

"There's always been a market for Munnings, but this, I don't know." She stood up, walking to the hallway. "Need anything?"

"No."

She walked the old polished floor, walked upstairs, then came down with a large book of Sir Alfred Munnings's work.

"Here. I keep this in my little room off the bedroom, along with my old nineteenth-century foxhunting books."

He opened the pages, found *The Ride to the Chateau*.

"Sidesaddle," she stated.

"So I see." He looked over to her, now seated again. "As long as this is confined to paintings. We can assume these works are insured."

"Money can't compensate for a loss like that."

"No. Strange as this is, as long as someone riding sidesaddle today is unmolested, people are probably okay. It's about money."

"Gray, that's perverted. Someone attacking women riding sidesaddle?"

"People are perverted. And sidesaddle is making a comeback. Hunt shows are putting back sidesaddle classes."

She ran her finger over her lips. "I can't believe they could be connected."

"Well, as long as no one is kidnapped or killed, they are not."

The good news of the day was that Sam rode Sugar, who was an obedient girl. The mare, so beautiful, could have been a subject for Sir Alfred Munnings. What a gift to be able to capture an animal or person's essence, one that would travel through centuries.

Sam dismounted, untacked, admired Sugar. He thought for a moment about someone painting her. Then he thought a bit deeper. Money is temporal power. Great art is eternal power.

C H A P T E R 8

February 13, 2020   Thursday

Welsh Harp, Jefferson Hunt's northernmost fixture, covered what old-timers called "Billy goat land." The poor soils discouraged corn, wheat, soybeans. Cow-quality hay could be grown but not horse-quality. For all that, the spectacular views held people spellbound. The small cottage, itself simple fieldstone, sat on a ridge eight hundred feet high, so the views spanned three hundred sixty degrees. So did the wind.

The pastures surrounded the well-kept place, beyond which the woods grew thick. Over years the trees had been thinned out, which meant what was left grew to an enormous girth. The owners, Vivian and Grant Chafee, spent winters in Tempe, Arizona, and the summers in Virginia. Sister kept an eye on the place, a courtesy most masters practiced for their landowners. Hounds found on the west side of the house but that fox slipped away after a bracing ten-minute run. A herd of deer blasted out of the woods, across the western pasture.

Sister didn't blink. She knew the hounds would ignore them, which they did. Tootie not out today because of a test at UVA meant

Sister was one whip shy. Thinking about it, she had asked Kasmir and Alida if they would consider whipping-in together.

Both jumped at the chance. So there they were on the left side, perhaps the tiniest bit apprehensive but also excited after that brief run. The whippers-in usually have the best seat in the house.

Weevil, none too familiar with this fixture, checked the wind, perhaps eight miles per hour. Not a problem but not a help either. So he called the hounds to him then slipped over the slight rise in this pasture down toward the woods.

"Get 'em up. Get 'em up," he called in a singsong voice. Dragon, out today, moved away from the pack.

"Dragon," Weevil called, for Dragon could hit a lick before you knew it, and he was right, but too far in front.

Keeping hounds together takes training. It's not that a hunts-man minds them in a line or even frets over some few hounds who will fan out a bit at the edges. If you know your hounds, you know who is young, needing more time, who knows the game. The young ones learn if encouraged.

If you don't trust your hounds, don't hunt them. Sister had that drilled into her by the late Peter Wheeler, a dear old friend, and a hunter of decades. Peter had hunted with the great Dicky Bywaters, as well as the Poe brothers, Fred Duncan, the greats of Virginia. He also had the pleasure of hunting behind the young Tommy Lee Jones, now in his fiftieth year hunting Casanova's hounds. Peter would knit his eyebrows together, fuss at Sister, "I'll make a foxhunter out of you yet."

She loved him. Who didn't?

She trusted her hounds and she trusted Weevil, young though he was. Weevil possessed a sure light touch with the intelligent, lov-ing animals. He loved the hounds and this was returned. Weevil was the one with the higher view, the good eyes. He had to borrow four legs. Hounds knew on two he was unfortunately slow and they knew his nose wasn't worth a damn. Well, their noses were superb. So they made a good team. They wanted the same thing: to chase foxes.

Dragon hit. *"Red."*

Fifteen couples, out today, put their noses down at the spot, roared, shooting into the woods.

Sister found a decent trail. The last time the club had been here was cubbing on a luscious October day, but the winds since then had knocked down trees, some big ones, so it was an obstacle course.

Betty, on the right, memorized territory after one visit. If she'd been dropped onto a fixture of Deep Run's outside of Richmond that she'd hunted as a guest in the 1980s, Betty would know exactly where she was. Uncanny.

Kasmir pushed into a narrow deer trail. Riding Nighthawk, a horse he had bought years ago from the late Faye Spencer, he stopped, listened. The music ricocheted off the trees. Alida, behind him, noticed a flash out of the corner of her eye.

"Tally-ho," she softly alerted Kasmir.

Kasmir turned to see the direction in which she was holding her cap. What he saw was the butt of a coyote, a big one.

Cupping his hands around his mouth, he shouted, "Tally-ho!"

Weevil heard him but did not interfere with his hounds running in the opposite direction. Sure enough, they paused fifty yards into the woods, furiously working, they turned left, south, to head in the direction where Kasmir and Alida stood fast.

Within a few minutes, battling low branches, Weevil appeared, hounds streaming before him. Alida had her cap outstretched.

"Coyote," Kasmir called out and Weevil nodded back.

Then the two newly recruited whippers-in moved farther to the left, charging forward as best they could.

Clever as a fox is, a coyote is not stupid. This fellow vaulted over tree trunks then dipped over an odd embankment that once was part of a man-made irrigation canal, dug during the Depression by the CCC. While it wasn't steep, horses would need to jump the canal, which was two feet deep, perhaps as wide.

Sister on Lafayette soared. Never look down. She did not.

This, however, did not apply to Dr. Walter Lungren, her joint master, out today on his day off from the hospital. He didn't throw his wonderful partner, Clemson, off but he threw himself off.

Father Mancusco, behind him, hollered, "Lay flat!"

In this manner, Walter could observe the bellies of the horses in the field. Once they had passed he scrambled out, mud on his right side, mud on his cap, which had flown off.

"Thank you."

Freddie Thomas, a good rider, stayed back, caught Clemson, who was in no hurry. Holding the sweet mare, she waited while Walter found a tree trunk, lots to chose from, stood on it, easily mounting.

"You tight in the tack?"

"Yes." Walter smiled at the attractive Freddie.

"We've got a lot of ground to make up."

They tore off just as the coyote broke cover at the edge of the woods, abutting property filled with old cars, rusted bedstands, plastic barrels.

Skirting this mess, the coyote came out behind it, turning back onto the Chafee's Welsh Harp. Again he used the woods, but this time followed a wide stream. Hounds sang in tune.

Fast though they were despite the difficult terrain, he knew he was faster. Making a tight circle he then headed back toward the small unused barn behind the house, burst past that, now flying due east, straight as a stick.

Hounds came out onto the pasture just as he disappeared at

the other end of it. Staff and the field saw the entire pack running together, a sight which foxhunters love. A few of the older hounds now ran tail but they weren't out of the pack, simply at the rear. Again they plunged into heavy cover then stopped.

"Dammit!" Dreamboat cursed.

Tinsel, a young fellow, tried not to go to the deer carcass, but what was left of it still emanated that heavenly smell to a hound.

"Leave it!" Betty rode over.

"Okay." Tinsel dropped his head.

Weevil pulled them away from the enticement. "Did you see him?"

Weevil's eyes followed her as she held out her crop in the direction of the coyote. Betty, long a whipper-in, knew no good would come from this. Coyotes take you right out of your territory a lot. They charged on to Showoff Stables.

The pack also ran behind the luxurious stable, then lost the line by the tractor shed complete with gas pumps. That powerful gas smell covers many an odor. They circled, noses down, trying so diligently as Parker Bell, red-faced, charged out from the end of the stable.

"What in the goddamned hell do you think you're doing?" he screamed at Weevil. "Get these damned dogs out of here before I shoot them."

Weevil put his horn to his lips, blew three equal blasts, then sang out, "Come along."

As he did so, Kasmir and Betty moved, now between the paddocks, to help him.

Seeing them, Parker bellowed, "Get out. Get out. You've got the horses farted up. If there's one scratch on any of these horses, you all are paying for it! Mr. Sabatini sues people for sport."

Alida rode back to Sister. "Kasmir said to stay away. So I'm coming to you."

"He's right. The last thing that idiot needs is an audience. Forgive the crude language."

Hounds, loathe to surrender their search, did return to the horn one by one. Trinity, a sweet little fellow, veered too close to Parker, who kicked him. That fast Weevil dismounted, knelt down to pick up the hound, and Parker kicked him. Weevil rolled over.

Kasmir vaulted off Nighthawk. Middle-aged, a touch of a paunch, he hauled off and hit Parker smack in the face.

"You goddamned Arab!" Parker punched back.

"Goddamned Muslim," Kasmir responded as Parker insulted him, then punched the worker in the gut.

While Kasmir may have been past his prime, he had boxed at Oxford. He was actually enjoying this so he crashed his right fist into Parker's jaw when the large man doubled over.

Weevil, holding Trinity, frightened but unharmed, handed the sweet fellow up to Betty, who draped him over her saddle.

"It's all right, sweetie. I'll put you down in a minute," she reassured the trembling animal.

A distant siren preceded the cursing. Alida had called the Sheriff's department just in case. Ben Sidell drove down the main entrance, lights flashing, which of course caused more equine consternation. He cut the motor, got out, beheld Parker struggling to his feet, Kasmir standing over him.

"Sheriff," Kasmir simply said.

"Trespassers! Trespassers!" Parker unsteadily stood up. "Goddamned hounds ran through here. These assholes ran through here. I want them charged with trespassing."

The sheriff, calm as always, handed him an envelope, which he'd pulled from his pocket. "The Goodloe law. These people have the right to come onto this property to retrieve hounds. It's the law in Virginia."

"My boss will change that. He can buy you and sell you."

Kasmir just smiled, for this field hand, which is how he thought of him, had no idea who he was or what he was worth.

"Here comes your boss now," Ben remarked as Sabatini strode from his house. He did not look angry but he did look concerned.

Ben snatched the papers from Parker, held out his hand to shake Gigi's, and with his left hand gave him the Goodloe law.

"Mr. Sabatini, I had hoped to call on you, but not in this fashion."

"Scared the horses," Parker sputtered, although it was dawning on him that this was not going to be an ordinary tribulation.

"Are you all right?" Betty asked Weevil, who nodded he was.

"Given the uproar, Sheriff, if you will permit me, I'd like to get the hounds out of here. For the record, this oaf kicked Trinity."

Gigi, whip smart, knew the minute the name was spoken that the sheriff also knew the hound. While he was not happy that a pack of hounds had roared over his farm, he was shrewd enough to not wish to make an enemy of the sheriff. These hunting people had pull. He was the new guy in town. New guy with a big ego, but he was smart.

"Yes, go on, huntsman. Before you go, do you wish to bring charges concerning the hound?"

Parker's face was now purple.

"No, Sir, I just want to leave." As Weevil mounted, Parker's dirty footprint on his side was visible.

Ben looked from Weevil to Parker to Gigi. "Mr. Sabatini, this place is beautiful. I can understand your concerns and I know that Jefferson Hunt did not willingly come onto your property. Hounds can't read. If the scent is strong they will follow it. I'm sure the masters of the hunt will call upon you to secure any damages, should there be any. I realize you've come from New York," Ben had the information before he drove down the driveway thanks to a terrific staff, "and I hope you learn to like it here. You should know that foxhunting is the state sport of Virginia and the foxhound is the state dog. I've given you the Goodloe law, which will make clear the rights of hound owners. I do hope this settles things." He touched his cap, got into the squad car, and slowly drove out.

Parker bawled his innocence but Gigi turned his back on him without reply. He had some things to think over, one of which was Parker's behavior. Gigi hired ex-cons. They were grateful and they were cheap. Unfortunately he had other things to worry about than foxhunters, but he did not want people hunting over his land.

Hounds reached Sister, the field, the woods behind.

"Master?" Weevil said.

"Are you all right?" she asked, for they all saw him get a hard kick.

"Yes, Ma'am."

"Weevil, you showed extraordinary discipline and I thank you."

Kasmir, touching his cap with his crop, apologized. "Master, I fear I evidenced no such discipline. That lout kicked a hound."

Weevil piped up. "He called Kasmir a goddamned Arab."

"I corrected him." Kasmir grinned mischievously.

Alida, now alongside him to ride back, said as they moved off, "Honey, you let him have it."

"If he had insulted you, my dear, he would now have no teeth."

She smiled, reached over to touch his arm as they walked the hounds back.

Once hounds were loaded, the small field of twelve, horses tied to trailer sides, hay bags also tied to trailer side, grabbed their food baskets and folding chairs to sit by the tailgate. Everyone poured over the scene.

Walter sat next to Sister. "We'd better get over there."

"Something tells me that fellow who I met at Kathleen's opening will do better with another man. I'll come along, naturally, but you carry the ball. I am sorry. None of us ever wants to run over territory we don't have permission to hunt, and in a way, Walter, we are at fault. We knew a big show stable was coming in here but we didn't come by before hunt season."

"Two reasons: One, we have never had a run like that from Welsh Harp in this direction. It's always west. And two, this place is now finally open and in business. Was over a year in construction."

"Seeing it, I can understand why." She took a deep draft of a hot tea handed to her by Betty, who also plopped down.

"Trinity is fine. Poor little guy." Betty sighed. "What's wrong with people?"

"What's always been wrong with people," Father Mancusco offered. "We are all God's creatures and they don't respect that."

Kasmir and Alida joined them. He came in for a ribbing but everyone was impressed.

"So, Kasmir, they didn't have anger management training at Oxford?" Walter teased.

"Oh, Walter, I'm so old, they didn't even teach psychology," he teased back.

"Do they now?" Walter asked.

"I actually don't know. I will say, no offense to your university system, that studying with a don made me come up to the mark. I had nowhere to hide. Oh, plenty of fellows didn't study, their families pouring money into the various colleges at Oxford, but I knew I had this one chance to learn before life filled up with obligations."

"You obviously learned." Sister adored him.

"I did." Kasmir stretched out his legs.

Alida changed the subject. "How about another Munnings painting being stolen?"

"Maybe it's a coincidence," Betty remarked.

"Those paintings, the smaller, are worth between six hundred thousand and eight hundred thousand. The big ones are worth millions, as in three or four million." Kasmir had become familiar with Munnings's work when he studied and lived in England, for so many of them are still there. His estate is a museum, The Munnings Art Museum.

"Sidesaddle," Alida added.

"So elegant. So feminine." Sister smiled.

"We all look pretty elegant right now." Walter grinned. "Of course, you ladies look better."

"Right thing to say." Betty laughed.

CHAPTER 9

February 14, 2020   Friday

S tanding in the bucket, lifted high up, Melvin Willis, called Willis, maneuvered the connector for the heavy optical fiber wire. The late-afternoon sun lent a shimmer almost blinding if one faced it. Oddly shaped, not quite round and not quite elliptical. The connection was necessary, as the high-speed fibers, thicker and heavier than an old normal telephone wire, had to be properly secured.

Broadband finally edged its way into rural areas. Two presidents had promised it. Nothing, but now Firefly, in cooperation with Central Virginia Electrical Cooperative, took on the task.

Heavy equipment sat by the road, tipped a bit inward as the roads, narrow, were not banked like city roads. The estimate that this would be finished by March was proving too optimistic. The territory alone would give people fits: ravines, swift-running creeks, larger feeders to the great Virginia rivers . . . in this case, the James ultimately and the actual foothills of the Blue Ridge Mountains. No matter how closely one read the topographical maps or checked with GPS, nothing truly prepared the man in the field for what he would encounter.

In this case it was a small pack of feral pigs. Willis watched as his crewmates ran for the cabs of their trucks. Until pigs could fly he would be safe. Glad of his perch he watched the small far group trot across Old Randolph Road and head into the woods. From the opposite direction a coyote slunk out of the woods . . . yesterday's coyote, as Willis and the boys sat between Welsh Harp and Showoff Stables.

The expanse of Showoff Stables impressed even nonhorse people. A center stable, as long as a football field, sat in the middle of a manicured field and a sensible driveway with a big circle for trailers.

The stable, two stories high, sported a wide center aisle with brick laid in a herringbone pattern. The stalls, open to the top, sat under a high catwalk, used to crank open a row of windows along the roofline. In good weather, fresh air flowed easily throughout the structure. Each stall's outside door, a Dutch door, could also be opened for fresh air. In the exact center of this long building a cross aisle led to the huge indoor arena. One had only to saddle up, walk into the arena in any kind of weather, and work one's horse or take a lesson.

Behind this structure an equivalently sized outdoor arena, a roof overhead but open otherwise, was another place to work your horse or take a lesson. Around all the large paddocks, three-board fences were white and now without lead in the paint, which meant you needed to paint them about every three years. Two if you were fussy.

Wide walkway between each paddock meant the horses couldn't reach over and bite another horse. Most of the paddocks contained three or four horses, all of whom got along. Every paddock contained its group of friends. The walkway kept the peace.

Every paddock had a run-shed, which the horses could repair

to in bad weather. But horses having an odd sense of weather as well as humor often happily stood out in a driving rain. You never knew why.

Around this, more open pastures met the eye, not yet greening up. Too early, but when spring finally did come the place would glow emerald green. Woods covered the remainder of the two-hundred-acre place, these being filled with trails, and some of these trails had natural jumps.

An office, semidetached, anchored the south side of the large stable. A covered walkway connected it to the stalls, for this way foot traffic could be controlled, keep owners at the stable. The main house could be seen in the distance, large yet simple. The design fit into the board and batten of all the wooden buildings, as did the color scheme, a deep mustard yellow with Charleston green shutters. The outbuildings all had white frames for windows but Charleston green doors, and if shutters, Charleston green.

All the supporting outbuildings echoed this color combination.

This color scheme flowed from generation to generation. Whether it came from England originally no one knew, but it was common in this New World. Hanover Shoe Farms, founded in the late nineteenth century then transformed in the early 1900s, used it for their Standardbred breeding operations.

The yellow was lighter than Showoff Stables.

One could find the colors in Maryland; Upstate New York; Lexington, Kentucky. Wherever there was a large population of horse people, this would occur.

Given that the trees with the exception of evergreens were denuded, the mustard yellow helped one focus. A wheelbarrow next to an equipment shed could easily be seen.

Willis, once the support ellipse was secured, took a moment to admire the setting. Down below, to the side of the outdoor arena, a small building, he didn't know what it was for, had the door open.

Squinting, it looked like a person's gloved hand on the ground. Given the position of the door, he couldn't be sure what he was seeing.

Intensely watching this hand, he counted to himself. After he reached sixty he thought he'd better hit the walkie-talkie and tell Foster to bring him down.

"Done."

"Roger." Foster began to lower the high bucket. Once down, Willis lifted one leg out then the other. "Foster, take a minute. Come with me."

"Yeah, sure." The young man with his four-day stubble cut the motor, wrapped his scarf tighter, opened the door, his feet touching the ground as he reached for his gloves in his pockets.

"Got your cellphone?"

Foster replied, "Always have my cellphone. You guys couldn't work without me."

"Right." Willis, now in the middle of the beige pea-gravel road, head down, walked fast.

"Slow down."

"Speed up. Something's not right."

"Willis, everything's fine. All the markers are set. We won't have trouble digging the cable from this point. Everybody wants stuff underground. Yeah, well, it doesn't last but so long. They'll have to dig it up again."

"Thirty years from now. Hey, maybe forty. Nobody really knows. Come on, Foster. Quit dragging your ass."

"I don't know."

Willis reached the outdoor arena; moving with purpose, he reached the shed. "Shit."

Foster, now beside him, looked down at a large man, forties at the most, arm outstretched. This was the hand that Willis had seen. "Jeez."

The man, lumberjack cap over red hair, eyes to the sky, had been strangled with a Fennell's lead shank.

Willis tersely ordered Foster, "Call 911."

Kneeling down, Willis didn't touch the corpse. It seemed to him the man had not fought for his life. Perhaps his attacker was too experienced.

CHAPTER 10

February 15, 2020   Saturday

Hortensia, snug in the big hay shed at Mill Ruins, Walter Lungren's place, listened to chatter far away. Her ears, sensitive, could hear sounds at a distance, which humans' could not. The rumble of rigs crunching stone as they rolled down the long drive alerted her to this Saturday's hunt. Walter put out food for the foxes at Mill Ruins, there were four in constant residence but others passed through. As it was breeding season, many a male shot through chased by James, the old red behind the mill, or Ewald, a younger red, who cleverly made a den under the back porch of the house. He also had another one at a more distant outbuilding. The house den, close to the smells of the kitchen, kept Ewald happy. Sometimes the other foxes would come by to investigate the garbage or whatever Walter threw out, but Ewald snatched up first pick being right there.

The other gray fox, the third on the property, lived acres away in the back, having a den under a large old storage building. All of the dens protected their occupants from the winds, fierce in winter. Each den had more than one entrance. There were other places to tuck in, in case of being caught unawares, that also dotted the large farm.

Yvonne Harris followed the field, driving Aunt Daniella and Kathleen Sixt Dunbar. The "girls," as they thought of themselves, especially liked Mill Ruins. The large waterwheel, turning, water flying off the paddles, seemed to transport them to another time, maybe a better time, or so they wished.

The mill, heavy gray fieldstone, built after 1790, testified to the wisdom of our forebears. Built to stand for centuries, it did. The two-story structure, grinding equipment intact but unused, had served generations of settlers. Everyone needs grain, corn, wheat, oats. Freshly ground grain also brought in foxes, other creatures, eager for the leavings. Corn kernels spilled being carried into the mill, oats scattered, and ground fine flour dusted the wide-plank floors. All a fox had to do was wait until nightfall, eat what fell on the way to or from a wagon, or wiggle inside. James, the crabby red living behind the mill, constantly reminded Hortensia and Ewald that they were newcomers. He couldn't do that to Grenville, living in the back at what's called Shootrough, for his ancestors had lived here since the eighteenth century as well.

Old blood was old blood, whether vulpine or human.

Hortensia thought the whole thing silly. She liked foxhunts. She rarely gave the hounds a run but when the people left they always dropped food, even gummy bears. She loved those gummy bears.

Once the people left, Yvonne slowly driving behind, Hortensia scurried to the trailers. Most of the riders closed their tack-room doors. A few did not, so she could pop in, rummage around. Freddie Thomas usually kept the door open. Hortensia recognized the trailers as well as the humans who owned them. She'd seen them for years. She caught a whiff of the gummy bears. Freddie's plastic bag proved no match for Hortensia, who sat there being a pig.

Ewald, slinking under a trailer, crawled out.

"Boy, there are a lot of them today. Hey, sweets!"

"The yellow ones are the best." Hortensia fished one out.

He jumped into the tidy tack room, a regular, heavy horse blanket lying flat in the space of the nose. Curious, he easily jumped up.

"Nothing better than a horse blanket," Hortensia said.

"People sleep in these things. Some of them have living quarters, but it makes the trailer way too big, I think. Sleeping in the nose must be okay. With blankets a human can keep warm. Hey, mind if I eat a gummy bear?"

"No. Whole bag full." Hortensia reached in for a grape one, placing it in her mouth. Very ladylike.

A stiff wind gust blew the door shut. The latch clicked.

"Uh-oh." Ewald pushed the door.

Hortensia scratched at it. *"Damn."*

Ewald looked at her then climbed up in the nose again. *"At least the hounds can't get in here."*

"No, but the human can," Hortensia fretted.

"She'll be tired. It's cold today, and bet you Grenville gives them a run. He likes to zigzag, cover rough territory, and see them fall off. Here's what we do. We sit tight. If we stay perfectly still when she comes back, she won't even know we're here." He slid under the blanket, only his black nose sticking out. *"Come on. This is warm. She won't be back for hours. When she turns her back we can go."*

"You're more hopeful than I am. I say she opens the door, sees us, and screams."

"You give the humans much too much credit. The last thing she will expect is two foxes in her tack room. Get under the blanket with me and when the door opens stay perfectly still."

"I hope you're right." Hortensia joined him.

All one could see were two black noses sticking out from under the blanket. One would need to look for them.

While Hortensia and Ewald snuggled in, Grenville, true to form, waited at woods' edge. Hounds walked on the left side of the farm road while he observed on the right side. To reach him all would need to take a stout coop. He wasn't worried. He could thread his way through the woods, giving everyone fits. He liked to hear the "Ommph" when someone hit the ground.

Giorgio, nose to the ground, moved slowly. He'd hunted here over the years, knowing that often Grenville left a signature on pastures. However, he needed to draw the pasture he was on, not the one across the road. Had to obey his huntsman.

Yvonne stopped to watch. "A lot of people out today."

"February is great if you can take the cold," said Aunt Daniella, short heavy coat on, her legs wrapped in a plaid throw.

Kathleen, in the back, learning about hunting, asked, "This is an old fixture. They must know where the fox is."

"Yes and no." Aunt Dan watched as Tootie disappeared into the woods on the left side.

"Sister, Weevil, and Betty, especially Betty, know where the dens are. Tootie does, too, because she started hunting Mill Ruins when she was at Custis Hall. But knowing where the dens are doesn't mean the fox was out, may not be scent." Yvonne had learned a lot in the last year.

Ribbon, her Norfolk terrier, sat in her lap, keen to see everything.

Grenville waited for hounds to reach the woodline across the farm road then he trotted into the open pasture, sat down, and waited.

The field passed on the road. Then Second Flight passed. The sheriff was riding tail that day and he noticed a flash of red.

Counting to twenty he called, "Tally-ho!"

Ben turned Nonni in the direction of Grenville, now heading into the woods. His cap off, arm outstretched, he said nothing. Betty, already in the woods, jumped back out, saw Ben, then waited. Tootie stayed where she was.

Weevil jumped the coop in the corner, crossed the road, jumped the coop into the right pasture. Sister, on Rickyroo, stopped, for she and the field were in the middle of the farm road.

Rickyroo's ears swiveled. Grenville waited for Weevil to clear the jump then he tore off into the woods.

Ben kept his hand and hat steady as Betty also held out her cap.

Weevil, seeing the direction, put hounds on what he hoped was the line. It was.

Not a second of being tentative, all opened, leaping over, under, and through the three-board fence. Weevil took the coop in that fence line.

Sister thought staying on the road paralleling the hounds might be the best choice. It was, but that road dropped soon enough, footing slippery. She slowed a little.

"Well," Yvonne muttered.

"They'll all back up at the stream crossing," Aunt Daniella predicted. "Wait. If we hear hounds going away we can cross the stream, too. Shouldn't be too high. But if not, I'd sit tight."

Although the stream flowed rapidly thanks to the rains and snow meltoff, the depth was only a foot. There had been times when the water rose higher than that. All the riders splashed through easily.

Yvonne crept down as the last rider, Ron Haslip, crossed, riding tail for Second Flight, which he didn't want to do but Bobby Franklin was desperate to give Ben Sidell a day up front.

"All right, girls." Yvonne put her vehicle in low gear just in case. "Any predictions, Aunt Dan?"

The older woman opened her window, a slash of cold air right on her face. "Wind is shifting. More westerly to east than coming right down from the northwest. He'll run with the wind at his tail."

"Why?" Kathleen asked.

"Blow scent away from the hounds. If Weevil turns his hounds into the wind, the scent will carry. Foxes know this, so if their scent gets picked up they'll zigzag to confuse the hounds. Then, too, if there's a stiff wind they'll use it to blow their scent yards away from its original path. They are cunning creatures."

"Tootie says the only creature that understands scent is the fox," Yvonne repeated her daughter's wisdom.

Kathleen noted, "People seem to find a buddy or a group they stick with."

"Sometimes that's due to the athletic ability of their horse. A person on a fast or long-strided horse will usually ride with like horses. Otherwise they'd need to be rating their horse," Aunt Daniella explained.

"I would have never thought of that," Kathleen confessed.

"All kinds of stuff going on out there. You can see Carter next to Buddy. Both on 16.2H, or thereabouts, Thoroughbreds. They'll stay up front." Yvonne was learning a lot from Tootie and Sam.

"Buddy travels a distance to hunt here," Kathleen noted. "He certainly pays attention to what I have in the shop when he's here."

Aunt Daniella smiled wryly. "Kathleen, he's paying attention to you."

A few moments passed then Kathleen said, "Doesn't seem like it. He only chats about the pieces."

"Ah well, his wife died two years ago. They married out of college. I suspect he has no idea how to date now." Aunt Daniella took a breath. "I knew them both. He's a good fellow. Took good care of Sophia. Men have a much harder time, you know?"

Buddy Cadwalder, tall and lean, did want to know Kathleen. Furniture gave him a reason to talk to her, overcome his shyness. Kathleen, polite and warm, seemed to have no interest in him, while other women threw themselves at him. This made her all the more fascinating. Being a man of a certain age, he wanted to make the first move but wasn't sure of himself.

Before Kathleen could comment Yvonne said, "Feathering. Just a few."

"That devil will make them work. He knows the territory. He knows the hounds. He'll make fools out of them," Aunt Daniella predicted.

Grenville, comfortably ahead of the speaking pack, trotted along the stream, heading east. Hounds picked up scent but it wasn't hot. They knew they were on but the wind at their backs created difficulties, blowing scent away from them.

Pickens, a younger hound but not a youngster, nose down, stopped a moment. *"Bobcat."*

Diana and Dreamboat came over, touched the earth, then Dreamboat pronounced, *"Not long ago."*

"We need to stick with the fox. It's Grenville. He's easy to track but once he decides to run, he'll do crazy things," Dreamboat counseled.

Grenville crossed back and forth over the stream, easily done, then he headed up through the woods to the Shootrough part of Mill Ruins. Broomstraw, golden and tough, covered the old abandoned pasture at the top. A rutted farm road ran alongside this, finally emerging onto a two-lane state road rarely traveled back here. A few round hay bales covered in plastic sat in two rows on the good pastures. Walter had rehabilitated the pastures on the sunny side of this part of the property, cutting good hay. The rest stayed broomstraw, which gave skunks, groundhogs, rabbits, foxes, and turkeys cover. Turkeys had been there early in the morning, for the soil was scratched to bits especially under the odd large sycamores, hickories, and black gum trees dotting the various pastures.

Walking out of the broomstraw, Grenville heard the hounds behind him. Picking up the pace he ran in the middle of the rutted road. He could hear Yvonne motoring toward him but from a ninety-degree angle. The nose of her expensive SUV would pop out of the farm crossroads in a few minutes. He decided to go in the other direction, straight for the row of hay bales.

Weaving through the hay bales he rubbed against them. Scent would be heavy. Then he climbed to the top, surveyed the countryside, leapt down, ran to a car so old it was abandoned in 1954. He walked through the insides, what was left of them, then he shot out, making straight for his den in the big storage building back there. Having time to dig entrances and exits, he was never far from a quick duck down thence upward inside, to enjoy whatever Walter had parked in this faraway building.

Hounds worked their way across the stream, back and forth, then threaded their way through the woods, emerging into the broomstraw. Working steadily they kept moving, crossed the rutted farm road just as Yvonne drove out from the crossing farm road. She stopped the car, cut the motor.

Hounds didn't bother to look, they were so intent.

"It's a clear track but fades in and out," Trooper remarked.

"Wind. Not strong but tricky. It's not staying still." Taz inhaled deeply.

"Shifting. I wouldn't be surprised if we get some wind devils. You never know back here. The lay of the land, with all those swales just over the ridge there, works to his advantage," Pookah sagely added.

Once at the hay bales they spoke louder, for scent was stronger.

Pickens jumped up on the hay bales, walking along the top rows. "Been here." Then he jumped off, moved faster, all with him, and they streamed to the large storage shed.

"He does this all the time. I hate it. Can't get him out." Thimble ran for the large building, found the entrance he used, began digging furiously, a plume of dirt erupting behind him.

"You'll never get me," Grenville tormented him.

"That's what you think," Thimble threatened.

Weevil rode up. "Good hound. Leave it, Thimble."

Thimble looked up, disgusted, but he stopped digging.

"Come along." Weevil knew Grenville had his fun.

Pickens followed his huntsman, as did the others.

The tails on the back of Weevil's cap, down, for staff wore their caps tails down, fluttered a bit. Weevil looked up, studying the sky. February played tricks. That being the case he thought all was well. The wind, not stiff, didn't carry moisture, so with that belief he pushed down the farm road, away from the storage shed.

The creek meandered, little loops here and there, as it was an old, old creek. Young waters run straight. Following the creek, which now ran close to the farm road, he headed south.

A wooden footbridge arced over the water perhaps six feet wide at that point, wide enough for a horse or human, since many humans on foot would not have been able to jump six feet as a long jump. Truly it wasn't that wide but the banks could be slippery and a child would not be able to span it with a leap.

Weevil on HoJo nudged the Thoroughbred across the creek. Hounds, forward, noses down, moved with deliberation. The thin water vapor hovering over the creek might intensify scent.

An old deer trail wound up, for the land rose a bit.

Yvonne couldn't go farther, as the farm road became impossible, deep ruts for decades.

"Hounds are headed for Birdie Goodall's," Aunt Daniella informed her. "The only way there would be to go out Mill Ruins, turn right, turn right again at Clinton Corners, way in the back there, and go down maybe two miles. A little white sign will hang on an old post. 'Goodall.'"

"God's little acre?" Yvonne laughed, using the phrase from the play.

"No, Birdie keeps it pin-tidy but it's not convenient. The old home place of the Goodalls still stands. Never was a Goodall had a gift for money but they work hard and Birdie manages Walter's medical office, the one he shares with the other doctors. If you sit still I am betting our fox will come back. This way we can warm up." She lifted a flask with the Jefferson Hunt insignia engraved on it, reached again in her bag, pulling out Jefferson cups.

"I like the way you think." Kathleen took the cup handed to her.

Yvonne ran her window down a bit to hear. Even though opened only a crack the cold air slipped in, wafer thin. She, too, was offered a libation.

"Ah." Aunt Daniella smiled, for hounds opened loud enough for them to listen.

The whole pack together ran down the rutted farm road, which widened just enough for them but not enough for riders to gallop more than two abreast.

Reaching a garage, slate gray with red trim, they stopped. The front door to the garage was open, the house within walking distance but not particularly convenient. Hence no car was parked safely in the garage. It sat instead next to the house, under one of those roofs propped up on four legs. Why people used these things was anyone's guess. Snow and rain easily blew onto the vehicle from the open sides.

Sister held up far enough from the house so as not to be a nuisance. She figured maybe Birdie just didn't want to walk to the bigger, wooden garage except when a terrible rain or snowstorm was predicted. Then the car would be protected, except one would need to dig it out. Then again, it didn't matter where you parked a car in a snowstorm, you had to dig it out eventually.

Pansy circled the garage, followed by Dreamboat. Not a tendril of scent assailed their noses. The fox didn't go to ground. He had vanished, just vanished.

Weevil rode to the edge of the garage, looking inside to see if by chance the fox had climbed onto a shelf. Not a thing.

Well, they'd had another run, short but still good music.

"Come along," he bid his charges as they turned back to Shootrough.

Leaning over HoJo's side, Weevil checked for tracks. Raccoon tracks dotted the creekside once he again reached it, but nothing else. Yvonne and her passengers sat on the road. Upon hearing Weevil's call, then seeing him cross, Yvonne backed up to a spot where she could turn around to park by the side of the farm road.

Weevil passed the storage shed, reached the intersecting farm road, and turned for the big mill itself, two miles off. The day would try the patience of all the giving saints.

Betty and Tootie shadowed him as the field walked far enough behind the hounds, so as not to disturb them.

As the temperature dropped people flipped up the collars of their coats, which protected your neck a bit. If a hunter wore a four-in-hand tie, wider and often thicker than a thinner tie, that helped cut cold. Sister, long in the tooth and wise in the ways of keeping as warm as possible, except for her feet after an hour, wore a cashmere stock tie. Since it wasn't fuzzy it looked like a conventional stock and blocked the wind.

Heading back onto the trail flanked by thick woods, Barrister, two years old, a young entry, stopped, tail flipping. *"Hey."*

Diana checked. *"Let's go."*

This fox, not anyone they knew, had walked in the middle of the farm road, which was helpful of him.

"Okay, girls, bottoms up." Yvonne shifted into drive.

The ladies held on to their empty glasses except for Yvonne, who handed hers to Aunt Daniella.

Young and strong, the healthy red heard the commotion so he stepped on it, as did Yvonne. She had to crawl behind the last flight, while the fox ran through the creeks between the two hills, charged up the western one, took the big coop in the corner, then ran for all he was worth to the mill itself, now a mile distant, but given its size, visible.

Tootie, now in the pasture, hollered, "Tally-ho!"

Betty, also now in the right pasture, caught sight of the fellow speeding toward the mill. Urging on Magellan, her second horse, she moved up to keep him in view. He was breathtakingly beautiful.

Hounds burst onto the left pasture, speaking as one. Then Weevil took the big coop, pushed HoJo, lengthening his stride so Weevil could close with his hounds.

As there was no coop in the middle of the fence, hounds easily wiggled under but Weevil had to hurry to the end of the pasture, where there was another big coop. By the time he was over and Betty and Tootie had also cleared their obstacles, the fox zigged toward the mill then cleverly ran around it to the front, where the big waterwheel slapped, slapped, slapped.

He weaved through the trailers, zoomed up to the house, moved around it, then hit the afterburner to reach the hay shed, where he spied Hortensia's den entrance, the one on the western side. He skidded right down into it, emerging in the hay shed, where the stored orchard grass and timothy hay bales smelled like heaven.

Hounds bayed outside. Pookah, Pansy, and Baylor, another youngster, dug for all they were worth. The entrance, cleverly angled, yielded no way in.

"Well done," Weevil praised them.

"Not fair. Not fair, I can get him if I can dig a little more." Baylor believed this was possible.

"Give it up, kid." Dreamboat deeply breathed in the fresh fox scent.

Sister rode up to Weevil. "We're here. Might as well put them up. They did very well on a spotty day."

Gray rode up alongside of Sister as they walked to the mill. "Not a bad day."

"No. Not a terrific day, but hounds did well, no one hit the ground. February baffles me. Always has."

"Was reading in the paper that many of our worst snowstorms

hit us in February. Well, sooner or later have to start shoveling." He noticed the hounds, sterns up. "Happy."

"They are. They ask for so little and give so much. Same with our horses."

Gray patted Wolsey's neck. "Right, old man?"

"Right," Wolsey replied.

Once at the trailers it seemed colder than when they began. It was. Temperature plays tricks on one and the spray shooting off the paddles made it seem even colder.

Weevil dismounted, as did the staff. "Kennel up."

The riders, now on the ground, tidied up their horses, removed bridles, tossed on blankets. Freddie Thomas saw to her horse then rubbed her hands. The cold felt so raw.

As hounds stepped up onto the hound trailer, the party wagon built just for them, Barmaid, young, lagged a bit behind.

Freddie opened her trailer door, foot on the running board, stepped into the room, carpet on the floor, her extra heavy jackets hanging on a rack, a saddle rack and bridle holder on the right wall.

Nose peeping out from the blanket, Hortensia waited until Freddie's back was turned. *"Now!"*

Ewald wormed his way out from under the cozy blanket. The two foxes blasted by Freddie, Ewald brushing against her leg. She looked down in time to see the red and the gray vault out of her tack room.

Barmaid, door held for her, turned to see the escape. The odor of fresh, very fresh fox reached her nostrils. She took off.

"Foxes!" she squealed, her young voice still high.

"What are we waiting for?" Tattoo shouted gleefully.

The entire pack exploded out of the trailer, with Trinity in the rear, still a bit shy from being kicked. Weevil stood there with the door open, feeling like an idiot, as he didn't quickly shut it.

Freddie, finally in possession of herself, yelled, "Tally-ho!"

Sister ordered Gray, "Leg up, honey."

He cupped her left foot in his hand, gave her a lift, then easily swung up on Cardinal Wolsey. The horses were excited.

People stood at the trailers, dumbfounded.

"Betty, Tootie, mount up!" Sister yelled as Weevil, young and lithe, was already in the saddle, passing his master; he could, being the huntsman. The two foxes, not lacking in speed or brains, streaked through the trailers, now passed the house to hit the open space, all pistons firing.

"Follow me," Hortensia called out.

The two magical creatures, out in the open, vulnerable save for their head start, blasted for the big hay shed.

"I see them! I see them!" Barrister, Barmaid's brother, babbled with joy.

The "B"'s, young entry, never knew foxhunting could be so unpredictable. At that moment, neither did the humans.

Freddie, back at the trailers, for she'd removed her horse's bridle, stared in wonderment then glanced down at her right boot to see a few slivers of red fox fur where Ewald had brushed her.

Others mounted back up but most had horses already tied.

Weevil, right behind his hounds, horn between the buttons of his coat, remained silent. Hounds needed no encouragement.

Hortensia reached the hay shed, slid into her entrance like a baseball player belly down trying to steal third. Immediately behind her, Ewald also skidded to safety. Thank the fox in the sky that Hortensia's den was so close.

Hounds crowded around the opening.

"There's gotta be a way," a frenzied Barmaid yelped.

Diana said, *"Good work, pup. No way we can reach them."*

Weevil dismounted. Betty hurried up, taking HoJo's reins while he blew "Gone to Ground," to everyone's delight.

"What good hounds. Barmaid, my clever girl." He rubbed her head then called each hound by name for a pat and praise. He could linger, for the day was done. Taking HoJo's reins from Betty, he and Hojo walked on foot back to the trailers, hounds close to Weevil, thrilled to be close to their huntsman, and high from the wild event.

In the hay shed, Hortensia and Ewald caught their breath while Reuben, who had sought refuge there, cocked his head. *"Close call."*

"I'll say," Ewald replied, then turned to the gray vixen. *"Thank you."*

"If I were you I'd stay until the last trailer leaves. We've had enough adventure for the day." She then looked at the handsome red. *"Who might you be in my den?"*

"I had to hide. I'm Reuben."

"Where is your den?" Hortensia asked.

"I don't have a permanent den yet. I'm still looking. Right now I live above the creek, under an old dead tree, at Kingswood. There's no one there. No other foxes, no humans. Squirrels."

"There are many good places here and there's a lot to eat. Tomorrow I can show you what's here, and this is a big place. Kingswood is falling down."

He smiled, dipping his head, which was vulpine good manners.

Ewald added, *"The old red at the Mills, James, is bossy and a crab but as long as you leave him alone, it's not so bad, but he wants the mill all to himself. Say, you didn't by any chance see us jump out of the horse trailer, did you?"*

"No, but I heard the ruckus."

Both Ewald and Hortensia eagerly told their story, which involved a human who couldn't smell and who had left a bag of gummy bears in her open trailer tack room. Every detail was expressed: the tastes of the different colored bears, the round tin of shoe polish, the coats hanging up, the wind blowing the door shut. It was a good story.

As there was so much food at Mill Ruins, another fox wouldn't create problems. In fact, another fox could add to the hounds' confusion.

It was also a good story back at the trailers when staff finally got the still excited hounds loaded. Barmaid wanted to check out Freddie's trailer but she finally did get on. Freddie, meanwhile, regaled whoever was around her with Ewald brushing her as he escaped.

Finally, the people made it to Walter's breakfast, everyone laughing, beside themselves with what had happened.

The bar saw a lot of activity. Aunt Daniella, in a chair, bourbon in hand, announced in all her nine decades she had never seen anything like that, never.

Kasmir and Alida, with Yvonne, Ribbon in her lap, and Kathleen, covered the event then Yvonne inquired, "Anyone read this morning's paper yet or see the news?"

They shook their heads.

Yvonne filled them in. "One of the workers at Showoff Stables was found murdered. Found at twilight by a Central Electric repairman up in the box."

"Did they say who it was?" Alida wondered.

"Next of kin has to be notified first," Yvonne answered.

The conversation moved on, as no one thought a worker at Showoff Stables had anything to do with them.

"It's an impressive place," Kasmir noted. "Carter, have you shown Gigi your jewelry yet?"

"No. You know, often when I hold the old jewelry from families, not all of them needing money, by the way, I wonder who wore the rings, necklaces, bracelets, pins? Jewelry is so personal and it's not all women's jewelry, men have rings, watches, of course, and for some even a bracelet. Whatever I'm holding in my hand was expressive of someone's personality, their years," Carter mused, grateful to be inside. "My work can be enjoyable. I see so much."

Buddy stood in the group.

"Marion Maggiolo gets a lot of the equine jewelry, studs, cuff links, wonderful stuff." Kathleen had seen Marion's jewelry case.

Carter spoke up. "When I go to England, if I see old equine jewelry I text her. It really is her market. To hold that jewelry, to see the workmanship, makes her want to get the stuff."

Buddy joined in. "I'm glad she doesn't sell furniture. She's too good at what she does." He paused. "Kathleen, you have that good eye."

"Thank you." Kathleen smiled.

"It's nice to see you, Aunt Daniella, and Yvonne out there. You must see things we don't." Carter spoke up as Buddy didn't know what to say next to Kathleen.

"I do but I don't know what I'm seeing." She laughed at herself. "Lucky I'm with the girls."

"You must be good at it. You're driving a new, three-horse Sundowner." Yvonne named his horse trailer, as Tootie had explained to her the various brands.

"How observant." Carter smiled. "Ladies, I don't have to pay rent on a store. I do not have any employees, nor do I have an employer. Marion has to be at the top of her game. Look how big her store is and loaded with pretty much the best of everything. I can carry my inventory in my pocket."

Kathleen nodded in affirmation. "I hate to think what the rent on the 1780 House would cost me. Harry left me a wonderful store, living quarters upstairs and a good business."

"But you give the store flair." Buddy worked up the nerve for a personal compliment, being rewarded with a genuine smile.

"I don't know how you can run a retail business. I couldn't do it. I don't have the patience," Yvonne confessed.

Carter looked at Yvonne. "Neither of us has to predict fashion, but you had to show it off walking down the runway in New York. You had to have hated some of that stuff."

Yvonne, still buzzed from the day's events, laughed. "I had to wear some things, rags that I wouldn't have used to clean the car. Fashion is a ruthless business. Look what happened to Halston or Yves St. Laurent. Poor Halston. He gets bought out then, in essence, paid not to create. Well, I'm not really creative, but when we were married I ran the media business with Victor. I began to understand the power of media for good and for evil."

"You could still command the runway." Carter flirted a little.

"Yvonne, he's right. Oops, let me grab our host. I've got to find out where he bought the coffee."

"He made it," Yvonne informed Kathleen.

"Made it?" Carter's dark eyebrows knitted together.

"He buys coffee by the burlap bag. Goes down to Shenandoah Joe's and tests what they have then orders a bag. He and Alida entertain a lot. Plus he bakes, as you may know."

"A man who bakes." Kathleen held her chin lightly. "That's a real recommendation."

Buddy smiled at her. Now he knew what to bring to the store. Something freshly baked. This would take some thought.

"Before we all go our separate ways, when summer comes please come out with me on my boat. Sailing the Chesapeake is relaxing. It's funny what happens when you leave the shore. You leave your troubles behind. It's a forty-foot boat, has a cabin and a kitchen," Carter invited them.

"Are you moored near where Crawford keeps his boat, that big sailboat? If you've been to his house you've seen the photo in the hallway," Kathleen mentioned.

Carter smiled. "That is more of a ship. He's got radar, a captain, a crew. Can you imagine the expense? He is moored down in Hampton Roads. He likes to go out the mouth of the James River and into the Atlantic. My boat is powered and more modest."

"A forty-foot boat wouldn't be described as modest," Yvonne noted. "However, not having to fiddle with sails seems like an advantage to me."

"People who sail love it. It's like foxhunting, a passion," Kathleen posited. "Not that I know that much about either activity, but I am absorbing foxhunters' dedication."

"Everyone needs something that makes them happy, something not driven by profit. Well, ladies, I am glad we could share the day, me on horseback, you all in the car. Best I get back home, but don't forget a day on the Chesapeake?" He slightly bowed then turned to go.

"No one can fault his manners," Kathleen remarked.

"As long as he doesn't try to sell me jewelry, I'm fine." Yvonne smiled sardonically.

One by one, the thrilled hunters finally did leave, driving back to their barns and homes, filled with wonderment at their unique experience.

Weevil and Tootie left early to take the hounds to the kennels.

Gray left with his brother to see the new mare at Crawford's, the stunning Sugar.

Sister drove the trailer while Betty rode shotgun. As they pulled into the Roughneck Farm driveway off the old state road, another sign was tacked to a telephone pole: "Stop Bloodsports."

Next to this, side by side, a large photo of a youngish man, big black letters underneath the photo: "Elect Jordan Standish."

Sister slowed. "What the hell is this?"

"I have no idea but I bet we find out."

In the kennel, everyone fed, boys in their side, girls in theirs, Weevil and Tootie finished up their chores.

Barmaid snuggled next to Tootie on the raised bench, warm air from the overhead vent, but not too warm, wafting over the girls.

Barmaid licked Tootie then put her head on Tootie's back. *"This is the best day of my life."*

C H A P T E R   1 1

February 16, 2020   Sunday

T he Episcopal church at Greenwood was the church of the
Langhorne family, the family famous for the four beautiful
daughters, one of whom became the first woman to serve in England's Parliament, Nancy Astor. Lady Astor was also a terrific horse-
woman, as were her sisters, Phyllis being quite famous for her skills.
Irene became the Gibson Girl, the personification of the "New
Woman." Nora, also beautiful, lived a quieter life. Beautiful, hard-
riding women drew attention in the hunt field. Almost a century
later their exploits were remembered in the United States and
Great Britain. They were the kind of women Sir Alfred Munnings
painted, the sheen of their skills apparent.

Driving home from the service, the air cold but clear, Sister
turned for the Lorillard place, knowing Gray, Sam, and Aunt Daniella would be there, having gone to their church service together.

She knocked on the back door, as an old friend would do. Sam
opened the mudroom door for her. They walked through the
kitchen door to the warmth of the old wood-burning stove, its iron
potbelly looking as though it had had a good meal.

Uncle Yancy watched them from his perch over the kitchen door. Flattened on the ledge over that door, the spoiled fox was missed by the humans, despite the whiff of fox scent. They attributed it to the old towels in the corner, thinking they had old cologne smell, even old washed-out dirt. Uncle Yancy lived quite well.

"The gang's all here." Sister smiled, for Yvonne was also there. "Yvonne, aren't you Catholic?"

"I am. I went to mass and like you dropped by here."

"We know where the good times are." Sister walked across the shiny old kitchen floor, the original, to kiss Aunt Daniella on the cheek, then Yvonne. Ladies in Virginia believe in kissing, so Yvonne had adjusted but she still sometimes raised her shoulders and grinned.

"Sit down here," Aunt Daniella ordered.

"I will but first let me put this in the fridge, shepherd's pie. Perfect for a cold day, and boy, it's cold."

"Good sermon?" Sam asked.

"Was. How about yours?"

He sat by the stove. "All those Sundays after Epiphany. I lose count. What really gets me is shifting the calendar to the Gregorian." He looked to Yvonne, sitting next to him. "These chairs are old kitchen chairs. Wouldn't you all rather be in the living room with the big fireplace?"

"Not a bad idea." Gray rose, preceded them into the living room, threw more logs on that fire.

The fireplaces helped cut the electric bill. The odor of pearwood, cured hardwoods, wonderful odors, made one relax and breathe deeply.

Sam walked Aunt Daniella to her favorite chair while Gray brought her drink. Sam then attended to everyone else's drinks. Although an alcoholic he had no trouble smelling liquor, creating mixed drinks. He poured himself a tonic water with lime, one for

Sister, too, and joined the others, who had encapsulated the sermons they heard.

"See the news this morning?" Aunt Daniella asked.

"No. I was tired from yesterday and overslept. What is the outrage du jour?" Sister smiled slyly.

"Not so much outrage, for which I am grateful, but the man killed at Showoff Stables was Parker Bell."

"Really?" Sister's eyebrows raised.

"Maybe he had it coming." Sam shrugged. "That's the creep that kicked Trinity then Weevil, right?"

"Yes. Ben later told us his name. He took statements to have a record should there be any legal proceedings."

"For what?" Yvonne wondered.

"Trespassing. That's what he was shouting about. We sat, oh, seventy yards behind one of the paddocks. I didn't go down those lanes because you could hear him screaming about trespassing. Weevil kept his cool. Well, anyone know how he was killed?" Sister was curious but figured Parker Bell got his due.

"Strangled with a lead shank, a brand-new Fennell's lead shank, the commentator reported."

Aunt Daniella filled in, "Here's the strange part. His right forefinger and second finger had been cut off at the first knuckle, the wound long healed. They discovered this when they removed his gloves."

"Probably an old accident. Farm work is dangerous," Gray wisely noted. "I think, too, many of those workers or anyone's workers do odd jobs for others for cash. One gets injured over years of labor."

"Oh, remember when Yugoslavia blew up after Tito died?" Sister thought back as the others nodded. "It was Muslim vs. Christian. I'm sure there were other hatreds as well but that was the one that made the news over and over again. It was quite savage."

"There is such a thing as an enlightened dictator, and I guess Marshall Tito was one. When he was alive nothing like that happened." Aunt Daniella relished her bourbon. "If there isn't some unifying principle or strongman, things fly apart."

"In our case the unifying principle is the Constitution," Sam offered.

"We hope." Yvonne smiled, as she had her doubts that people even read the Constitution anymore.

"Well, we took you off the track," Gray apologized.

"That's what happens when we all get together." Sister opened her hands, palms up. "We are all over the map."

"Then let's go back to the former Yugoslavia." Sam untied his shoes, slipping them off.

"Lots of killing. I saw a photo, it was in *The Manchester Guardian* newspaper. I remember that and it showed Christian dead soldiers, facedown. Their forefinger and second finger had been cut off. Everyone."

"Why mutilate a corpse?" Yvonne shook her head lightly.

"You keep hating them after they're dead." Gray was right about that. "That's why law enforcement people study the victim as they do. Was it a clean killing? Get them out of the way. Or was it hate?"

"Gross but human, I guess." Sister then added, "The point of the mutilation was that they couldn't make the sign of the cross. Also a signal to other Christians that the Muslims would give them no quarter. This hatred was well repaid by the Christians when they got their hands on any Muslims. Never ends, does it?"

"No," Yvonne said with finality.

"Didn't the murdered man call Kasmir an Arab?" Gray frowned. "I remember Kasmir laughing about that and saying he corrected him. He wasn't a goddamned Arab, he was a goddamned Muslim."

"No way Kasmir would kill the lout." Aunt Daniella appreciated the odor of the pearwood.

"Of course not, but people being who and what they are, some will gossip about it." Sister shrugged. "Let's forget Showoff Stables. What about the signs popping up? 'Stop Foxhunting,' 'End Bloodsports'?"

Sam said, "I've seen the signs. Just a thought, but what if Gigi Sabatini is behind this? It was his man who was killed, his man who blew up when hounds crossed into the farm."

"He couldn't be that stupid." Sister's voice rose.

"No doubt, but Parker Bell was his man. Perhaps there is anger there," Gray remarked.

Yvonne thought a moment. "Tootie said Ben Sidell called Weevil to ask some questions."

"To change the subject, how about those two foxes in Freddie Thomas's tack room?" Sister laughed.

This happy subject delighted them for nearly an hour until finally Sam couldn't stand it. He heated up the shepherd's pie and they all ate a shepherd's dinner, a perfect meal for a cold day.

Sister didn't get home until five. Gray stayed with Sam and Aunt Daniella was driven home by Yvonne. Sister heard her car drive down to Tootie's place after that. She thought it good that mother and daughter were becoming close.

"Where were you?" Golly indignantly asked. *"I could do with something from the refrigerator. No canned food."*

"O la." Rooster rolled his eyes.

The complaint evaporated as Sister actually heated up leftover chicken soup, pouring it on the dogs' kibble as well as Golly's. Two shepherd pies rested on a refrigerator shelf for the next day. Sister shared her food with her pets. Not all of it but enough to spoil them rotten.

The phone rang.

"Sister."

"O.J. How good to hear your voice. Have a good hunt yesterday?"

"I did, but I'm calling you about something else. This is, I don't know, perplexing? Anyway, last night the Munnings painting of Mrs. Oliver Filley was stolen from Delores Buckingham's. Her mother was a friend of Lady Astor. She and her husband would take a hunt box in England for most of the season. Anyway, her mother and father became friends with Sir Alfred Munnings. I think they met him shortly before the First World War. Became fast friends. This is bizarre. Delores inherited the painting decades ago, upon her parents' death."

"Funny, I was thinking about Nancy Astor today because I go to her church, the one she grew up in. It's so simple. Nothing extraneous and Mirador is across the road almost." She named Lady Astor's childhood home, kept in fine condition. What was missing was the nonstop activity of those days: all the people, horses, long parties since distances took so much time to cover. Once you got somewhere you stayed a few days if not weeks. People drew close together and those four girls met so many people, played games constantly, and like most children of the time, especially girls, economic and political conditions were not explained to them. The marvel of it was that Nancy Langhorne became so political and so wisely married Waldorf Astor.

"I remember. So here's the thing," O.J. said, using one of her common expressions.

"Is this about Munnings?"

"Is this some kind of obsession with foxhunting?"

"Munnings foxhunted," Sister calmly replied.

"Not sidesaddle."

"Not that we know." Sister had to smile.

"The black market. Has to be some kind of black market," O.J. mused.

"I agree. And it is peculiar that these thefts are taking place so close together. So if it is the black market, perhaps the work is going to the same place. Best to take them all at once."

A pause followed this. "I don't know. What if this is someone obsessed with either Munnings or women riding sidesaddle?"

"The only answer to that will be if another artist's sidesaddle painting is stolen."

"Well—yes." O.J. considered that.

From there they compared Saturday's hunt notes. O.J. loved the story of the two stowaways in Freddie's trailer tack room.

Then Sister gave her the story of Parker Bell kicking Trinity, and then being murdered.

"If my father were alive he would have something to say about those missing fingers. Has to mean something."

"I suppose, but not to us. Here's an unrelated thought. Ready?"

"I'm always ready." O.J. egged her on. "Never know what you'll come up with."

"Joint meets are a lot of work and you need to prod people to travel or you need to prod them to host guests. It's great fun but I think the Leishmaniasis scare kind of damaged that."

This was their response to a Mideastern disease that attacked dogs but could pass to people. The uproar was back in 1999. All clubs had to get blood drawn, and depending on the results hounds were supposed to be killed or removed from the pack. Apart from some hunts putting down good hounds, it was a kind of panic that played itself out. Is there Leishmaniasis? Yes. Is it under control? Yes, and foxhounds are not singular vectors for it, although some did have those titers.

But the scare was intense. The Master of Foxhounds Association's vigilance killed joint meets because people feared putting their packs together. There are still joint meets but not like in the old days because packs aren't often blended for the day. New foxhunters have no memory of that and don't realize how important joint meets are.

However, Sister and O.J. had those memories and they mourned all those fabulous joint meets where packs could be put together, sometimes three or even four packs at a time. The music was stupendous.

O.J. agreed. "Everything changed and I still draw blood."

"I do, too, but let's do this: We won't call this a joint meet but we will call our stomping buddies and go to one another's hunts. If anyone wants to come they have to tell us so the hunt can prepare. But laid-back."

"Okay. Who do you have in mind?" O.J. asked.

"Deep Run, Red Rock, Bull Run, Big Sky, and the two of us. Maybe Marion Thorne at Genesee Valley if she can get away. That's the real difficulty, getting away, and Marion hunts the hounds. She is gifted."

O.J., knowing the Upstate New York huntsman, readily agreed. "Don't you think huntsman are born, not made?"

"Yes, but I feel that way about so many things, be it the arts or medicine or being called to God. Priests and pastors feel called. One should never mock that."

"People do that. Can you imagine if a schoolteacher suggested people are called?"

"You can teach people some things. I mean, you can give people the demands of hunting hounds and a reasonably intelligent person will do it, but that doesn't mean they'll be good at it and in time the pack will unravel. Same for a congregation, I suppose."

"Boy, is that the truth. Takes a couple of years to pull hounds back together. How did we get off on this?"

"The way we get off on everything. So let's just ask our girl-friends, a girls joint gathering, and go for it. I'm not being sexist but I do think it would be so much fun if the hunts get together. All of us women masters."

"That's a good idea. But I don't think we should advertise that this is girl power."

"Of course not, O.J. Anyway, men like to look at women. Those ladies are good-looking. The boys won't know what hit them."

"What might be easier is to all convene without our packs, think of the hauling distances, at one hunt. Each year we change the location. Something a little different," O.J. suggested.

"Good idea, sugarpie. It's always a great idea to dazzle men."

Peals of laughter followed this, then O.J. inquired, "And how is Gray?"

"One of the sweetest men who ever lived. We don't meddle in each other's lives. We enjoy what we do together. Then again, it helps to be older."

"Does. Okay. I'll call you back tomorrow and we can make a list of who calls whom."

"Such good English," Sister teased her.

"After all the money my father spent on my education, I'd better be correct." The Kentucky master smiled, remembering her father, a powerful and driven man who loved his children.

"Okay. We're on," Sister said.

"We're on."

C H A P T E R 1 2

February 17, 2020   Monday

President's Day seemed like a cheat to Sister. When she was in school, Lincoln's birthday, February 12, was a full holiday, as was Washington's birthday, February 22.

Sunrise sneaked in earlier about a minute a day. She hated to rise in the dark but like most country people, she did. Then again, those people sitting in traffic often got up before the sun.

Today Tootie and Weevil fed the hands, cleaned the kennels, then had the day off. Sister would check at sundown. She enjoyed being with the hounds just as she enjoyed hearing the horses in their stalls rattle their buckets because they wanted to be fed right that minute. Sometimes they'd rattle their buckets for play. Keepsake had a large rubber ball hanging from the beam across his stall. He'd bat it around with his nose, making her laugh.

Having finished up in the stable she flipped up the sheep fleece collar on her ancient leather jacket, also lined in fleece, to walk back to the house flanked by Raleigh and Rooster.

The three of them happily entered the kitchen, the warmth enveloping. Mondays, errand day, gave Sister the chance to visit friends as well as pick up noodles, cat food, what was needed for the house.

Her cellphone, on the kitchen table, beeped. She couldn't get into the habit of carrying a phone with her but she did remember to put it into the car when she drove.

"Hello?"

"Sister, Marion." Marion Maggiolo's distinct voice filled her ear.

Marion owned Horse Country in Warrenton, Virginia, a store filled with treasures, be it old silver or a tweed coat that could protect you from the wind on those bye days.

"Good to hear your voice."

"O.J. called me about the theft of the Mrs. Oliver Filley painting. That makes three."

"Without any idea what's going on."

"I called Nancy Bedford first." She named the head of the Museum of Hounds & Hunting. "She said she'd talked to each of the painters that the museum highlighted in 2018. Larry Wheeler, Linda Volrath, Booth Malone, Sally Moren, Reverend Michael Tang, Christine Cancelli, Joanne Mehl, Morgen Kilbourn. Just out of curiosity she wanted to talk to working artists. The one idea that seemed to be paramount was given the price of Munnings's work, this has to be about money. She also asked did they know of modern sidesaddle paintings."

"And? You are so smart, I wouldn't have thought of that." Sister was so often surprised by Marion's creative intelligence.

"The Andre Pater one. It's quite large, of Catherine Clay-Neal on her horse, Dude. He's 18.1 hands."

"Wish there were more modern sidesaddle paintings," Sister said.

"Yes, but then again, nobody is selling their work for millions." A pause followed this. "Linda mentioned Heather St. Clair Davis, the late English painter. Given that Davis passed in 1999, Linda did say her works were fetching higher prices. No surprise, but also no sidesaddle. All those wonderful hunting scenes but no focus on a lady riding sidesaddle."

"Not many paintings of people driving carriages either." Sister walked to the stove to turn on water for tea. "That is a beautiful sport. Can you imagine the cost for the tack and harness alone, much less the carriage?"

"That's why only rich people do it." Marion laughed. "You know the rich are going through a period of being demonized, but so many old beautiful things are saved by people with great resources. You'd think others would have the sense to be grateful."

"Envy is a low emotion." Sister pulled a heavy mug out of the cupboard. "Envy and spite, which reminds me, before I forget: Someone is putting up posters against foxhunting."

"There are people out there against just about any sport involving animals." Marion laughed. "Back to the thefts. Do you know anyone at Sotheby's? They might have an idea?"

"No, but I'll tell our sheriff. They'll talk to him and I expect someone on Sotheby's staff knows these works well, an early twentieth-century expert, sporting art expert. They have everything. Gives me an idea. I'll ask O.J. to call Cross Gate, the art auction house in Lexington."

"I'll call The Jockey Club, I have an old friend there, and you call your sheriff and then O.J. There has to be some tiny idea, some odd fact that can help us figure it out." Marion's brain was spinning. "Well, who is getting the most money right now? Sporting art, I mean?"

"Munnings."

"Sorry, Sister, I meant a living painter. Horses, not dogs, although some of those paintings are rising in value. I guess that's why the American Kennel Club now has a museum. I really don't know."

"A living painter." Sister thought. "Andre Pater. Much of his work, depending on the size of the canvas, sells for six figures. His draftsmanship is superb, as is Heather St. Clair Davis's, but that's my response, someone else might differ."

"Andre Pater paints silks that look as though you could touch them. Kind of like the great Renaissance painters. They all were in thrall to fabrics." Marion relished fine painting and fabrics, especially fabrics, which is why she made two trips a year to Europe, for fabrics.

"Booth Malone is pretty good with silks, but you know more than I do, Marion. For one thing, everyone comes into the store. But you know the first theft was that extraordinary painting of Munnings's wife, standing next to Issac, the dappled gray. And it was owned by Crawford Howard, who unfortunately bragged about it. Whatever this is, it started right here in central Virginia."

"If it had simply been Crawford, I would hazard a guess that he offended someone so this would be elegant revenge, but now we're up to three. Whoever this is has impeccable connections. One has to know where treasures rest."

"Marion, if this were just money, why not steal one of those breathtaking Munnings of the racetrack? Why sidesaddle?"

"It is peculiar. Well, let me track down my calls, you track down yours. Get O.J. to go over to Cross Gate. Those gallery owners surely have some ideas."

"Right. Hey, if you have a navy blue stock tie with tiny white bird's-eye dots, send it down."

"Okay."

Sister hung up, poured the hot water over the tea ball she'd filled with the phone tucked under her chin, no mean feat.

Raleigh and Rooster curled in their large fuzzy beds. Golly patrolled the counter.

"*Yellow Bronco. Betty,*" the cat announced.

Not three minutes later, Betty opened the mudroom door, knocked on the kitchen door, then opened it. "Your favorite person."

"Indeed." Sister walked back to the stove to boil the water, which was still hot. "English Breakfast? Irish? Name it."

"Whatever you're having." Betty opened the cabinet, took out a mug with a rabbit painted on it. "Where did you get this?"

"Ashland Bassets; Diana Dutton sent it down."

Once seated, Betty wrapped her hands around the cup. "Spring is close but it's so cold."

" 'O, wind, if winter comes/can spring be far behind'?" Sister quoted Shelley.

"Do they teach Shelley in English anymore? I read him twelfth grade."

"Something tells me if it's difficult or exceptionally beautiful, no, it won't be taught; then again, we should ask Charlotte Norton at Custis Hall. Anyway, you aren't here to talk about poets or spring. What's cooking?"

"News." Betty beamed. "Will be on the news tonight but I have my sources."

"I'm sure you do, which means you ran into Ben."

"Don't spoil my moment." Betty took a sip. "The oaf that was killed at Showoff had a criminal record."

"Did Sabatini know?"

"That's who told Ben when he questioned him. Sabatini hires former prisoners, nothing vile, but stuff like petty theft, growing dope, stealing cars. No armed robbery or murder."

"And shall I assume his record will be discussed or printed in the paper?"

Betty nodded. "Illegal gambling. Cards. Betting on football games, the spread, that sort of thing. Anyway, he served his time. That's the story, or that's the story I heard."

"Was he married?"

"No mention of that or next of kin."

"What about the severed fingers?" Sister's curiosity was climbing.

"Now, that's what is perhaps significant, or what Ben knew but kept from others until he spoke to Sabatini."

"Betty, as our sheriff he is not obliged to tell us anything."

Betty thought about this. "No, but he does have to ask questions and he did. It seems the amputated fingers may be what one did as a young man once accepted into a gambling gang. It was the mark of belonging, so they always wore gloves. Gangs often have some mark or tattoo."

"If gambling had been his road to prison, you think he might have made money or the gang would take care of him. Those crime families do take care of their own, I think in the old days and maybe even today."

"You would think so, but Mr. Sabatini . . . I can't get used to calling a man Gigi . . . anyway, he believes this is a warning. He never mentioned Parker Bell except to Ben."

Neither woman spoke, then Betty said, "So maybe he fell back into illegal betting? Being choked to death is violent. Whoever kills you has to get close."

Sister grimaced. "Get close and carry a lead shank."

"Maybe it was someone who knows horses."

"Maybe, or maybe he grabbed one off a stall hook. Parker Bell could have been killed in the morning or anytime, and the person who did it could have gotten away easily. Like our coyote, maybe he slipped through the woods. And what if the killer wore a hoodie? Wouldn't see his face. If a person has time to plan a murder I expect it's easily committed. Again, all those TV shows about killers being caught makes for good TV, but I think the number of unsolved cases is . . . well, still unsolved."

Betty nodded then took another long sip. "Ben had to thoroughly question Kasmir, of course."

"Dot the i's and cross the t's. Don't you think so much of police work is tedious?"

"It would be for me, but I do think we won't be hunting from Welsh Harp anytime soon."

"No," Sister agreed, then relayed her conversation with Marion.

"Certainly seems to be an eventful February." Betty shook her head. "Fortunately, neither Crawford's painting or Bell's murder have anything to do with us."

"No," Sister again agreed. "It is a little unnerving that these events have happened here. So close."

C H A P T E R   1 3

February 18, 2020   Tuesday

Pattypan Forge, thick stone walls still intact, the windows long ago broken, had stood since the end of the eighteenth century and would stand for many more. The forge was in use until shortly after World War II, when roads improved dramatically as well as needs changing. Fewer and fewer Virginians, or Americans wherever they lived, needed a wheel well beaten out or a broken axle either replaced or made anew in the heat of the huge furnace. The hand skills, the ability to fix such large objects, faded.

The forge, part of After All Farm, remained untouched. The woods grew around it. The old farm road could be discerned mostly because those deep old wagon-wheel ruts also survived the centuries. The forge provided good living for owls, nesting birds, and one older vixen, Aunt Netty, who had transformed the huge interior to her liking. Exits and entrances both inside and from the outside to the inside dotted the floor, for portions of the slate floor had cracked up. Thick slate can withstand weight but harsh weather damaged the floors under those huge windows. Aunt Netty, fastidious, pulled old towels, some stolen dog toys, and even turkey feathers into her underground rooms. The wind might slide through the trees, rain blow through the broken windows, but that well-built roof and the thick walls made Pattypan desirable. Her towels and other finds kept her den warm.

Sister Jane thought Pattypan Forge a brooding presence. The story-high paned windows provided light critical before electricity. A few still had the heavy shutters to protect them.

Those shutters kept out rain, snow, and wind. This was the most desirable place to have a nest or a den. Most of the broken windows were on the west side, the glass bits long pulverized. The sound of wind slicing through the windows sounded like an eerie whisper or scream depending on the force.

The path to the forge, even though opened at the beginning of hunt season, right after Labor Day, closed up quickly enough thanks to creepers that grew while one slept, fallen branches, whatever was blowing in the wind, literally.

Sister never liked Pattypan Forge, it reminded her of how good work can be forgotten, and she didn't like it much today as she sat on Matador, a former steeplechaser. He's seen it all and done it all. They got along famously.

Diana, nose down in one of Aunt Netty's entrances, chided her. *"Come out, Aunt Netty. We can talk."*

"You can jump out that far window. I gave you a run. I'm not giving you another."

The pack, surrounding the entrance, sniffed; Tinsel dug a bit.

Weevil, dismounted, stood over the hole and blew "Gone to Ground!"

"Stop that infernal noise!" the old red vixen complained.

"Good hounds. Good hounds." Weevil tucked his horn between the top two buttons of his heavy coat, walked out, the pack following.

Dreamboat turned and yelled, *"You're a step slow, Aunt Netty. Better watch out."*

"I can outrun you, but you all are stupid. I will always win."

"You are mean as snakeshit," the dog hound cursed her.

Fast as a flash, Aunt Netty popped her head up and spit at Dreamboat.

It so surprised him, he turned and quickly rejoined the pack as Weevil called. He kept his humiliation to himself.

The small weasels . . . minks, really . . . observed all this from their dens.

Aunt Netty heard them giggling. *"Why don't you all go back to Hangman's Ridge? It was so quiet when you moved out."*

Hangman's Ridge, the high plateau behind Sister Jane's farm, she owned it, was where the colonists hanged those convicted of serious crimes: murder, rape, or large theft. The minks thought of it as their summer home. The forge offered better quarters during the winter.

Weevil, mounted, pointed toward Broad Creek, which would take a bit of bushwhacking to reach. The trail, narrow, finally opened onto a wide, cleared trail above the creek, flowing vigorously thanks to the recent rains and snow. He turned the pack south, toward the big estate's mansion and outbuilding. He'd hunt the hounds back to the trailers, all parked on the far side of the covered bridge. This fixture, full of game, proved a treasure, plus the Bancrofts, the owners, having hunted for most of their eight decades, appreciated hunting. After All was a fox-friendly fixture. Rabbits, skunks, bobcats liked it, too, along with the occasional traveling bear.

"Get your fox," he called in his deep baritone, a sonorous voice.

Pansy moved with more determination, her tail flipping. Trident, next to her, mirrored her behavior. Within a minute all the hounds pressed but didn't open. A huntsman's hopes are raised with this behavior, so, too, for the riders who know hunting. Hounds have something, but what? Is it a fading line that grows stronger? Is it fox scent or something else? Foxhounds can and do hunt coyote, bobcat. Deer, rabbits, skunks, raccoons, and groundhogs should be ignored. A bear presents a judgment call. While legitimate game and game that can move faster than a city person, one would think that bear can climb a tree, fine but not so fine; bear can also stop, wait for hounds, and then swing. The creature is so powerful it can snap a neck with one blow, break a human's rib cage with one blow. Best to respect bears.

When hounds do not speak but continue with determination, the huntsman must follow. No one truly knows what hounds are tracking until the hound opens. Then the line is heating up, the game is legitimate. Off you go.

Sister watched a few "J" youngsters out today doing great, working with the pack. She allowed time for mistakes in the first season. Same as first-graders missing a letter in the alphabet, you calmly wait. They'll get it right.

"A visiting fox. Let's go." Cora pushed Pansy and Trident on, as they were still a bit hesitant.

Trotting forward, the hounds moved as one. Just where this was leading was anybody's guess; but then, it's always anybody's guess.

Nothing enticing, as all rode along the creekbed. Reaching the covered bridge, hounds stopped then dropped down to Broad Creek.

"Maybe a half hour," Diana stated as a first snowflake lazed down.

All, noses down, worked to decide in which direction the fox, Comet, who they knew, was traveling, for he had doubled back.

Finally, Trident called out, *"Heading home."*

This meant the hounds' home as well as Comet's, who had a den under the dependency in which Tootie lived.

Hounds opened, now on the west side of Broad Creek. Weevil trotted through the covered bridge, dropping down to the right onto the pasture. He squeezed Midshipman, a young Thorough-bred he was training for Sister, a gorgeous fellow with a sensible mind and that great Thoroughbred heart, and they surged.

Sister followed through the bridge, waited a moment for Weevil to decide whether to follow closely behind his hounds or to follow the farm path through this pasture, which then turned into a cleared path in woods abutting Roughneck Farm, Sister's property. At that point a stiff hog's back jump allowed one to get over handily into her wildflower meadow, all dormant now but decent footing.

If he followed hounds closely he'd wind up in the woods, fighting his way through. Hounds knew they were on Comet but Weevil did not. As three foxes lived at Roughneck Farm in relative splendor, there were three destinations. The young huntsman felt certain it had to be a Roughneck fox but he wouldn't know which one until hounds hit the wildflower meadow. One fox lived in the apple orchard behind the kennels, Inky. Comet luxuriated under Tootie's small house. Georgia would go over Hangman's Ridge to the schoolhouse at Foxglove Farm if she had time. Hangman's Ridge creeped out everyone, even the foxes. But if weather impeded progress or high wind came out of nowhere, and it seemed to do that around Hangman's Ridge, Georgia would race to the back porch at the main house, under which there was a den for just such purposes. The problem with that was it set off the hounds in the kennels, the two house dogs carried on, and the cat sat in the window discussing canine shortcomings at a high decibel level.

One time, a friend of Georgia's during cubbing miscalculated the territory and hounds' speed, having been asleep under one of the apple trees when hounds came out of the kennels. Knowing the den, he made straight for it, but not before running through the garden shed by that porch. Tools fell off the walls, a wheelbarrow was knocked over, and a few highly motivated hounds smashed right through the paned-glass windows.

Much as a huntsman tries to keep his or her mind on hounds,

such memories or stories of same do intrude. No one wants hounds with cut pads, or worse, a wrecked building that belongs to your boss or any landowner.

Midshipman and Weevil flew as the tiny snowflakes grew fatter. As the cold bit his face he realized this storm was not predicted on The Weather Channel but it was here and growing stronger.

Such thoughts filtered through Sister's mind as well. The open pasture lent itself to a hard gallop, which came to a severe slow-down once into the woods. She could make out Betty's black coat as Betty was on a deer path winding due north. Tootie, on her left, raced in the open, heading for a jump at the far end of the wild-flower meadow. If hounds and fox turned left she would be there. If they turned right she could make up the ground.

Comet, comfortably ahead, wasn't taking chances. He picked up speed, forgoing evasive measures. Just get home.

Giorgio, the fastest hound along with Dragon, who was in the kennel, ran perhaps two hundred yards behind the sleek, healthy gray, full winter coat attesting to his well-being.

A few yards behind Giorgio ran Bachelor, a first-year entry. He had the engine, so no reason to hunt behind an older and wiser hound. At least that's what he thought.

The hogs' back loomed ahead. No problem for hounds, even though the footing was beginning to get slippery, not evil but slip-pery. The snow fell heavily but one could still see.

All the hounds leapt over the hogs' back. Given the pace, no hound wanted to wriggle under the three-board fence. Jump and go. Weevil did just that as Betty, ahead of him on the right, negoti-ated a fallen tree, slowing her down, but she then made it over a simple thin three-rail fence. Outlaw, her hunter of many years, did not favor an airy fence, but she squeezed, clucked, and moved her hands up his neck. He figured this wasn't the time to have a mo-ment, anyway; hounds were in full cry and he was a true hunt horse.

Comet streaked across the wildflower field, easily viewed by hounds, staff, and the field, his tail straight out behind him. Reaching the other side of the big field, he easily scrunched under the lowest board on the fence, blasted to the back of the clapboard cottage, a small covered porch leading to the back door, and shot under the latticework under the porch floor first, ducking into the big den under there.

"What are you doing?" Target, the red who lived there as well as Comet, asked, then he heard the hounds really close. *"You have no sense."*

"How was I to know they'd hunt on a snow day? The pickings were great at After All. And those garbage cans are a cinch to open."

Target cocked his head. *"Humans can't tell the weather. They only know what's happening when it's on them. And as for the treats over there, you'll lose your hunting skills. You can't live off human largess without getting lazy."*

This conversation was interrupted by Giorgio, nose under the base of the porch, white-painted lattice hiding the open space under the outside porch.

"Almost! I almost had you."

All the hounds, now there, hollered at once.

Target growled. *"Shut up. I can't hear myself think."*

The field, standing only ten yards away, heard the furious barking from the fox.

"Drama." Sister laughed.

"Okay, let's kennel up." Weevil walked to the kennels, where Betty and Tootie quickly dismounted to open the big draw pen doors. They'd have to go back to pick up the hound trailer, but no use going all the way back when hounds had run to the kennels.

"Folks, that's our day," Sister announced. "If you want to put your horses in a pasture here or tie them to the hitching post, we'll have breakfast in the house. You all know Edward has the flu, so there's no breakfast at After All." Looking up at the sky she added, "If you want to ride back then drive your trailer here, that's fine, too. Won't take you all that long and this stuff doesn't look like it will let up. Maybe it's best to go while you can still see. You can also leave your horse, borrow my truck, drive back, and drive your trailer here. You can pile in Betty's Bronco, too. We'll fit everyone in."

Betty helped put hounds up then came outside to take her horse and Tootie's into the barn. Tootie, still inside the kennels, looked out the window.

"What do you think?" Weevil asked.

"Better I put Midshipman in his stall now. I can drive you back to After All. I'll call the Bancrofts to see if they mind if we leave the hound trailer there. Driving the hound trailer back then getting back yourself might not be so great, especially if the wind picks up."

He agreed, so Tootie walked out, taking Midshipman to the barn.

Within forty minutes most of the club members had arrived for the breakfast, their trailers now parked around the barn. A few people not wishing to brave an increasing storm loaded up to drive straight home.

The house, full of people in tweed coats, as was proper for a hunt breakfast, talked, drank, ate, and did not observe Golly snagging a morsel from their plate if their backs were turned.

Raleigh pretended to be appalled. *"One of these days you'll get caught."*

"Never," the calico bragged.

Gray acted as bartender, with Sam making sure all the ladies had seats. He drove Yvonne today, as he wasn't riding a horse for Crawford. The two of them chattered the whole time. Sam, marvelous on a horse, answered all her questions and told her if she felt ready they would ride closing hunt together.

Yvonne enthused, happy with the day. "Don't the grays have sweeter faces?"

Sam nodded in agreement, tonic water with lime in hand, and sat next to her as they recounted the hunt. Other men, including

Walter, felt Sam was falling for Yvonne. Walter wondered if Yvonne felt an attraction to Sam. Then again, Yvonne was only a year out of a hideous divorce.

Buddy Cadwalder, tall, lean, moved among the group. He'd come down from Philadelphia to meet with Carter Nicewonder about potential clients for his exquisite furniture, but also to hunt with Jefferson and see Kathleen. He didn't want to be too obvious. Carter teased him.

As the gathering grew warmer, more laughter, many on their second drink or second hot coffee, a knock on the front door took Sister away from the group.

"I'll get that, honey," Gray offered.

"I'm halfway there."

Opening the door, the cold, stepping over the threshold, she beheld John Wickline, Animal Control, whom she knew from his kennel inspections once a year.

"John, come in here. Have a drink, a sandwich. Helps you to fight the cold."

Embarrassed, he shook his head. "Sister," he handed her a paper, "you've been cited for cruelty to animals. I must inspect not just the kennels but every single animal on this farm. County regulations."

"Good Lord. Come in, anyway."

He stepped in as she called for Gray. "Gray, get him something warm to eat and drink then meet me in the library. If anyone asks, tell them I won't be long." She smiled at John. "Everybody in the room knows you anyway, especially those who put in hours at the animal shelter. Come on, John. Whatever this is, we can work it out."

Gray joined them, plate in one hand, a hot toddy in the other. "This isn't really an alcoholic drink. The alcohol is burned off. It just keeps you warm." Then he sat in a chair while John took a sip.

"I shouldn't really be here but I wanted to give you time, so I could return tomorrow. I'll bring my new assistant. We really must inspect every single animal on the farm. County ordinance." He repeated this fact. "It will take most of the day."

"Yes, it will," Sister agreed. "At least you will have inspected our kennels, which you do once a year."

"Because you call me and ask me to do it." He looked from Sister to Gray. "I know your practices are the best, but if I'm given a summons I must follow up. I am sorry."

"Am I allowed to know who filed the grievance?"

"No. County rules. Anyone can accuse anybody and not have to come forward, the idea being you would retaliate."

"They are right about that, John. I'd slap them right across the face." Then she laughed.

Finishing his drink and his sandwich in two bites, John asked, "What time is convenient?"

"Whenever you get to work. Call me, though, in case the roads are bad. We have no idea how long this snow will last."

"If it's bad, we'll reschedule." He stood, as did Sister and Gray.

Both walked John to the door, Gray took his coat off the hook. "You'll need this." Then he held it so the bulky fellow could slide his arms in.

Waiting a moment, John couldn't help himself. "You know, there's no common sense anymore. New people. New people in love with rules. Just no common sense."

"I couldn't agree more. Don't worry about it, we'll have a good time. As you know, my animals have vivid personalities."

As he left, Sister and Gray looked at each other. Then she touched his hand as they turned to go back to the gathering.

"It's possible. Usually there's an element of revenge in something like this. All anyone has to do is come down the drive to see how healthy and happy all the critters are."

"You know, honey, I wonder if we can take foxhunting for

granted anymore. Can we take anything for granted? Even dog shows?"

"If Miss America has been demoted, I suppose anything can be," Gray responded.

She laughed. "Was the old bathing suit parade demeaning? I don't know. Men like to look at women. Never did a thing for me, but then again, if there were a male equivalent, I'd be riveted." A pause. "I would compare every man to you. He couldn't possibly come up to the mark."

They walked back to the dining room, arm in arm. Sister would call Betty, Tootie, and Weevil, asking them to come, be ready tomorrow for whatever. No point taking a chance of someone overhearing about the summons. That old game of telephone demonstrates human nature better than decades of university studies.

Carter was telling Freddie the best small art museums in England. She responded with good small ones in the United States, like the Brinton Museum in Big Horn, Wyoming. She then looked out the window, excusing herself. Best to get home.

As the breakfast unwound, people leaving three or four at a time, each time the door opened, the snow was deeper.

C H A P T E R   1 4

February 19, 2020   Wednesday

"I remember him." John Wickline smiled, bent down to rub Asa's ears.

"Retired now. My 'A' line is a great one. So now his job is to teach the youngsters their ABC's. He goes on, walks with them." Sister looked down at the hound senior citizen. "He crawls into your heart."

Tootie and Weevil stood at a distance while Sister walked John through the kennels, showed him the outer runs, all of which he knew, but she figured better safe than sorry. Both of them walked outside the high chain-link fence. The Animal Control officer could clearly see the condos, now outfitted for winter. The condos, large boxes, twelve feet by twelve feet by twelve feet, sat up on heavy raised posts. Each condo was insulated as well as being filled with deep fresh straw. The straw was changed weekly. The roofs were peaked. They, too, were insulated inside. In winter a heavy door reduced the opening size to retain heat. A sloping walk-up, thirty degrees, had inch-wide raised strips across the grade to make getting in and out easier, especially if icy. All had a wraparound porch.

The outdoor runs fed into the indoor housing but many of the hounds preferred their condos; there were two in each big run. Part of the appeal was a hound could easily walk outside under the stars and inhale deeply. All those night hunter scents filled the air.

The snow, three inches, fluffy, contrasted with the white condos, a bit of green trim around the doors for effect. Tootie and Weevil picked those yards clean as the sun came up.

Although picked daily in the afternoon, they wanted the yards to be as clean as possible, which they were.

Now inside, Sister reminded John of the medical room as she opened the door. "When we do suffer an injury or need an operation, say having a tumor removed, it can be done here. Our vet comes out. If it's complicated, we take the hound to Dr. Ligon. Rarely do we need to do that."

"I remember when you remodeled the inside of these kennels. I'd just taken the job. You could operate on a person in here."

Sister laughed. "Cost a lot less. I remember you wondering why we would put in a steel operating table, purchase instruments, an oxygen mask, the big refrigerator. Over time, seeing what can happen to anyone's dog, I realized not having to transport an animal in distress really helps. Then again, Dr. Ligon really helps, too.

"She's the best. Don't know if you recall my now-deceased hound, Lilybee. She had gotten caught between two tree limbs, tree on the ground after a storm, and dislocated her hip. The poor girl was in so much pain and we had to take her to the clinic. This would not be a simple fix. Well, Jessica," she named Dr. Ligon by her first name, "wired her back together, reattached ligaments, then we had to keep her from running around, so Lilybee came here to the recovery room, and recover she did. What a sweet girl. Anyway, a hound can run sixty miles on a fast day. No more hunting for her once the bandages and supports came off. I used her for a schoolmarm. And . . ." Sister opened the medical room back out to the indoor girls' dormitory. "Look here. Come on and show yourself, Tootsie."

John looked down at Tootsie, who looked up with her soft brown eyes. "Hello, Tootsie." Then he chuckled. "Do you ever call Tootie Tootsie?"

Tootie and Weevil, steps behind them in case a hound needed to be brought out, giggled.

Sister turned around. "If I did that to you, would you hunt on all fours?"

"I do whatever my master tells me. That's foxhunting, right?" The beautiful young woman grinned. "Mr. Wickline, here." She handed him a small treat, as both she and Weevil usually carried a pocketful.

He took the treat and held it as Sister opened the door. Tootsie daintily took the treat then scampered back through the door to the larger living quarters, the indoor ones with raised benches.

"Granddaughter on the male side. The boys look a great deal like Lilybee, too. While you're here, would you like to see the medical records?"

"Show me where they are. I don't need to read anything. And I apologize again for the time this is taking."

"You're the one who has to write this up. It will take you more time than it takes us. Which reminds me, I thought you were bringing an assistant."

"Didn't show up for work. No work ethic anymore."

Sister beckoned Weevil and Tootie to her. "And here I have two young people who live to work."

"Madam," Weevil always correctly addressed the master in public as "Master" or "Madam." "This isn't work."

"Thank you." She did love those two.

"I think we've covered the kennels. Did I miss anything?"

"Come on, let me show you the records, then we can go to the stables." She walked him to the office, warmer than the actual kennels.

Kennels should have some warmth in cold weather but if a

master allows the kennels to be at a temperature comfortable for a human, they risk hounds not being able to effectively work in cold. The other consideration is that hounds and horses' ideal outside temperature is lower than what a human likes. Most humans feel best in 68–72 degrees. That's way too hot for hounds and horses, although they can work outside in the heat, but not for hours on end. It's cruel to them, even if it feels okay to the human. This is why cubbing calls for judgment based on the animals, and not the people. Also, when the temperature rises, a huntsman must allow hounds to drink whenever they wish.

By now John Wickline had learned things. He'd read, studied, asked questions over the years.

"Wow," he exclaimed when he walked into the inviting office.

The Louis XV desk sat in the middle of the floor, where the old clunky school desk once sat.

"You weren't born when Uncle Arnold's Louis XV desk was in here," she teased him, as he was in his late thirties. "About twenty-two years ago it was stolen. Never found it, couldn't imagine anyone doing such a thing. Harry Dunbar, the antiques dealer, willed me this. An overwhelming gift." She dropped into the chair. "Do I look royal?"

"Always." John smiled.

She opened the middle drawer, handed him a sheaf of papers. "These are the bloodlines I am currently studying." She rose, walked over to the bank of wooden cabinets along an interior wall. "This cabinet contains all the medical records for the last thirty years. The stuff starting in 1887 is in the next room. I have everything. My late husband's uncle was obsessive. I hasten to add that I really am not, but Weevil keeps me on track, as does Shaker."

She mentioned her huntsman of many years, currently on a medical leave.

"Well, I have no worries. I've taken photos of the hounds. Hard to argue with a photograph. Stables?"

Sister pulled on her gloves, was helped into her coat by Weevil. Tootie and Weevil stayed in the kennels as Sister and John walked across the snowy path to the stables, where Betty Franklin waited. Betty didn't work in the stables but she kept her two horses there. The stables, like the kennels, sparkled, smelled fresh.

The two women brought each horse into the center aisle, removing the animals' stable rug, lighter than the outdoor blanket, so John could take photographs.

Betty lifted each hoof so the officer could inspect the hooves. This operation used up almost two hours, because they then showed him the feed, the quality of the hay, and the shelf with supplements for those horses needing them.

One more station remained, the house. The two women and John walked to the house, where Gray had not only spruced things up, he'd actually groomed the dogs. Golly, of course, was impossible.

After this, a half day had passed.

"Sure you don't want lunch or a sandwich for the road?" Sister asked.

"No. Again, I apologize, but I must obey the ordinance. I can't promise that this is nipped in the bud and you know I can't tell you who lodged the complaint, but I can hint that there are those who are anti-hunting, more and more of them."

"Well, I'm glad we got to visit a bit, no matter what the circumstances. This does seem like so much exhaustive effort burned to deal with something that is a deep part of our history."

John shook each person's hand then left by the back door. Gray, teapot at the ready, poured tea.

"What a host you are." Betty thanked him as she put cookies on the table.

"Cookies. I wouldn't dirty my mouth with a cookie," Golly complained.

"I would." Rooster sat by Sister's knee, the picture of devotion. Raleigh leaned on Betty, who gave in.

"How did it go?" Gray asked.

"He saw everything. The odd thing is, we have a record and now a recent visual one, for he took pictures. Actually, I believe masters should have an animal control visit at least once a year. Doesn't have to be like this, but John had no choice and neither did we."

"It's the new people." Betty pronounced this with gusto.

Gray broke a peanut butter cookie in half. "Betty, maybe, but even without this new influx flooding Virginia, there have always been people opposed to hunting. Some are adamant about not killing animals."

"We don't," Betty interrupted.

"Of course, Betty, but who knows that? Foxhunters have been rotten about educating the public." Gray, having worked in Washington, D.C., for years, possessed insight into the urban and suburban mind.

"He's right, Betty." Sister turned to Gray. "But remember we were taught that our names should only appear in the newspaper when we were born, when we married, and when we died. Anything else was considered vulgar."

"It is." Betty stood up, poured herself more tea, and topped off Sister's and Gray's cups. "It truly is."

"What about Facebook?" Gray's eyebrows rose.

"You don't see me doing it. Exposing yourself in that way is vain. Why would anyone assume they are that interesting?"

Sister laughed, dropping her forehead into her hand for a moment. "Betty, you have just offended millions of Americans, plus whoever else in the world is taking a selfie at this moment."

"Betty, you're younger than we are. I'd think you'd be part of this," Gray teased her.

Betty leaned back in the kitchen chair. "I suppose writing a letter is a form of exposure, but that's private, and if you take the time to actually write using good paper, which my husband and I carry, in case you forgot," she smiled mischievously, "you think a bit. Simply going to your iPad or your computer and firing off what comes into your head without reflection, I believe it does more harm than good. I need time to think things through."

"Not when you're whipping-in." Sister meant this as a compliment.

"That's different. That's action. We think on our feet out there. Actually, we think on four feet."

"You'd imagine that people would find that a challenge." Sister liked running after an animal who could think and turn at a ninety-degree angle, who could make a complete fool out of horses, humans, and hounds. Who could and did.

"They don't grow up in the country. A house on a two acre lot is the country to them. Riding on a lawnmower that costs five thousand dollars is doing your chores. They live in a different world. They could care less about country people, if they even know we exist."

"Well, Betty, they do, or they wouldn't be passing anti-barking ordinance laws." Sister sighed as the phone rang.

Gray walked over to pick up the landline. He listened. "She's right here." He held out the phone, whispering, "O.J."

Sister took the phone while Gray seated himself and the two dogs kept pressing for cookies. Betty noticed the look on Sister's face.

"I am so sorry. I know she was one of your oldest and most supportive members. Let me know if there's anything we can do. I know you have a lot to do. Let's talk when you're not so pressed." She listened then said, "Bye. Love you."

"What's going on?" Betty held her cup midair, focused on whatever the news would be.

Sister returned to the table. "Remember me telling you about the Munnings painting being stolen in Lexington? The painting of the beautiful Mrs. Oliver Filley riding sidesaddle? It was owned by Delores Buckingham. She'd supported the hunt club for years, was in her eighties. Well, she was strangled leaving her house. No one saw a car or a person. Or no one says they did. Oh, another lead shank. Fennell's."

Gray said, "It may be the old story, who has most to gain? The lead shank method seems unnecessary."

"Quite." Sister added, "But there are different kinds of gain. We're focused on money. What if this is about something else?"

Later, settled in the library, dogs asleep at their feet, Golly snuggled next to Sister on the sofa, both humans finally home, each reading a magazine that interested them.

On the coffee table, Michael Hicks's detailed biography of Richard III lay, the bookmark at page 93. Sister would tackle it again tomorrow. Mr. Hicks's knowledge, deep and wide, impressed her, but she had to rev her mental energy to read it. At this moment her engines were slowing down. It had been a long day.

"What are you hmming about?" she asked as she glanced up from her *Garden and Gun* magazine filled with enticing photographs.

Looking up from his *Economist,* he replied, "This bug in Wuhan, China. Spreading."

"Bugs do that. Then again, China has so many people crammed together, has to be a field day for bacteria and viruses. A form of pestilential paradise."

He folded the magazine in half. "Doesn't matter where something starts, all those things travel easily. It's creeping into Italy, Europe. Think of Ebola."

"I'd rather not," she teased him. "I remember the day the polio vaccine was hailed; 1955. Mother said it was a miracle and it was. I remember one of the boys at school coming down with polio.

He lived but was crippled. Think of all the diseases that have been conquered or greatly reduced."

"You're right. I take a lot for granted. I eat good food, there's an abundance of it. We have central heating and air-conditioning. We can move about freely. I think restoring the home place has made me appreciate what my ancestors did. Tough people, the Lorillards and the Laprades."

"Still are."

He placed the folded *Economist* in his lap. "I wonder. Think how our ancestors worked, used their bodies. Even baking bread takes effort, and women did it every morning. If rich, they had a cook who did it. Can you imagine getting a toothache? When we worked on the flue . . . well, there are two of them, in decent shape, but you can't fool around with a chimney . . . it reminded me that twice a day the fires needed to be stoked. The only insulation was horsehair. Honey, they were tough. No wonder men started splitting wood in the middle of the summer. Then you had to stack it, it needed a year to cure. The cured wood from the prior year had to be brought into a woodshed near the house. No one wants to fetch wood in a blizzard, so there had to be places inside the house that were safe to store flammable material, and I haven't even gotten to food storage."

"Not much. Well, canning, and if a family built a smokehouse, that helped with meat. We are spoiled. On the other hand, most people unless disgustingly rich had fabulous bodies."

He laughed. "Vanity. I expect some of the disgustingly rich had pretty good bodies, too. How did we get off on this?"

"China."

"Oh, well, how is your *Garden and Gun?*"

She sighed. "One temptation after another. I am so glad my mother curbed my impulsiveness or I'd buy most of what I see in the magazine."

"Uh-huh."

"What's that supposed to mean?"

"The Louis XV desk."

"Now, Gray, Harry Dunbar willed me that."

"If he hadn't died, you would have found a way and snookered me into helping."

"Well—maybe. I mean, what's the point of loving someone if you don't spoil them a little?"

He left his chair by the fireplace, leaned over her as she sat on the sofa. "You can spoil me anytime you please."

C H A P T E R 1 5

February 20, 2020   Thursday

"When was the last time you had contact with Delores Buckingham?" Ben Sidell questioned Carter Nicewonder.

Both did not hunt this Thursday.

"A year and a half ago." The slightly overweight Carter replied, then leaned forward. "The woman possessed sophisticated taste. I knew her preferences, of course, and I had acquired from a Richmond estate a perfect pair of sapphire and diamond earrings and a bracelet to match; 1890s. Couldn't be made today."

Ben couldn't help a half smile, for Carter was always selling if he could. "Did you go to Lexington?"

"I did. I brought some other jewelry, as I have clients there. Delores tried on the earrings and bracelet. For an eighty-something woman, she looked good."

"Your card was in her secretary. When the chief of police called, I volunteered to question you."

"That secretary, French, was remarkable. Buddy Cadwalder,

the Philadelphia dealer, knew Delores, too. He would kill for that secretary." Carter stopped. "Sorry."

"An expression. Do you remember the Munnings?"

"Who wouldn't? Once seen you never forgot Mrs. Filley."

"Did Mrs. Buckingham ever mention her painting?"

"Only that Mrs. Filley was such a great beauty in her day and a strong rider. We focused on, uh, personal adornment."

"Delores Buckingham was a good client?"

"A delight. Yes, she was good. The great wealth of her family diminished over the generations, but she lived at ease, don't get me wrong. She inherited the farm, the furniture, everything, but she was careful."

"How so?" Ben smelled someone making coffee in Carter's home in Ivy, a sort of subdivision west of Charlottesville itself.

Carter smelled it, too. "Would you like a cup?"

"No, thank you."

"That's my houseman making it. What the English might once have called a batman. I have him and a maid. Given my odd schedule I need to have the house covered."

"Odd?"

Carter smiled. "People often think a long time before selling family jewelry. It's so personal. It represents the deceased. Either that, or they sell the minute Momma has died. Greed," he said with a little smack of his lips. "When they call I need to get there."

"The seven deadly sins." Ben closed his notebook.

"Accurate," Carter agreed.

"Can you think of anything, a conversation? An offhand comment? A feeling?"

"With Mrs. Buckingham?" Carter put his fingers to his lips. "She had two daughters. Well married or married well. Once she said the oldest daughter would take over the farm. The younger, sixty-something by now, would remain in Phoenix. They all seemed to get along."

"Can you think who might have stolen her Munnings?"

"No, but as you know, the value is astronomical."

"Crawford's painting as well as the work stolen in New Jersey were, too. Have you any idea why she was killed?"

"No. It was after the painting had been stolen. She wasn't in the way."

"She was killed in the same manner as Parker Bell. We're at the point where we have to consider some connection. It is possible Mrs. Buckingham knew too much. For Parker, a blank. A total blank."

"Yes." He then sighed. "Fennell's makes indestructible leather tack. This is dreadful proof of that."

"The chief has questioned the Fennells. Kit, her son, and his wife, Marguerite. They are sick about it, of course. The chief said they are part of Lexington. People adore them, his exact words."

"Well, I don't doubt that they are sick about it, but I guarantee you, sales will go up."

Ben tucked his small notebook in his pocket. "People are funny that way. There is no such thing as bad publicity. I bought one of their bridles for Nonni and a lead shank with a brass plate with her name on it. I know how good they are." He stood up, asked one last question. "Let me come back to Mrs. Buckingham. Is it possible Mrs. Buckingham figured out who stole her Munnings?"

"Well . . ." A long pause followed this. "She was a woman of high intelligence. It is possible."

C H A P T E R   1 6

February 21, 2020   Friday

"It was one of the best-attended events ever," Claudia Pfeiffer, the George L. Ohrstrom, Jr., Head Curator at the National Sporting Library & Museum, said to Sister as they walked through the museum. "We had hoped it would be a success but it exceeded our dreams."

Sister noticed a small Dorothy Chhuy painting, work she liked very much and was glad the National Sporting Library did, too.

Ms. Pfeiffer was referring to the "Sidesaddle" exhibition, which ran from September 8, 2018 to March 24, 2019.

"Wonderful. The two women riding sidesaddle from Colonial Williamsburg certainly were a smash hit. I had never truly seen habits from the early eighteenth century, the beautiful dark blue and the other red with facings like military uniforms. The woman in blue wore a tricorn hat. You know, women look dazzling in a tricorn hat with one's skirt flowing over the left leg.

"I'm sorry you missed Dr. Ulrike Weiss's lecture. She flew from Scotland to present it and she helped us with the research for the exhibition. She's at the University of St. Andrews and she studied here during her John H. Daniels Fellowship in 2016. We're quite proud."

"You have every reason to be. What surprised me is that people, and I mean people in universities, don't realize that one of the best ways to approach a culture or a century is through sports and fashion. Well, in sidesaddle you have both and I thought your bracketing the exhibit with the years 1690–1935 opened a door."

"You're kind." Ms. Pfeiffer smiled. "We love what we do. There isn't a day that I come to work that something new, insightful, possibly exhausting isn't happening."

"You are good to see me. I know you all are preparing your 'On Fly in the Salt' exhibit. We have so many highly skilled and interesting sports here, so much water, fly-fishing isn't for the lazy although it looks calm. Well, it is calm, but you know what I mean. My father would cast in the backyard just to keep his hand in, as he would say."

"You saw that great movie with Brad Pitt, *A River Runs Through It?*"

"Did. What a way into a brotherly and paternal relationship, alcohol and real racism. Some people, well, some truly talented people like Norman Maclean can pull that off. I'm babbling on here."

"Not at all. We're always glad to see you." Claudia sat on a bench in the museum; Sister sat beside her. "You called me about the Munnings. The theft of the first painting, which as you know we have exhibited here thanks to Crawford's generosity . . . we do have the best people around us . . . but well, it was a shock, and then another and now another and a murder."

"Which is why I wanted to drive up here. Was there anyone who kept returning to the sidesaddle exhibit? Anyone who began to attract your attention?"

"We've all talked about this. When we hosted the roundtable on sidesaddle horsemanship, you may recall the speakers were

Devon Zebrovious, Amy Jo Magee, and Sarah O'Halloran, which was great fun since they compete sidesaddle against one another. I thought the audience would be only women but there were a few men, but not anyone who seemed at all suspicious, questioning. I don't know, I mean I don't know what we would have been looking for at the time."

"Given the attractiveness of the three ladies, I don't wonder that a few men showed up. I'd like to see them try sidesaddle."

"Interesting you should say that because I think our 'Sidesaddle' exhibition, more than anything we have ever done, highlighted the position of women without being politicized, if you know what I mean?"

"I do. I remember Laura Kramer, Penny Denegre, and Amy Webb, now Walker, competing what, twenty-five years ago? The men certainly hung on the rail but I doubt they thought about the demands to be feminine, where it started, how a lady could only ride in the hunt field if so attired. No one really talked about those things."

"You know Penny is out there competing and beating people now, riding astride."

"I do. Some people just have it, you know? Look at Ellie Wood Baxter, still rides at ninety-nine. She's mostly blind, still going. Flawless on a horse, as are the ladies we are discussing. Kay Blassic, Betty Oare. Effortless, and then you think about sidesaddle. They say Phyllis Longworth, and Lady Astor, her sister, were unbelievable on a horse, sidesaddle."

"Or the Empress of Austria, Sissy," Ms. Pfeiffer added. "Again, think of the politics and the pressure."

"Do you have any thoughts about who's behind all these crimes? I've been thinking all this is connected to the value of Munnings's work." Sister folded her hands in her lap, the space was conducive to quiet and thought.

"In 2016 Sotheby's auctioned *Winter Sunshine: Huntsman by a*

Covert, which was painted in 1913. Not an especially large work, it went for two hundred seventy-five thousand dollars. The sidesaddle paintings that have been stolen . . . well, all three of them, the bidding would begin above that. And if sold on the black market, it wouldn't be any less."

"Is it possible some obsessed person of wealth would pay more?" Sister queried.

"I suppose if you have billions, what's a million or two? We've talked about this here, who of today's billionaires would have the acumen to know Munnings? It's a bit like interior decorating. Few of the new billionaires would know who Nancy Lancaster was, Nancy Astor's niece."

"Colefax and Fowler." Sister named the great interior decorating company that rose to great prominence after World War I and is still going today. The impetus for this success was Nancy Lancaster.

"It's an instantly recognizable look but I am willing to bet not one of these wealthy people would know who Stéphane Boudin was, the legendary decorator of Maison Jansen."

"They have wealth but no breeding. I know that's not a nice thing to say but in the old days those with great resources had a trained aesthetic sense. Your vice chairman, Jacqueline Mars, apart from being generous, has an exquisite sense of the arts. Well, your entire board of directors is exceptional."

"Sister, most museums do have glorious boards, as does the New York Public Library, but few members are even in their forties. My fear is when they go, who will be there to take up the reins?"

"Ms. Pfeiffer, regardless of the institution, that's a concern. I feel it's as though someone put the film of history backward on the projector."

"Ah, interesting way to put it. By the way, please call me Claudia. Okay, back to the Munnings. Only Munnings."

"Is it possibly a family relation? Someone who feels cut out of his work?"

"There's never been any criticism from that quarter, and Violet, his wife, was above reproach. A good marriage, I think. No outside children. No one seething at being left out of wills, at least where art is concerned. His first wife, Florence Carter-Wood, committed suicide in 1914 after two years of marriage. No issue there either."

"Let me try another tack. Before women had the vote in England, remember the woman, Emily Wilding Davison, who threw herself in front of the king's horse at the 1913 Epsom Derby? She was killed. There have always been fanatics and often their sacrifices provoke others to make smaller ones. Women got the vote in England in 1928. It's only been a hundred years here. Is it possible this is some sort of feminist motivation? Sidesaddle as an emblem of distorting the female body for male pleasure? I know I'm grasping at straws, but to have three thefts of major art in less than two weeks and then Delores Buckingham's murder, I'm trying to think of all manner of things. Sidesaddle may not be the key except for rarity. Munnings painted fewer of them than his other paintings, as fewer and fewer women rode sidesaddle as he aged and, well, it is making a comeback, but how many hunts have active ladies who ride sidesaddle?"

"Not many. A lady might do so for one of the High Holy Days but it's not like old times. I still think the key is the value."

"It makes the most sense," Sister agreed. "You must know who owns Munnings's paintings, the works in private hands."

"We do as does Turner Reuter at Red Fox Fine Art. Some are in our country on the East Coast, as you would expect. There is a massive Munnings in the Virginia Museum of Fine Arts. Interestingly enough, a few great corporations own Stubbs's work but not Munnings's. And there is The Munnings Art Museum in England, of course."

"Those extra decades must add a patina." Sister smiled. "Has anyone expressed concern?"

"Curiosity more than concern, because the people we know who own the great hunting paintings, or racing paintings from even the early eighteenth century, feel secure. As this has been focused on sidesaddle, no one has pressed the panic button."

"And I assume none of the sidesaddle ladies including the ladies of Colonial Williamsburg have been discomfited, stalked, stuff like that?"

"Not that I know." Ms. Pfeiffer asked Sister, "Have you ever ridden sidesaddle?"

"Yes. When I was young I tried. I liked it but thought I could do better astride. I've taken up so much of your time. Let me let you get back to work. You've been very generous."

"It's always a pleasure to see you. When you come up for the fly-fishing exhibit, call me. I'll take you through it. You must come, you know. Your father would want you to." She smiled broadly.

"Yes, he would."

Ms. Pfeiffer walked Sister to her car, which she'd actually washed, given that she was driving to Middleburg. Even though there was mud in Middleburg, she wanted to drive in a clean car, or as clean as it could be in this weather.

Sister opened the door and Ms. Pfeiffer said, "There is a Side-Saddle Chase Foundation. You could call them."

"Thank you for reminding me. You all worked with them for the horsemanship roundtable, right?"

"Did. It's the only thing I can think of and I'm sure you spoke to Nancy Bedford at the Museum of Hounds and Hunting?"

"I did. Everyone is in agreement that the value of the stolen works is enormous. Other than that, well, we are all outfoxed, forgive the expression."

Driving the two and a half hours home, Sister turned over in her head all they had discussed. The only thought she had was she should reread Sir Alfred Munnings's three volumes of autobiography. He mentioned the sidesaddle paintings. Perhaps there is a running thread. It occurred to her as she reached Culpeper, the mountains visible before her on the right, that Delores Buckingham rode sidesaddle at Piedmont Hunt in the late forties. Her maiden name was LeCoq, she married Buckingham, moved to Lexington. Sister met Delores first when the woman was in her sixties, no longer riding sidesaddle but riding astride. She pulled over, dialed Jane Winegardner.

"O.J., I was just up at the National Sporting Library and Museum to talk about the 'Sidesaddle' exhibit they had last year and am driving home; I'm pulled over on 29. Anyway, Delores rode sidesaddle in the late 1940s and 1950s."

"That came out in the Lexington newspaper. I never saw her ride sidesaddle." She paused. "No leads. Catherine Clay-Neal, a member at Woodford Hunt before we merged with Long Run, rode and still sometimes does ride sidesaddle. I asked her. She is as confused as the rest of us and she runs the Headley-Whitney Museum. It is possible Delores was killed for another reason."

"It is."

O.J. replied, "It's my understanding that most murders are solved pretty quickly if they are to be solved. You know, the killer is standing there or has blood in his car. So, let me say this," she said, using one of her expressions. "No one knows anything. The first theft was in your territory. It might not be such a good idea to be obvious in your questions. There must be a great deal of money at stake. Who is to say that this person isn't someone you know or at least in Virginia? Think of Virginia's coastline. Pretty easy to sneak something out of the country using the Atlantic. No planes. Just a thought."

"Right. My curiosity has got the better of me."

"You know what they say about curiosity and the cat," O.J. mentioned.

CHAPTER 17

February 22, 2020   Saturday

Crackenthorp, not yet under construction save for the farm road, rested above the church at Chapel Cross on the northeast side. The fox headed north although he didn't show himself. Scent held, for it was a raw day, maybe thirty-six degrees, if that, and fog refused to lift. Fortunately the staff at Jefferson Hunt knew the territory well, but even with that, a shape could loom ahead, spook you more than your horse, so one rated one's mount and slowed.

Hounds did not slow but they negotiated frozen footing in some places and the beginnings of slick in others. Fortunately, the pack, in peak condition, leapt over, crawled under, or circumvented any obstacle in their path.

Sister Jane rode her old Thoroughbred, Lafayette, tried and true. A dedicated but small field rode behind her, perhaps twenty people, small for Jefferson Hunt on a Saturday, but conditions kept people home. In the old days members rode through anything but in those days one didn't need a van, you hacked to the meet. Parking when the fields were muddy and deep was a sure way to upset a landowner, unless it was an area he or she didn't fret over.

As the people who bought the land for Crackenthorp still lived out of state, leaving few good pastures to rip up, Sister rode straight as she could, bits of mud and some snow flying off her gray's hooves.

Hounds turned left, crossing North Chapel Cross Road, now heading west.

The paved road, scraped, mostly thin ice, meant slow down. Rating Lafayette, Sister walked along the road listening intently, for sound bounced around. This northern expanse, above Old Paradise and the old Gulf gas station, tested one's balance, for the ridges quickly dipped into low fields or narrow valleys, only to rise again. The lower ridges stood at two hundred feet above sea level and then the next set doubled that, and so on until you had the choice to climb one of the true Blue Ridge Mountains or not. This was if heading straight west. Given there were so many dens, outbuildings, good places to duck in, few foxes took the direct mountain route.

Hounds again turned due north; she could hear them well enough to take the coop ahead, which put her into Close Shave, a newer fixture and a good one. Then nothing, nor did the fog lift.

She held up, waiting again. A toodle told her that Weevil and hopefully the pack had run to a collapsing shed that the owners had not yet time to remove. Given that they were restoring much of this old place, that would come. Giving Lafayette a little squeeze, she walked toward the horn notes.

Finally the outline of the shed, part of the roof sagging down, appeared, as did Weevil, the pack, and Betty and Tootie.

Yvonne, Aunt Daniella, and Kathleen weren't following in the car this morning because they wouldn't have been able to see a thing.

"Master, what do you suggest?" Weevil asked.

"We turn back. We might pick up another fox, but this fog isn't lifting and it feels to me, at least, as though the temperature is starting to slide."

"Madam, do you mind if I walk through the fields where we can walk? I'd like to avoid the road. A driver might not be able to see us until right upon us. There are three jumps between here and the crossroads. Mr. Franklin knows where the gates are."

"Of course. I'm glad you thought of that." She pulled her white-dotted navy blue stock tie higher up on her neck, thinking the dots might soon be covered by tiny snowflakes. It felt like snow.

Hounds, horses, and the field turned south. The old Gulf station, no longer open to the public but still used by Arthur Du-Charme, the son of Binky, one of the brothers that used to own Old Paradise, sat near the crossroads. His cousin, Margaret DuCharme, M.D., rode out today with Ben Sidell. The two liked each other, an affection that grew into a romance, which surprised the old guard. Sheriff Sidell came from Ohio, from a working-class family, whereas Margaret was a DuCharme, once one of the richest, most powerful families in Albemarle County. Both Margaret and her cousin hated blood snobbery, plus their fathers never made a penny but sure spent them. Both sat in jail mostly, because they really wouldn't do an honest day's work.

Kasmir rode up to Sister. "From time to time we see Arthur. It's a shame the Gulf station and little café are closed. I'm sure once it was a place for people to be together, like the old post office in the train station."

"Once it was. Millie, Binky's wife, made the best grits in the county and her hamburgers filled you right up. Margaret says her aunt, now that Crawford bought everything, doesn't have to work, doesn't want to work, and is ashamed of her husband's behavior. She's more or less hidden away."

"Understandable." Kasmir nodded.

As they rode past the station, the garage door was open. The rest of the building remained closed up.

Kasmir noticed this. "Arthur must be working on someone's truck or car. He'll do it for his buddies."

"I'll bear that in mind. When I take my truck to the garage it's Ali Baba and the Forty Thieves."

They laughed, finally reaching Tattenhall Station, a few twirling snowflakes lazing down.

The small group eagerly trooped into the station for warmth and food. Along with the fox's route through Crackenthorp and winding up at Close Shave, the next exhausted topic was the weather. As the members left in small groups, Margaret walked out with Ben. He had trailered his horse on her gooseneck two-horse trailer.

Climbing into the driver's seat, he clicked his belt as Margaret clicked hers.

"Ben, drive over to the station for a minute. Let me see what Arthur's doing and if he can get me floor mats cheaper than I can."

Ben did, waiting for Margaret to come back after she stepped out.

She ran back. "Ben, there's a dead man in there."

Cutting the motor, the sheriff followed her inside. The driver in a Dinken's Plumbing truck sat bolt upright in the seat. Given the temperature, decomposition would be delayed. At first sight, time of death was difficult to determine.

Before calling in a team, Ben walked around the back as Margaret turned on lights. Both wore their gloves because it was cold and so as to not leave fingerprints. The rear of the small box truck was empty but Ben noticed a small glitter on the floor. He walked back to Margaret's truck, picked up his cellphone from the seat, and called headquarters. Then he took the flashlight out of the side pocket on the door, walked back to the plumbing truck. He shined the light on the glitter.

Margaret joined him.

"A gold chip a bit like something off one of the frames at Kathleen's antique store."

"Could be."

"Doctor, any idea how long he's been dead? Of course the body will go to the Medical Examiner's but what do you think?"

"It's hard to tell, given the temperature. It would need to be bitterly cold to freeze a body like this. I'm no pathologist. He's cold but I doubt he's gone into rigor and come out. My hunch is, he's been here long enough for his body temperature to plummet but he hasn't been here, say, for even six hours or so."

"No attempt to hide the truck. The door was open to the garage. Given my work, I try to think of possibilities."

"Of course." Margaret found Ben's work fascinating.

"The body isn't on display but it's not exactly hidden. Yes, it's out here where there's little traffic, but my first thought is, this is a killer very sure of himself. Never a good sign."

The driver had been strangled with a leather Fennell's lead shank left in the truck. There was no doubt he had been murdered.

CHAPTER 18

February 23, 2020   Sunday

S ister, Betty, and Bobby stood in the small, pleasant vestibule of the Episcopal church in Greenwood. Each Sunday Gray and Sam took Aunt Daniella to her church, the one in which she was baptized. Sister never minded that Gray escorted his aunt. It was the proper thing to do and he loved her, although from time to time Aunt Daniella could drive him crazy. But then Sister figured she could do that to him, too. She mused to herself that heterosexuality had a few built-in land mines, but then, perhaps all relationships do.

"I had no idea." Sister slipped her arm through Bobby's as Betty did the same on his left side. "It wasn't on the news."

"Margaret called to ask me if I'd seen Arthur. You know he's been working part-time at the press with us. Arthur was home, so Ben reached him. He knew nothing about it. Didn't know the victim when Ben showed him a photo."

"Not even who it is? I mean, he was in a Dinken's Plumbing truck." Sister thought it strange that an unknown person would be driving the truck of a well-established business.

"Margaret said Ben called Lionel Dinkens straightaway. He said all his drivers were accounted for but then Ross Stirling called back and declared his truck was missing. Lionel allows the drivers to take the trucks home if they worked late."

"Shall I assume Ross tied one on?"

Bobby smiled. "Is there a Stirling who doesn't have a hollow leg?"

"Well, there is that," Betty agreed.

"Sometimes I wonder about Chapel Crossroads. So much has happened there over the centuries." Sister inhaled the cold air as they stepped out of the church.

"Come on back for breakfast," Betty invited her. "You never eat before the early-morning service and you know once Aunt Dan has her audience, she will be loathe to let them go."

Within twenty minutes, part of that time on back roads, they arrived at Cocked Hat, Betty and Bobby's small home built about the same time as Roughneck Farm got started, 1787. Unpretentious, inviting, it had a warmth that Sister always felt, imagining that it had been filled with centuries of love.

If not, it was filled with love now, for the Franklins complemented each other in good times and bad. Their bond never weakened but grew stronger, deeper. Sister admired them as well as loved them, for she knew their sorrows as well as their joys.

"You sit there. Bobby, fetch our master a cup of English Breakfast, her favorite morning tea. I'll take black coffee. Just sluggish today." Betty smacked an old number 5 iron skillet on the range, chatting away as she did so.

"Here you go. Barefoot, as always." Bobby poured her the tea then started on the toast as he and his wife talked.

"I think so much happened out there at Chapel Cross over time because it's right up against the mountains. Easy to hide or hide stuff. Neither the Brits nor the Federals could quell the goings-on there, nor can the revenue man from the government. Good old tobacco, firearms, and booze." Betty giggled. "Must drive those three-piece-suit types crazy to be fooled by what they consider a lower life-form."

"Deplorables?" Sister slyly grinned. "Ah yes."

"Here's the thing," Bobby pushed down the lever on a huge toaster, "raise a tax, create a criminal, if you think evading taxes is criminal."

"Depends on the tax." Sister felt the bracing tea warm her throat. "What else did Margaret say?"

"Only that this is two unsolved deaths in the county in just over a week and Ben is fretting, since now a woman was killed the same way in Lexington, Kentucky. She also said the discovery will be on the late-afternoon news. Maybe by then the body will be identified.

"Ben takes his job seriously. He's a good sheriff. If you'd asked me when he was hired, I would have been doubtful. Virginia remains Virginia, which means you need to listen very closely to what is being said. Of course, that's why people from the north think we are hypocrites. They don't know the code."

"True," Bobby agreed. "We learned and so can they."

"Well, we learned the Ten Commandments, too, does that mean it sank in?" Sister raised a silver eyebrow.

"Too hard." Betty turned off the flame, scooping her signature omelet onto three colorful breakfast plates.

The Franklins' Manx cat sauntered in, sat down waiting for a piece of bacon, which he received to thunderous purrs.

"Have you all weighed Roman Bold?" She named the fat fellow, a typefont name.

"Don't be ugly." Betty buttered her toast.

"His butt is so big you could show a movie on it."

"Don't you fat shame my cat." Betty pointed a fork at Sister.

"Roman, forgive me. I am an insensitive human," Sister apologized while Roman devoured the treat. "Have you all ever wondered how we landed where we are now?"

"Plenty. Our problems are the problems of plenty," Bobby answered authoritatively.

"Honeyman, not everyone in America has plenty." Betty didn't argue, simply made a statement.

"I know, but the great majority of our people live very well. Someone of modest means would be rich in Venezuela."

"Has Central America ever been stable? Guatemala, El Salvador? Those people get battered by the right then the left comes in and it's nastiness, if not death, from the other direction. Maybe disarray, violence is the human condition. I mean, here we are in one of the most beautiful places in the United States if not the world and a man is found with a lead shank tied around his throat at Showoff Stables."

"Not while I'm eating," Betty suggested.

"*I don't mind.*" Roman's ears perked up. "*You should see me kill mice.*"

Bobby assumed the feline chat was a request for more food so he slipped the cat a piece of his bacon. No wonder Roman was huge.

"You met the Sabatinis. What did you think?" Sister asked.

"Attractive. Rich. But there were so many people at Kathleen's grand opening, hard to say."

"True."

"Delicious, as always," Sister praised her friend and whipper-in.

"You feed me enough. After walking hounds in the off-season. After working the horses."

Sister smiled at Betty. "Odd how food brings people together."

"*Yes,*" Roman enthusiastically agreed.

"It's brought us the cat." Bobby loved his fat cat. "Back to the dead man in the old Gulf garage. He had to know Arthur's schedule. So I suppose Ben has questioned Arthur, plus Margaret would tell him whatever or whoever she knew. When Binky ran it, everybody out in Chapel Cross took their trucks and cars there."

"You would think, but the station, although closed, is known to many of us. Also what if the dead man had been driven there by someone who knows the area? Easy enough to do. The old Gulf station is hardly a secret."

Betty nodded. "Margaret said as much."

Bobby jumped in. "Why would he be there? Why not just dump him by the side of the road?"

"Parker Bell was killed where he worked. So it's a bit different, the body at the gas station." Betty leaned back in her chair.

Sister rejoined, "Who did these men offend? Think about Parker. His forefinger and second finger missing at the first knuckle, an old wound, long ago healed. Ben asked me did I think there was significance?"

"Do you?" Betty wondered.

"I don't know. They were old, healed injuries."

"Before I forget, have you picked the dates for the girls' meet, for lack of a better term?" Betty stood up to collect the plates. "You could change the last week of the season so we could travel. A thought."

"O.J. and I are working it out with Deep Run, Red Rock, Bull Run, and Big Sky. I much look forward to that. We're working toward one meet with all hunts. Then in the coming years each hunt will host same. That's a lot easier than trailering horses to all those separate hunts in one year."

"Good idea." Bobby got up, poured Sister more tea while Betty brought some cookies to the table.

"For your sweet tooth." Betty smiled.

"I am trying to throttle my sweet tooth."

Betty flicked Sister's shoulder. "You never put on weight. Eat them all."

"Oh, great. Sugar gives me such a buzz. I really am trying to cut back." She reached for a small rich chocolate cookie, popped it in her mouth. "On the other hand."

They talked hounds, fixtures, people, kept returning to the two dead men, then Sister glanced at the wall clock.

Bobby followed her eyes. "Hey, stay all day."

"I lose track of time when I'm with you. Need to get back and check on everyone. Gray should be back soon, full of Aunt Daniella's tales." Sister brushed crumbs into her hand, rose, and dumped them in the trash can. "My focus is blurring. Too much going on. We're so close to the end of the season. I've got to clear my head."

Betty and Bobby smiled then Betty said, "I think we all feel that way. Nobody ever knows what tomorrow will bring but things seem especially confusing."

CHAPTER 19

Hounds fanned out over a pasture rolling down to a meander-ing creek. O.J., sitting next to Catherine Clay-Neal, riding sidesaddle, observed the chase.

"That coyote always loses us down there."

Catherine nodded, her silk top hat catching the light. "This wind isn't helping."

"No, but at least it's warm. Bad for scent but good for us." O.J. urged Blossom forward at a trot.

The two women, riding as silent whippers-in today, watched everything. Spencer, the huntsman, asked them to sit on the hill-tops, watch. This particular coyote drove the man to distraction. In ways the animal eluded them like a fox.

Down at the creek the field waited patiently while the hunts-man cast again. O.J. and Catherine, a bit to the side and behind them, saw hounds make good every inch of the ground down by that creekbed. Nothing. Truly, it was uncanny.

"You know scent lingers a bit stronger near water," O.J. whis-pered. "And water is wider than we see. Depending on the size of the creek or river it's also under the ground on both sides of the creek. Good for scent."

"Bottomland." Catherine smiled, a longtime foxhunter.

They'd been out for three hours. Had a decent run but the high-pressure system, the sun with a light wind made for a great trail-riding day but not a great hunting day.

The senior master, Dinwiddie Lampton III, rode up to the huntsman, chatted, hounds turned for the trailers, a wise decision, as it would only grow warmer, dissipating scent.

O.J. and Catherine walked at a leisurely pace.

"Snow last week. Look at that." Catherine pointed to a handful of daffodils, happy faces turned up to the sun.

"I don't even try to predict the weather anymore." O.J. smiled at the daffodil faces. "I heard that the police pulled in a suspect, Delores's murderer."

"We'll see. The police came to the museum to question me, this was yesterday and I kept my mouth shut . . . well, until it was made public, but they wanted to know, did we ever use a window service or any repair services?

"I gave them the names. Nothing much was told to me or any of the girls." Catherine called her assistants "girls." "But I asked was there thought that this is related to some sort of international art theft? I mean, should we worry at Headley-Whitney?" She cited the museum of which she was the director.

"And?"

"The authorities didn't know. I mentioned that if it is an international art ring, one would think they would be wiping out England, where much of Sir Alfred's work remains." She added, "Stealing paintings is one thing. Killing a fine old lady is another."

"Obviously you didn't catch the news this morning, but the man apprehended drives a truck for a big window company. No explanation offered, but the truck had been parked down the street. No one in the area had window work done."

"The question is, what did Delores know or did she get in the way? Her Munnings was taken. She wasn't home, so the thief or thieves knew her routine; then why come back and kill her? It's a terrible thing."

"It is. Let me switch to a happier subject. I volunteered Long Run Woodford to host the first hunt with Red Rock, Blue Sky, Deep Run, Bull Run, and Jefferson Hunt, and you know why?"

"No, but I'm ready to hear it."

"We could have them all here for the opening of the Andre Pater exhibit."

Catherine, a terrific-looking woman, broke into a wide smile accentuating her warmth. "O.J.! How wonderful of you. Just what we need, a museum full of people, and of course the press will have to come." A pause. "Have you told Dinwiddie, Joe, or Paul?" She named the joint masters.

"No, but Catherine, have you ever known them to pass up a great party?"

Catherine laughed. "No, but this means the women of the club will have a lot of work to do."

O.J. slyly said, "And so will you."

"Throw it at me."

"The evening after the big hunt, which will be at Shaker-town, of course, what about a formal dinner preceded by a gathering at the museum? Evening scarlet. If we can pull it off that will even get the TV people out there for the opening and the fashion drama."

"Do you ever stop?" Catherine turned to smile at her.

"Whatever do you mean?"

"Pulling rabbits out of the hat and in this case it's my hat."

"Well, Catherine, you are wearing a top hat."

As Tuesday was also a Jefferson hunt, Sister and the Tuesday faithful sat on folding chairs at Heron's Run. Like in Kentucky, the day proved warm, so everyone sat outside after the hunt, horses munched their hay in the bags, the hounds on the hound trailer sprawled in the trailer loft, an area taking up half of the trailer; it had an indoor ladder leading up to it so hounds had an upstairs and a downstairs. As the day had proved surprisingly fast they ate a cookie then flopped on their sides. Soon most of the pack was asleep.

Ben Sidell, sitting between Sister and Walter, fielded questions about the discovery at the Gulf station last Saturday.

"It wasn't grisly. Unusual, but not grisly. He was gone. Still no word from the Medical Examiner, but that can take time unless there's pressure."

"People being afraid bring pressure." Alida had figured that out.

"So you still don't know who was in the truck?" Bobby Franklin mentioned.

"No. No one has come forward to claim him."

"What about Bell?" Sam, who had ridden one of Crawford's horses, Trocadero, asked.

"He was an ex-con. Served time for illegal gaming and gambling. Gigi Sabatini knew that and said he had had such good results hiring former prisoners to help with the horses. He's heard about the James River Horse Foundation. Although Parker served time in Kentucky. It's funny to think of gambling being a problem there because of the casinos on the Indiana side of the river."

Kasmir, happily settled in a comfortable folding chair that Alida had brought, shrugged. "Gambling, prostitution, drugs, illegal liquor, the so-called sin crimes. Do the laws solve anything?"

"No," Sam forcefully said as his brother stared at him for a moment. "All it does is keep people from seeking help. As you know, I'm an alcoholic. Even though what I drank was legal it didn't mean I wouldn't drink what wasn't, and would I seek help? No. Had I been on drugs I truly wouldn't have gone into rehab. Be on my record forever. I thank God for my brother and my late cousin."

"Do you mean we legalize everything?" Weevil, being Canadian, found some American ways odd.

"No, but decriminalizing isn't the same as legalizing," Ben answered. "Can I take a position as your sheriff? At this time that wouldn't be wise but do I think we need to change a lot of this stuff? Of course I do."

"Where would you start?" Alida asked.

"That's a tough one. Either drugs or prostitution. The violence against prostitutes by their johns or pimps beggars description. No one much cares, and of course so many of the women in the life are on drugs. I will follow the law. That's what you pay me to do but it doesn't mean I believe those laws all work."

"This is what I love about our tailgates." Sister put her feet up on an overturned red bucket. "We tell one another the truth. We don't have to agree but we put it out there."

"I think it's because foxhunting can be dangerous. We draw close to one another in a way perhaps tennis players don't," Betty pondered.

"Any hunt where you dismount, can walk away, your horse is fine, that's a good hunt." Kasmir laughed.

"I can tell you something strange." Ben held his glass. "When we took off Parker's glove on his right hand, he was missing his forefinger and second finger to the first knuckle. An old wound. When we took the glove off the right hand of the unidentified man, same thing."

They looked at one another, then Walter spoke. "Surgically removed sometime in the past?"

"I would have to say yes. Clean amputation."

"What in the world?" Betty exclaimed.

Sister, taking this all in, clearly stated, "That's too unique not to mean something, not for those two to be connected in some fashion even if they didn't know each other."

"Well, Sister, how can two missing fingers be connected?" Betty exhaled. "That's too bizarre."

"Bizarre, yes, but I say trust your instincts and don't expect life to be logical." She held her glass up to the others as a toast.

CHAPTER 20

February 26, 2020   Wednesday

"Sure is a lot of suds." Tootie sprayed the power washer on the walls and floor of the kennel.

"Could peel the paint off a car, there's so much force, but I've yet to find anything that can clean a kennel like a good power washer, or as inexpensively."

"Once a week." Tootie nodded.

"Well, I did go over the top when I bought two. Thought it would save time. Just have one with the cleaner in it and the other with clear hot water. I maybe saved some time but probably not enough to justify the expense." Sister stood by her clear water power washer while Tootie finished up with the sudsy one.

The two women worked side by side and had been at it since nine that morning. Weevil and Betty walked hounds without them so they could do the indoor runs first. The outdoor runs were picked up, the poop thrown into a manure spreader, which also had straw bedding in there, which was changed whenever needed. Sister, a stickler for proper kennel practices, might let the straw go a week if the weather wasn't awful but that was it. Every outdoor condo, as they called the big boxes on stilts, was rebedded once a week in winter. No straw in summer to help keep hounds cool. Some mornings in the winter, Sister would walk out to see what looked like steam rolling out of the condos' small open doors.

The condo runs, huge, narrowed to a chain-link walkway to the main kennel and a push-open door, should hounds prefer to be in the kennel. However, the animals exhibited strong likes and dislikes so some kept to their social group in their condo, sort of like a sorority or a fraternity. Others enjoyed the camaraderie of the indoor housing. Best to let them tell you which, was Sister's attitude about all animals. Golly, the long-haired cat, would sashay down to the kennels, parade along the outside runs, and denigrate the hounds within. They ignored her, which Raleigh and Rooster could not. As it was, she now reposed in the kennel office, fire crackling in the fireplace, for it had been built before indoor heating, later added. The roar of the power washers disturbed her equilibrium.

This did not disturb the two humans, happy with how the kennels sparkled. After the washing was done each woman pushed a large mop so the floor dried out quickly. The mops, carried to the industrial sink by the storage closet, were rung out, not such an easy task, then placed inside the closet, mop-head up. Both women washed their hands, dried same, then rubbed cornhusker oil on their hands.

"Stuff works. My hands don't crack, I hate the cold on my hands and feet. Feels worse if your hands are cracked."

"Hate it, too," Tootie agreed, then added, "they're on a long walk."

No sooner had she said that than the iron gates to the outdoor draw run could be heard opening. The two women had also washed that concrete floor.

"Come along," Weevil's voice rang out.

"Barmaid, skiddle, daddle, do," Betty urged the youngster to hurry up.

Then the door opened to the inside of the kennels, girls first into their side of the kennels then the boys. Everyone finally settled, the door opened into the large feeding room.

"Brisk." Weevil rubbed his hands together. "It's sixty degrees one day then thirty the next. I don't know if I will ever get used to it."

"Weevil, I was born and raised in Virginia and I'm not used to it," Betty teased him. "Girls, this place looks practically perfect."

"Those power washers do the job," Sister replied.

"Given what you paid for them, industrial strength as I recall, they should. What was it? Three thousand dollars, and that was five years ago. God knows what they are now."

"Let's go into the office. Warmer there. Both of you are cherry red." Sister placed the back of her hand on Betty's extra-rosy cheek. "Cold."

Once inside the office, a nice room with the Louis XV desk in the center, they sank into chairs.

"Where did you all go?" Tootie inquired.

"The huntsman here," Betty nodded Weevil's direction, "thought a climb to Hangman's Ridge would be good for their engines."

Betty called the hindquarters of any animal the engine, which included humans. Those glute muscles drive one.

"Well?" Sister raised her eyebrows.

"My engine knows I climbed that grade, as do my calf muscles. Usually we ride up there. It's a haul but hounds enjoyed it."

"I suppose, but that place is creepy," Weevil admitted. "It's the steepest grade we have but when I get up there on that plain, the thick branches of that hangman's tree sway and it kind of gets me," he confessed.

"Gets all of us," Betty agreed.

Golly, stretched on the leather top of the gorgeous desk, lifted her head. *"The dead men are still there, unquiet. We can sometimes see them. You humans can't. It's not a good place."*

Sister, sitting behind the desk, rubbed the cat's ears. "Eighteen people were hanged there, men. Each one had a trial even then, rule of law although it was harsher, of course."

"Do you think people believe in the law?" Tootie, often quiet but always thinking, asked.

"They say they do," Betty replied, "until they get caught."

"Doesn't matter what country, what century, not much changes on that issue and the laws are made by those who can read and write and we take that for granted." Sister thought about this then changed the subject. "Shaker called last night from Cleveland."

"How is he?" Betty missed their huntsman of decades who had suffered a neck injury last winter season.

"As long as he doesn't pound himself, his words, he'll be fine. He won't talk about it right now but if he hunts that's a pounding. Even a smooth canter is a pounding. Once he gets home I'm hoping Skiff can talk sense to him. He won't listen to me, I know it." Sister pressed her lips together.

Skiff Kane, Crawford Howard's huntsman, had become Shaker's girlfriend. They spoke the same language. He had flown to Cleveland for the expert medical diagnosis and care there, and stayed with friends. Jefferson Hunt paid for this, of course. He was reluctant but he did go, as it was his last chance. Six months ago, neck still out of line, Sister sent him to a specialized clinic in Houston. They felt he was as good as he would be. Since he couldn't accept that, burning to once again carry the horn, Sister sent him to Cleveland.

"You're the master." Tootie obeyed a vertical hierarchy but she knew Shaker and all who hunted understood.

"I learned a lot from him." Weevil had whipped-in to the big hunt outside Toronto, before that, then wound up in Virginia, serendipity.

"Weevil, much as we all admire and even love Shaker, I don't see how he can ride hard. It would scare me half to death," Sister admitted. "No one necessarily wants to see a great huntsman give up the horn due to age and injury, but it's how it works. We all are happy with your work and hounds love you."

"I don't want Shaker to think I'm conniving behind his back," Weevil said.

Betty quickly responded, "He's not like that. Stubborn, opinionated, but he is fair-minded, and remember he took over the horn when Ray died. It's the way it happens." She named Sister's late husband, who died in 1991.

"You know what I've been doing?" Betty waited for all to ask then continued. "The missing fingers. Well, missing from long ago. I've been researching this on Google. Nothing really, then Bobby, sitting at the table playing solitaire, piped up 'Cards.' 'Cards! What?' I turned at him."

"Cards?" The other three looked at Betty.

"You have a deck in there?" Betty leaned over Sister to open the long thin middle drawer in the desk. "Most everyone has a deck of cards somewhere."

"I don't, but I bet there's a deck in Shaker's desk. He would play cards with the boys once a week down at Roger's Corner." She named the country convenience store miles down the road, which had not been altered since after World War II. Betty opened the drawer in the old schoolhouse desk. "Aha. Now watch carefully." She walked back to stand in front of Sister.

Weevil and Tootie watched as Betty flicked a card from the bottom of the deck with her forefinger.

"I don't get it." Weevil furrowed his brow.

"You saw me do that, right?"

"We all did." Sister stared at the cards in front of her on the desk as Betty kept flicking.

Stopping, Betty remarked, "If my forefinger and second finger, my middle finger, were cut off at the knuckle, squared off, a proper operation, you would never see me flick a card from the bottom." As they stared at the cards, then her again, she explained. "Whoever those men were or even what they did now, we may never know, but they knew cards. They were probably cardsharks. Wasn't Parker Bell imprisoned for gambling? As I recall, Gigi Sabatini mentioned he had had good luck with men who had not committed violent crimes. You know, stuff that isn't violent."

"Everyone deserves a second chance but I truly believe there are no victimless crimes. Think of the people ruined when Enron tanked." Sister folded her hands over the cards.

Betty looked at the two younger people. "You all were probably too young, but Kenneth Lay, head of Enron, misled people, probably the easiest way to put it, falsified profits. He also promised millions to the University of Missouri. Can you imagine the shock? The school had budgeted those millions."

"So there is no victimless crime." Sister handed the cards back to Betty. "Actually, in some ways entrenched stupidity creates its own victims. It's not a crime but, well, I don't know. How did we get off on this?" She looked at the cards in Betty's hand. "Okay. What's your theory?"

"My theory is those deaths are part of a crime network. So Parker Bell and the man in the truck either ran afoul of whoever they were working for or got greedy. They had to be in on the take. As for Delores, killed in the same way, her death is connected to all this."

"But what take?" Tootie's voice lifted up.

"If we knew that, we'd know what this is about." Betty walked back returning the cards to the drawer. "So here's what crosses my mind. Gigi Sabatini, we don't really know him. He's thrown his money around and he hired an ex-con. Maybe he's pulling the strings. He can't be happy about the incident on the farm. But I don't think that's why Parker was killed. Maybe Gigi does."

"Gray said Gigi made his money producing then distributing

high-grade plumbing fixtures. His products are sold all over our country."

Betty laughed. "A royal flush."

Sister appeared appalled. "Do you eat with that mouth?"

Weevil's eyes widened then Tootie, who had known the two older women since seventh grade at Custis Hall, quietly reassured him. "They're always this way."

"Okay." He smiled.

Betty patted his arm. "Weevil, when you've been friends with someone for decades, it all comes out . . . the good, the bad, the ugly. You know, ugly with shoes."

"I beg your pardon?" He blinked.

"I don't know if it's a Southern expression but it's an American one. Another one is 'She doesn't wash her fruit.' "

"What?" He laughed.

"Means someone is crazy." Betty laughed with him. "Come on now, Canadians must have silly expressions."

"Mrs. Franklin, we are totally reasonable people." He busted out laughing and they all laughed together.

"Well, Betty, you and Bobby have given us something to think about."

"My thought is, there's money to be made and money at stake." Betty then changed the subject. "We ought to leave fifteen minutes early tomorrow to get to Kingswood." She cited a newer fixture.

"Right." Sister then suggested to Weevil, "Leave the youngsters back. We don't know this place that well and even though we have the tracking collars, let's wait until next time."

"Right-O." He grinned. "British expression."

Betty fired at him, "I thought you were Canadian?"

"I am, but we're closer to the Brits than you are." He smiled.

CHAPTER 21

February 27, 2020   Thursday

S wirls of sleet demolished hope of warmer weather. Sister, leading the small Thursday group, picked her way down a steep hill made sloppy by the sleet. Sam and Gray rode immediately behind her, as did Kasmir and Alida. Freddie Thomas followed them, along with the treasurer, Ronnie Haslip. Most members had watched the early-morning weather report and snuggled back in bed. Staff does not have that luxury.

Aces led the pack, now at the foot of the hill. Young, he was coming into his own.

"Fading," Diana alerted them.

Dasher, her littermate, nose down, trotted determinedly. *"Here."*

The older hounds paused for a moment. Aces knew better than to forge ahead. One respects one's elders, regardless of species . . . well, some species.

"Got to be Charlene and she's heading home." Dasher recognized the red vixen's signature scent.

"What's she doing over here at Kingswood?" Barrister wondered.

"*Hard to say, but I wouldn't be surprised if she found something good to eat.*" Zorro sniffed then walked over to an opened sardine can, which made his point. "*Bet you Cindy Chandler put these out, including on the border between the properties. Good way to get foxes to travel.*"

Charlene was traveling at a faster pace, for she knew the sleet somewhat intensified scent. Any moisture gives scent a bit more tang unless it's a driving hard rain or blizzard. In the prime of life, the beautiful red vixen had heard the hounds before she smelled them and they her. So she gobbled the last of the sardines, a delicious treat, then started for home, but home was After All Farm. Given the drive of the pack, she'd need to duck in somewhere closer.

Heads down, the riders trotted across the unkempt meadow on the Kingswood side of the large open space. Made by alluvial deposits over the centuries it, too, held scent. Not that the humans could smell it, but the old human hunters learned a bit about scent over the years. Mostly they learned that nobody knew what the hell it was. Sure, it's the odor of one's game, but why on a day like today is it heating up just enough, whereas on another day, seemingly the same weather, nobody can find a thing?

Betty now rode in the unkempt field on the north side of Hangman's Ridge. Tootie, thinking ahead, galloped to the far side of the ridge, footing awful, but was ready for a run that might head east. Weevil hung right behind his hounds, who now ran, speaking loudly.

By the time Sister and the field reached the narrow deer path on the north side of the rough stuff, everyone felt grateful to still be mounted. Footing proved awful.

Charlene crossed the high flat plateau with the enormous hangman's tree in the middle, scooted across it to shoot down the south side, scattering minks who had come back too early, being as fooled by the weather as the humans, as she ran. The minks hurried to their dens. Opportunists, they liked coming down the ridge to the Roughneck Farm side and snapping up leftovers, but they needed to be careful of the house dogs. If weather turned dreadful, there were enough outbuildings to duck into that no little thief need be inconvenienced. These minks descended from the minks at Pattypan Forge and returned there for most of winter. Aunt Netty proved such a boor, the younger ones left early.

The branches of the trees shivered in the wind. The lower ones, three centuries old, massive width, didn't bend as the high branches did. But the wind, powerful across this expanse, could move them a bit so it looked as though they shivered.

Baker, one of the two "B" girls, stretched out, ran hard. As the hounds reached the path down the south side, the first-year entry jumped sideways as a mink shot across her path.

Weevil, now on the plateau, squeezed Showboat. The sleet stung, his hands in his thick string gloves throbbed. Like the animals, he disliked it up on the ridge. Within minutes he, too, slowed a bit to descend at a forty-five-degree angle.

Charlene knew better than to flash across an open meadow and the only way to After All was to do just that until she reached the fence line between the two farms. She cut left to duck under Tootie's cabin, squeezed through the hole in the lattice hiding the dirt underneath the porch, crawled into Comet's den.

"Sorry, Comet. Getting bad out there."

"Is. There's room enough for two." The slender gray fox, accustomed to pressed visitors, curled up on a pile of old towels, leaving the dog bed that he had saved from the garbage, for Rooster had chewed it. Charlene nestled in the dog bed while the pack carried on at the latticework.

"You'd think they'd have sense enough to know it's hopeless." Charlene rested her head on her front paws.

"They're bred to run around and make noise." Comet couldn't grasp why any creature with the canine mind could be so useless.

"Cheater," Baker called out.

Weevil gathered his hounds together. Having only been out over an hour he thought he might cast to the Old Lorillard place. As he turned to jump the coop, a loud crack and a crash made people pull up their horses. A limb from one of the apple trees tore off in the wind. Fortunately, no one was in the orchard, but they stood on the farm road next to the orchard.

"Weevil, think we got lucky there," Sister said as she turned toward the kennels in the distance. "Let's put hounds up."

Once horses were settled in the trailers, the staff horses in the barn, the small group gathered in the tack room for hot coffee and tea on the hotplate. Everyone brought sandwiches, cookies, and brownies, enough to fill you for the drive back.

As they talked, Sister's cell rang; she intended to ignore it but something made her look. She put the phone to her ear, walking out into the colder main aisle.

Listening intently Sister said, "Thanks for calling. I'll tell our sheriff. I'll call you later. We got back from a so-so hunt, not bad, not great, but a decent run. The diehards are in the tack room."

As she clicked off her phone, Gray walked out with her fleece-lined old bomber jacket, which was hanging in the tack room, draping it over her shoulders.

"Thank you, honey. That was O.J. There's been another theft. In Louisville. Another Munnings, but the thief didn't make it. As to the suspect in the Buckingham theft, he was cleared. He had truck trouble near the house."

"They caught the thief this time?" Gray's eyes brightened.

"Yes, but he was dead. They found him in a truck, another small box truck. The police were called by a neighbor who saw the truck pull out of the driveway. A construction company name painted on the side. Someone followed him and killed him. They got the painting. He may have stolen it but he was killed."

"This couldn't have been in the city. Someone would have seen something." Gray stroked his chin.

"Shelbyville. He made it as far as Shelbyville to turn onto the back road to Springfield. At least that's how I know it. You go inside, I'll be right there. Want to call Ben right away and he can call his counterpart in Shelbyville."

"No one else was harmed? Not killed like the Lexington lady?"

"Just the driver, strangled with a Fennell's lead shank. And oh, the painting was *Why Weren't You Out Yesterday*. Two ladies sidesaddle."

Gray shook his head as he opened the door to the tack room.

CHAPTER 22

February 29, 2020   Saturday

Father Mancusco rode with Reverend Sally Taliaferro, a Catholic and Episcopalian trotting toward a part of Beveridge Hundred, the farm abutting Tattenhall Station to the south. Yvonne, driving as usual with Aunt Daniella and Kathleen in the car, marveled at the change in the weather. From cold, high winds it transformed into lowering skies, a mercury in the mid-forties, yet a bitter chill remained.

"No speaking." Aunt Daniella cracked her window slightly.

The temperature, cold, made her face tingle. She listened intently while wrapping a heavy cashmere shawl tighter around her shoulders.

"I thought low clouds, cool temperature but not too cold nor too warm was best." Kathleen was determined to learn.

"Usually it is, but even on a good day it might take time to bolt your fox. It's easiest when you catch scent of someone going home or, given it's breeding season, a gentleman fox visiting a lady. You know, breeding, convincing a mate is a lot of work." Aunt Daniella smiled.

"My feeling is, let men do all the work. I'm not chasing any-one." Yvonne slowed, as a big jump loomed up ahead.

"Oh, when did you ever chase anyone?" Aunt Daniella teased her. "Fess up."

"In high school. There was this guy in music class. I thought he was wonderful but he wasn't interested in me. I was crushed."

"Had to be gay." Aunt Daniella laughed. "Before you have a moment, Kathleen, my son, so handsome, was gay."

"Why would I have a moment?" Kathleen's eyebrows raised.

"I suppose someone could take that remark as anti-gay. One doesn't know what to say anymore," Aunt Daniella remarked.

Yvonne laughed. "That is hardly your problem."

"Well . . ." Aunt Daniella trailed off. "Back to high school. Was he gay?"

"He was." Now Yvonne laughed. "We became best friends and he was the one who told me not to marry Victor. I should have lis-tened. He declared a man can see through a man easier than a woman can."

"I think he's right. Desire clouds one's judgment," Kathleen declared. "Not that I have bad stories to tell. Harry and I simply grew apart."

"Victor and I didn't grow apart. I wanted to kill him."

"Oh, Yvonne, no man is worth killing. I ought to know." Aunt Daniella leaned forward, turned to stare out the now rolled-up win-dow. "Listen." Then she rolled the window a crack.

"They've hit." Yvonne stopped, for hounds crossed to the west side of the road, bounding onto the southernmost part of Old Par-adise. "They are flying."

Back at Tattenhall Station after a hard hunt, for some riders, when their boots touched the ground their legs shook. The trail-ers had parked at Tattenhall Station. The hounds walked to Bev-eridge Hundred for the first cast. There wasn't enough space to park at Beveridge Hundred, plus Cecil Van Dorn was in poor health, fighting a nasty flu. So was Edward Bancroft. The two were friends.

The usual wonderful repast awaited the people. There wasn't one person who didn't sit down. Fortunately the long tables accommodated the field and the gentlemen even with shaky legs did fetch drinks for the ladies.

"Thank you, sweetie." Sister took her tonic water with lime from Gray, who damn the hour had a scotch for himself.

He left her after putting his drink next to hers so then he and Sam could serve Yvonne, Aunt Daniella, and Kathleen.

The fire crackled in the fireplace, for even though not a bitter day all had worked up a sweat, so on the way back the sweat turned cold, seeping into their bones. A few people took a chill, so that fireplace was welcome.

The drinks and food revived most folks, including staff, who Sister insisted come inside and take care of themselves first. The hounds had cookies, were snuggled in the straw, a few extra minutes in the hound wagon wouldn't hurt anyone.

"The best! Just the best!" Betty glowed as she sat down next to Sister.

"Was," Sister agreed as Ben now sat across from her.

Carter, next to Freddie, handed her the small box in which nestled the one-inch-square inlay of Artemis; the stone, onyx, was surrounded by intricate red gold.

She discretely handed him an envelope. "This will be prefect on my hacking jacket, the one I wear to breakfasts."

"Freddie, anything on which you pin Artemis will be perfect."

"Carter, you flatter me."

"Simple truth." He slipped the envelope to his inside pocket in his tweed jacket. "Great day."

She nodded. "The weather has been so rotten. This spring huge temperature bounces, rain, snow, and too much of it, and now," she snapped her fingers, "bingo. Terrific hunting."

"Is. Buddy Cadwalder called me from Philadelphia. He says Radnor's last few weeks have been terrific. Then he drives down to Fair Hill. Good hunting."

"Let's cross our fingers that our luck holds." She opened the box to admire the beautiful pin.

She rather liked that the Greeks worshipped women as well as men.

Carter looked across the table. "Thank you, Master."

Freddie echoed the sentiment.

"I hoped we'd see Crawford, even if in one of his expensive trucks or cars."

Ben answered, "He is determined to find his painting. He's called museum directors. He's even called the director of The Munnings Art Museum in England."

"Anything?" Carter asked.

"A few thoughts. The sidesaddle ladies were known to Munnings. Usually the painting was a commission. Some of the sidesaddle paintings, not the ones here in America, he did on his own. Fascination with beautiful women and horses, I guess," Ben replied.

"He rode, himself," Carter responded. "I'm sure I read that somewhere."

"Couple of photos of him on horseback." Sister supplied the information.

"You've been on this." Carter smiled.

"Curiosity." Sister shrugged.

Freddie piped up. "Maybe this really is all about money."

"Most things are." Carter finished his drink.

"Yes, of course, but something nags at me about Munnings, the time he painted. I can't put my finger on it."

Carter teased her, "Maybe you should keep your hands to yourself."

"Oh, I'll get over it. Ben will solve the thefts and that will be the end of it." Sister smiled at the sheriff.

"Thank you for your faith in me. Whoever this is is smart. Smart and can convince people, is probably quite likable."

Carter swept his hand outward. "Ben, that's everyone in the room."

Back in the stable, horses cleaned up, wiped down, blankets on, a bit of warm mash for them, too, as well as those delicious soaked alfalfa cubes along with flakes of hay, Sister, Betty worked alongside each other while Gray popped into the kennels to see if Tootie and Weevil needed anything.

"No more signs." Betty noticed the telephone poles driving back. "The old ones are torn off. Maybe our disgruntled person has given up."

"You know it's Sadie Hawkins Day." Sister remembered.

Betty laughed. "That means no bachelor will answer the phone or his email until tomorrow."

They both laughed.

Sister asked, "Did you want to get married, you know, like it was a goal?"

"No, but it was expected of me," Betty honestly answered. "When Bobby asked me I cried I was so happy. I picked the right man."

"You did. I never thought about it. Big Ray chased me for a year. I wouldn't even date him, then I finally did. We went to a production of *As You Like It* in Richmond. Don't know why, but we clicked. So when he asked me one year later to the day, I was ready to say yes."

"Maybe we should say yes more often to all kinds of things."

"Betty, you're right." Sister rubbed Midshipman's muzzle; he didn't hunt today.

"I really like Sadie Hawkins Day. I like the idea." Betty stepped into the tack room, glad for the warmth.

Sister, following, agreed. "I do, too. Why shouldn't a woman ask a man if she's so inclined?"

A devilish look crossed Betty's face. "We should call Ronnie Haslip."

"Only if you pay his medical bill. Heart attacks aren't pretty."

They giggled, laughed, threw out every single man's name they could recall, just silly stuff. The stuff that makes you love people.

Back in the house, boots off, Sister sank into a kitchen chair. "I'm too tired to move."

Gray joined her. "Know the feeling."

"It's Sadie Hawkins Day."

He paused a moment. "So it is."

"Betty and I were laughing that no bachelor will answer his phone or email today."

Gray looked solemn. "Does that mean you aren't going to ask me to marry you?"

"Ha." She laughed.

"So it's four more years?"

"You're full of the Devil." She blew him a kiss. "It's one of the reasons I fell in love with you."

CHAPTER 23

March 2, 2020   Monday

"Pretty terrific." Sister craned her neck to look up at St. Paul, the golden weather vane on top of the stables. "Thought putting the horse weather vane on top of the big hay shed nice, too. Let's take a picture and run in to the 1780 House. I need to pick up some odds and ends at Foods of All Nations. If we stay here we'll wind up doing more chores."

Gray put his arm around her shoulders. "Every now and then it's a great idea to escape chores. And it's a sunny day. That's a surprise."

Sister admired the beautiful weather vane, close to two hundred years old. "I seem to recall a conversation in the library where you questioned my impulsiveness, my discipline when it came to beautiful objects."

He put his arm around her waist. "Well, now, not exactly. All I did was remind you of your desire to buy the Louis XV desk."

"It really was lust and a kind of reckoning because of Uncle Arnold's stolen desk but I didn't buy it."

"No," he dragged out. "No."

"Oh, Gray, sometimes one can't be but so practical, and apart from horses I'm fairly reasonable. Although I must say Carter Nicewonder is forever pushing antique jewelry under my nose. Haven't bought any pieces but I do notice, my angel, that if there is a tool you need, you buy it."

He quickly said, "Sam and I are rebuilding the house."

She put her arm around his waist now, too, and squeezed him. No point questioning tools even if they cost thousands of dollars. A good compressor can set you back.

"I did jump at St. Paul." He sounded almost confessional.

"Baby, I'm glad you did. St. Paul brings back a wonderful memory of your mother and that silly rooster. Graziella and St. Paul, what a combination. I remember your mother well. Apart from her stunning beauty, which, of course, Aunt Daniella also has, your mother was quiet and kind, very kind, even when people were not kind to her. And those who should have been slapped usually wanted to go to bed with her."

"After our dad died, Sam and I became protective of Mom. If she could see this fellow up there now she would laugh." He took a breath. "It's a funny thing but when you paid for half of the rooster, I can't explain it, I could relax."

"You don't have to explain it. Gray, we're in it together. Not that we see everything eye to eye. You're a high-powered CPA and I'm still a geologist whether I'm teaching or not. I'm much more drawn to the natural world than that of people. But even if I do something not particularly fiscally prudent, I try to listen to you."

He kissed her cheek. "I didn't fall in love with you because you're prudent. I fell in love with you because you have a big heart and you let me be me. I never had to prove anything to you. Well, maybe I had to take some big fences early on that I might have gone around, but you're the only woman close to me who accepted me as I am. I don't know, honey, my experience is women try to change men."

They walked out to the car continuing the discussion.

"They try to change women, too. But I know exactly what you mean, which is why I am glad St. Paul is looking down at us. He's helping us talk about the important things and maybe, maybe, your mother is looking down, too."

Pulling into the parking lot of the 1780 House, Gray noted, "Yvonne. Those two are becoming good friends, and isn't that Carter's car?"

"Every year that man buys a new car or SUV. The antique jewelry business is good, or his is, anyway."

They walked into the door to a rapturous greeting from Abdul and Ribbon. Aunt Daniella was also there. The people, not as rapturous as the Welsh terrier and the Norfolk terrier, were nonetheless glad to see them.

"Kathleen, what are you all studying?" Sister asked as a stack of nine-by-eleven papers rested on the coffee table and everyone was looking at one, passing it around.

"Michael Lyne's work at the various auction houses." Carter glanced up as the two pulled up chairs.

"Can I get you all anything to drink?" Kathleen offered.

"No." Sister took up a sheet of paper with four colored representations just about one and a quarter inches by one and an eighth, small but clear. "I quite like him."

"Some of the studies, the line drawings, are offered at two hundred to four hundred dollars. The larger works, so many in watercolor, are priced at three thousand to eight thousand." Kathleen handed a sheet to Gray.

"Are you thinking of offering his work?" Sister was very curious.

"No, but Harry has two here. I like this work and Lionel Edwards's work, too. Watercolors are affordable, but I'm not an art dealer."

"Maybe not, but you have a good eye," Carter complimented

her. "Which reminds me, Buddy Cadwalder bought the entire contents of a townhouse at Rittenhouse Square in Philadelphia. There are still townhouses despite the high-rises."

"He's in the right market," Aunt Daniella commented, as she knew Philadelphia from her youth. "Well, Carter, is he prudent? I mean, according to the papers the young people have no interest in exquisite furniture."

Carter smiled. "Aunt Dan, there's so much money in Philadelphia and the Main Line, he'll always make money. Those people in their forties and fifties will snatch it up. But an entire townhouse!"

"Well, we came here to show you St. Paul." Gray handed Kathleen his phone. "We thought you might be able to use the image."

"St. Paul? Graziella's rooster?" Aunt Danielle loved to watch that silly rooster strut behind her sister, who would pick him up and the damn bird would coo.

"In honor of St. Paul." Gray smiled. "When Kathleen had her grand opening he was on the table. I couldn't help it. I thought of Mother, so Sister and I bought it and see . . ." Kathleen handed Aunt Daniella the phone. "Perfect. Wouldn't Mother love it?"

"She would." Aunt Daniella handed the phone to Yvonne, who smiled as she handed it to Carter.

"A most impressive rooster. I've always wondered why the rooster is the symbol of France. Usually nations use eagles or lions or bears. Why a rooster?" Yvonne wondered.

"That's a good question." Carter rubbed his forehead for a moment.

"*Gallus* is *cock* in Latin and the rooster is a symbol of bravery, regeneration. I vote for that," Sister said. "This is when we realize how young we are as a nation. Most of Europe was ruled at one time or another by the Romans. Anyone who wanted to succeed learned Latin as well as their ways."

Aunt Daniella added, "Anyone here who wanted to get ahead learned Latin. Started in ninth grade at our little school, and segregated though it might be, we had such good teachers. I think if the teacher is good, the students learn because they like the teacher. I deeply mistrust sitting children in front of computers."

"At Custis Hall Tootie needed a computer, as did all the other students, but this wasn't to supplant teachers. But you are right, Aunt Dan. A teacher can inspire a student. A computer won't inspire anyone," Yvonne replied.

"Kathleen, if I come across any drawings, all reasonably priced, of foxhunting scenes or dogs, would you like me to put those people in touch with you? You'd be surprised what you see when you buy old family jewelry," Carter suggested.

"Well, I suppose it wouldn't hurt. I don't want to represent myself as anyone who knows sporting art, but prints or watercolors on the walls are in keeping with the items in the store. And I can learn. I'll enjoy learning."

"If I see anything, what is your limit?" Carter got right to business.

"I think I had better stick to drawings, maybe a small watercolor. Mmm, a hundred fifty to two-fifty. I know the figures on what we are looking at are a bit higher but they are already retail prices or parameters for auction bids." Kathleen looked at Sister.

"So you would double your price?"

"Most times, but one can always negotiate. The important thing is to get people in the store. I'm not an art dealer, but if I please someone and the price is right, they'll be back."

"Now, there's a retail mind." Carter laughed then turned to Sister. "Are we going to the joint meet? Last hunt you mentioned it in passing. The season is about over."

"Our season ends March 14. Jane Winegardner, O.J., suggested all the other hunts come for the March 14 weekend. We'll get two hunts off. She said there would be a big Andre Pater exhibit at the Headley-Whitney Museum."

"Yes, I've been reading about that. Ought to be something a

little different. Old Frankfort Pike in Lexington is lovely. Big farms, big money." Carter glowed with the thought.

Yvonne inclined her head. "You must know where all the money is?"

"Not really. Harry, Kathleen's late husband, had contacts to the old families in Virginia, old furniture. Well, it's the same for antique jewelry. The money splashed around starting mid-nineteenth century. A wife became a man's advertisement, if you will. Most of my contacts are east of the Mississippi just as most of Buddy's are east of the Mississippi and north of the Mason-Dixon line. Lexington bursts with treasures." He smiled slyly. "And remember, George Headley was a jewelry designer. Not what one would expect from the scion of a great family, but he was both creative and rebellious. I will never get any of his pieces, that I know. But I do okay."

"Indeed you do." Aunt Daniella smiled her seraphic smile.

"Aunt Daniella, you honor me. You all may not remember, but in 1994 the museum was robbed of much of Headley's creations, to the tune of $1.6 million. Took them five years to nail the thieves, a gang in Ohio. Much of the jewelry was broken up, melted down, and sold. That was the end of that."

"I would expect the Munnings stolen from Mrs. Buckingham, that one painting, would exceed the value of the jewelry?" Gray asked.

Kathleen shuddered. "Can you imagine owning a piece of art worth that much? However would you protect it?"

Abdul chipped up, *"I'd let her know if anyone was around."*

Ribbon, eyes bright, replied, *"You have to bite them. Really hard bites."*

Yvonne stroked her Norfolk terrier, not knowing the conversation.

"It seems to be the problem. Crawford spent a huge sum on

his security, not that I ever asked, but he must have." Carter held his hands palm upward.

Yvonne turned to Aunt Daniella. "Let's go to Lexington. You, too, Kathleen, we could use a road trip."

"Sounds good to me." Aunt Daniella grinned, ever ready for adventure.

The door opened and a man, maybe in his early forties, walked in, holding some flyers in his hand. He looked at the gathering.

Kathleen stood up. "Can I help you? I'm Kathleen Dunbar, owner of 1780 House."

"I'd like to leave you some flyers. I'm running for county commissioner." He reached out to shake her hand, which she took. "Jordan Standish."

No one said a word as Kathleen took the flyers. "You're the one putting posters on telephone poles. You're against foxhunting."

"A cruel sport for rich people. Elitist. If you read my materials you'll see I'm for free college, healthcare, representation, and mandatory birth control in insurance."

Gray, looking at him, said, "You would prefer people play football?"

"Well, no, but foxhunting is wrong. If you look at my positions, you'll see I am for income redistribution."

Kathleen read his list. Some things she agreed with, some she didn't.

Aunt Daniella read aloud, pausing when she reached . . . "Reparations. How interesting."

"Well, I've got many places to visit but I invite you to any of my campaign meetings." He turned and left.

When the door closed, Aunt Daniella purred, "I just love it when white boys talk about reparations."

CHAPTER 24

March 4, 2020   Wednesday

"Look at the fixture card." Walter sat with Sister at the Keswick Sports Club Grille.

"We usually end on the Saturday closest to St. Patrick's Day. What's the problem?"

"I'm not sure, but today at the hospital after surgery the head of the department called all of us into his office. As you know, there's the virus that had appeared in Wuhan, China. Coronavirus-19 is devastating Italy, in Germany, moving globally."

"I can't say I've paid a lot of attention to it because I never know if what is reported from China is the truth."

"The virus is the truth. The statements that it's not serious are not. There is no First Amendment in China, as you know, so no one will admit anything until this thing is totally out of control."

"Meaning it will arrive here?" she questioned.

"Thanks to air travel, Sister, it probably is already here. We just don't know it. In a healthy person it seems like sniffles, a bit of fever, and being sluggish, but that passes after a day or two. There are people getting off planes at all our international airports who have traveled to China, to Italy, etc."

"No one has said anything."

"That's why the department head called us in. He warned us that we are woefully unprepared. We don't have enough of what we need, and that includes healthcare workers. The virus has to make its way across the Mideast and Europe before it erupts here full scale, but he advised us to prepare. He and the other department heads will meet tomorrow. We'll need more beds and ventilators. Shortness of breath is a primary indicator."

"Can hounds and horses get it?"

He smiled. "I knew you would ask that. So far no to horses, but if an infected person coughed and a hound inhaled the droplets, perhaps."

"Do you think this will affect hunting? Our fixture card is operating for another eleven days."

"It might. I don't worry about you or staff. Nor the members. We are out in the open. Tailgates could be a problem if this hits before we think it will. But I don't see how the virus can miss us."

"Well, Walter, how fatal is it?"

"Depends on age and robustness. Older people, those over sixty, are vulnerable. You, probably not. Let's say someone who has diabetes, any age, or someone who has suffered a stroke or has a chronic condition. Anyone who has had an organ transplant better be careful. The percent of death relative to age is beginning to become clear, but no one knows how long the virus can live, say, on a table. It's what we don't know right now that is the problem."

"Let's wait until things are more clear. All any communication to members can do at this point is frighten people. But if the time comes, I will send a letter out after you read and sign it." Sister paused. "So you will be exposed no matter what, don't you think?"

He nodded. "Don't worry about me. I'm a doctor. I'm exposed to stuff every day."

"Sister." Carter Nicewonder came in wearing a bespoke sports coat with a silk lime green tie, which worked for him, Mrs. Redmayne at his side.

Sister smiled. "Mrs. Redmayne, how good to see you."

"And you, Sister and Walter. I don't get out much anymore. When I do I am happy to see everyone, and everyone looking so well."

"Tomorrow's hunt can't be as good as Tuesday's. What a barn-burner." He grinned.

"Isn't it peculiar to partake of a sport where your star never tells you anything? For all I know, tomorrow might be another wild one. I hope so."

"I do, too."

"Good to see you, Mrs. Redmayne. Please come out with us anytime. We have our followers, and you know all of us."

As they walked to their table near the fireplace Sister watched Mrs. Redmayne, a woman twenty years older than herself, an elegant woman. Age slowed her down but she still turned out like a star.

"Carter always knows who has the best jewelry." She smiled. "It's not me."

"The engagement ring Ray gave you is stunning and I hardly know about jewelry, but that is one monster diamond. Plus you have those painted crystals, the hunt ones."

"Every now and then my late husband did come through." She waited for the waitress to place her salad in front of her. "Carter is a patient man. He keeps relationships fresh. He's much like Harry Dunbar that way."

"After that grand opening I think Kathleen will make it."

"I do, too, plus Aunt Daniella will steer her in the right direction and to the right people. And possibly she and Buddy Cadwalder can share customers, special events." She thought a long time. "Walter, you know I am not a conspiracy theorist."

"I do."

"But what if whatever you call this corona . . ."

"Coronavirus-19."

"What if this was something being worked on, a kind of germ warfare and it got away from the Chinese or an unbalanced person let it loose? Is that possible?"

"It is," he quietly replied.

"What a strange world. Strange to even think of that." She grimaced.

"Any news on the stolen Munnings?" Walter switched gears.

"No. O.J. visited Fennell's. The police had been there to look at sales of lead shanks. Well, Fennell's sells hundreds of them each year to the stud farms, as well as foal halters then regular halters as they grow. No way to keep track of all the new lead shanks. The only murder victims that have been identified are Parker Bell and Delores Buckingham," Sister answered. "The other drivers remain unknown."

"If this virus really takes off, what a cover for the thieves! Everyone will be distracted." Walter had just thought of that.

"Thieves are clever. There are a fair number of Munnings here in our country. You'd think they would have hit Great Britain first."

"True. I expect this is the work of Americans." Walter speared an artichoke. "As long as the thefts involved Munnings, I guess that is some form of clue."

"There's logic to it somewhere, along with the value of the work. The problem with logic is what's logical to you may not be logical to me." Sister sighed.

"If you want an exercise in logic, be a doctor. People do the damndest things to their body or ignore their body. Then again, there must be comfort in denial."

"To kind of change the subject. Do you think most criminals get caught in the end?"

He shook his head. "No. The smartest criminals are white collar. Every day they steal from the companies they work for, or if elected steal from the people or suck up whatever lobbyists give them.

"Actually, I'm not against lobbyists presenting their case. But I am against money under the table or other vices perhaps far more interesting than money. While I'm at it, any progress from Crawford's private detective?"

"No." Then Sister said, "I'll make you a bet. Fifty dollars. I bet whoever the thieves and the killers are, they are part of the show world or the racing world."

Walter smiled. "I'll take that bet and double it. I bet whoever this is in some way is involved in the art market or a museum."

They shook hands. "You're on," both said.

CHAPTER 25

March 5, 2020   Thursday

Two fixtures, abutting each other, filled five hundred acres on the opposite side of the ridge from Crawford Howard's Beasley Hall. As Crawford maintained his own pack of Dumfriesshire hounds, Jefferson Hunt feared rolling up over the ridge and then down into Beasley Hall. Although Sister and Crawford had made amends over the years, no one ever wants to wind up on land not granted to them to hunt. It would set his hounds crazy. The master doesn't live who hasn't had some offended, red-faced landowner screaming at them, or worse, passing a shotgun over the master's head. Crawford would forgo the shotgun, which he considered red-neck. Lawyers were his shotgun. He could make your life miserable. He might not flame out these days, but why take the chance?

To this end he allowed Sam Lorillard and Skiff Kane to hunt with Jefferson Hunt today. Sam rode Sugar in Second Flight. The horse, trained, had not been trained as a foxhunter, and much as Sam wanted to go slow, Crawford, not a horseman, wanted to know if he had made a good purchase. Sam's idea was to keep the gleaming animal in the rear, keep calm, and if she became overfaced turn back to the trailers. Skiff rode with him on Czapka, Crawford's made hunter, a warmblood who mostly tolerated his master's squeeze-and-jerk method of equitation.

The group parked at Fairies Bottom, the day held promise, the mercury remained in the low forties and a heavy cloud cover pressed down chimney smoke as well as scent.

Fairies Bottom, so called because when the temperature lifted, that first night of late May or early June, the fireflies appeared in massive squadrons of light. Back in the mid-nineteenth century one of the children thought they were fairies and the name stuck. Next to this simple, well-maintained farm nudged, in a northwesterly fashion, Pitchfork Farm. Built in the 1920s, the buildings appeared modern compared to Fairies Bottom. And as is often the case in the country, the owners of Fairies Bottom had to sell the land when times grew hard. Soon after they did, the crash of '29 plummeted everyone down with it. The owners of Fairies Bottom seemed pre-scient. As for Pitchfork Farm, drama swirled about it. The next own-ers, having bought it in the last six months, seemed easy enough. They gave Jefferson Hunt permission to hunt, but as yet they had not availed themselves of the social life of the club.

A few trees, buds swelling red, offered hope against the de-nuded trees. Spring would come.

Weevil, Betty, and Tootie surrounded the hounds, eager to go. Weevil couldn't sleep last night because he wasn't sure which way to cast. The last thing he wanted to do was create an uproar with Craw-ford Howard.

"I'll cast in the first meadow. If we don't find, I'll swing toward Pitchfork Farm," Weevil informed his whippers-in.

If hounds hit a hotline and kept running northwest, they would eventually land in Mousehold Heath, fifteen miles away. Healthy, that distance on a hard run will push close to an hour. As they had just hunted Mousehold Heath, Weevil hoped he could find something on these two fixtures without going too far afield.

Weevil cleared a simple coop in the middle of the fence line directly across from the house.

Noses down, the pack moved forward. Pookah slowed under a hickory, branches reaching to the sky.

"Old."

Cora, out today, checked the younger hound's line. *"Doesn't mean it won't heat up. Let's see."*

Sterns swaying, all the hounds shifted over to the tree line at the edge of the pasture, still brown but a hint of green peeking underneath. On and on they worked, steady. This was not a sight to thrill those people who hunt to ride but it did excite those who ride to hunt. The younger "B" hounds quietly worked alongside the older hounds. Indeed the line did heat up. Hounds trotted, as did the field behind them.

Sugar, in Second Flight, followed the other horses. Her ears swiveled, her nostrils opened wide. She didn't know what this was but everyone moved off so she did, too.

Czapka, next to the Thoroughbred, reassured her. *"We might run, we might not. We have to do what hounds do."*

"What about the horn noise?" Sugar thought it brassy.

"I'll teach you the calls. Right now it's one long note and three short ones, kind of in ascending order. The huntsman is telling the hounds to draw the covert. If they find anything, he might scream. He's not hurt."

Sam possessed hands that transmitted confidence to a horse. Sugar relaxed because his rider was relaxed, plus Czapka knew everything. Not two minutes later Tinsel opened. They were off.

"Stick with me. You're gonna love it." The big warmblood broke into an easy canter, the sounds, the smells, the pace lifting all spirits.

As Sister and Jefferson Hunt broke into a run, O. J. Winegardner and Catherine Clay-Neal admired Andre Pater's paintings in the gallery of Headley-Whitney Museum.

"Nobody paints jockey silks or jockeys like Andre Pater." O.J. admired *Fox Hill Farm Silks with Ramon Dominguez*. The jockey, a handsome man who radiated thought, glowed resplendently in silks, the body divided into four red and white squares in front, the sleeves white with three red hoops, the cap red-billed with pie wedges of white and red silk. His wedding ring shone on his left hand. All the paintings of silks provoked amazement, but this one showed you something of the man's character.

"You see fabric handled this way in paintings from the sixteenth and seventeenth century, but after that, with the exception of John Singer Sargent, we seem to have lost it." Catherine stood before the work. "Or maybe we no longer value that kind of beauty or seem to realize that clothes really do make the man. Think of the representations of Henry VIII or Elizabeth I. Their clothing was a statement."

"I fear we've become slothful, mmm, or we're distracted by obvious things. We no longer look at jewelry, fabrics, colors, you name it, as tiny trails into a personality. Then again, so many of those who now have fame wear so little." O.J. burst into peals of laughter.

"If you've got it, flaunt it." Catherine crossed to the other side of the gallery.

"If I spent as much on my body as those women have, I suppose I'd flaunt it, too." O.J. stopped before a painting of a German shorthaired pointer with a pheasant. "Gorgeous."

The two longtime hunt friends strolled through the exhibit, each painting drawing them in.

"I like that he paints African American jockeys." O.J. stood before a painting of a turn-of-the-century jockey in green and pink silks, an unusual combination that was stunning; then again, the jockey wore the colors with nonchalance.

"What was it, the first three Kentucky Derby winners were African American jockeys?" Catherine remarked. "So the men in charge passed a rule that black men couldn't ride the big races. And you know, now we don't have nearly enough African Americans in equine sports."

"Well, the men go into baseball, football, or basketball. Big bucks. I can't help but believe working with horses is a better life. Then again, I couldn't imagine a life without horses."

"Me, neither." Catherine turned. "Do you think we could make this work?"

"One minute. I want to stare at Andre's painting of you and Dude." O.J. walked to a thirty by thirty-four painting of Catherine, sidesaddle, on a large, well-made flea-bitten gray, the flecks tiny specks of chestnut. She faced the viewer, a soft smile on her face, her top hat with a thin veil, almost transparent, over her face. Her right hand, white glove, rested on her hip and her left gloved hand held her crop. Her vest peeking out a bit added a touch of mustard. Her tack, perfect, down to the sandwich case, would impress even people who knew nothing about tack.

Catherine stood next to her friend. "Dude is the perfect gentleman. Everyone needs at least one great horse in their life."

"This really is one of his best paintings, and I'm not saying that because we hunt together." O.J. smiled broadly.

"Thank you. Then again, Andre has a way of capturing you. This exhibit has been a smashing success. And the timing is right for the joint meet, or the movable feast, however you think of it."

The two walked back to Catherine's office, passing one marvelous painting after another, into the center hall, thence to a tidy office. The two sat near each other as O.J. pulled her chair closer to Catherine.

"My idea is to have a formal tea here after the Sunday hunt. Given the distances people are traveling, I do think we need back-to-back hunts."

Catherine replied, "If we get on one of our marathon coyotes, I don't see how someone can go out the next day on the same horse."

A pause followed this. "Sister and probably Deep Run may well bring their own horses, so that leaves us, Big Sky, and Red Rock people. I called Bull Run, too. I expect some of them will come. But they can trailer their horses. I know we can find stalls for them."

"I don't doubt that, but we have enough trouble finding mounts for visitors and now we will need two per person. We'd better think this through."

"Okay." O.J. looked down at her hands a moment, mind whirring. "But what about a tea? We can't really do a dinner in here but a tea in the center part of the museum, we might can do that."

"Hear me out." Catherine leaned forward toward O.J. "If it were May or June we could have a high tea in the garden but March can be filthy. If we have it in here we almost have to ask people to leave their shoes at the door. You know, it will either snow or rain and, if not, the temperature may be twenty degrees Fahrenheit."

"Or sixty-four Fahrenheit."

"Yes. So why don't we allow everyone to go to their hotel, shower, change, come here to savor the exhibit. Then we can either go to one of the halls at University of Kentucky or to the big room at Embassy Suites."

"Why University of Kentucky?" O.J. wondered.

"Some of our guests will have children ready, or soon ready, to go to college. If they see our university, meet a few people, a few might enroll. When people think of University of Kentucky they think of basketball and there's so much more to it than that."

"You know, I never really thought of that. The Maxwell H. Gluck Equine Research Center is one of the best in the country."

"We have a lot to offer."

"Well, if we do as you suggest, then we should provide a dinner. They'll be hungry by the time they get to the venue, whichever one it is."

A knock on the open door captured their attention.

"Mrs. Clay-Neal, you might want to turn on your TV. Louisville channel." Her assistant then walked over to turn on the TV and she left the room.

Both women sat without speaking. When the report ended Catherine turned off the television and sat back down.

"I don't know what to think." O.J. finally spoke. "I would guess some people here already have this virus and don't know it. Have shaken it off."

"A few, probably. If it's in Italy and Germany, probably more than a few. How many Chinese have traveled here and back before China took harsher measures? Does anyone know anything?"

"Like what?"

"How long does the virus live? Say, on a table? Hours, days? How long does it gestate? The speaker didn't specify anything."

"Catherine, do you expect the media to pass up the opportunity to have us glued to the set, interrupted by ads for great discounts on new trucks? They'll keep this thing going as long as they can."

"Up to a point. If this truly is serious, they have to provide sensible, calm information. If not, then I suggest everyone in America cut their cable contract, shut down Facebook. People need to know the truth."

"Yes." O.J. thought for some time. "If it's spreading, as that fellow said, then we're in for it."

"I hope not, but you're going to have to decide. I wouldn't hit the red button yet but you may have to cancel the meet."

"Oh, dear." O.J. was crestfallen.

"You'll know what to do," Catherine reassured her.

"I don't see how anything good can come out of this," O.J. fretted.

That depends on one's definition of good. If one is a murderer or thief or both, a coronavirus pandemonium could provide opportunities.

CHAPTER 26

March 6, 2020   Friday

"I told Buddy you would make him a better deal than anyone in Philadelphia." Carter sat at a table at Franklin Printing Company examining paper colors and weights.

"We'll certainly try." Betty sat next to him.

In the next room, door shut, they could hear the printing press.

"If he is going to attract the right kind of client, then he has to send out a proper card, and believe me, in southeastern Pennsylvania, Delaware, and Cecil County, Maryland, they know." Carter rubbed a fine grade of paper between his fingers. "Right weight. If it's too heavy then it's like a recipe card."

Betty smiled. "Well, it's not that bad, and heavier paper is now the thing for note cards. I wouldn't use it, but I see the point. Doesn't wrinkle or bend. This is to invite people to see the new collection? The stuff he bought from the Rittenhouse townhouse?"

"All four floors." Carter picked up another paper sample. "I like laid bond, not for a card, of course."

"One could trace history through papyrus, vellum, the advances in creating papers. Well, don't get me on that. Let me make a suggestion. Everyone deals with an avalanche of white paper. Buddy would do well to use a cream, light gray, or even a medium shade of tan. Something to stand out when the recipient puts the invitation in the 'to answer' pile. Another option would be a thin strip, a border, and that could be in, say, a more youthful color. Can't do black. And gray, imminently respectable, can be drab. If he has the moxie, go for something a little flashy, a hot aqua, or if that's too much, a rich burgundy. Did he give you any instructions?"

Carter sighed. "No. He dumped it on my lap. He said I was better with color than he, plus I'm gay, so therefore I have innate artistic abilities."

"Carter, you aren't gay." Betty burst out laughing.

"I know. He's just trying to tweak me into it. Buddy can be a devil. Well, being a Cadwalder, he can get away with murder. So, if I pick a color, can I use white for the paper?"

"You can but I still counsel cream at the least. It's hard to go wrong with cream; for one thing, it's warm. Cream and a hunter green border, although that's a combination used a lot by hunt clubs."

"Why?" Carter's eyebrows raised.

"So many of them have green in their colors because since medieval time green is the color for hunting. Another beloved hunt-club color is blue, blue facings. For instance, Glenmore over the mountain uses a marvelous Yale blue. So I say, go for it. Even metallic orange or a hot bronze. Metallic borders are fabulous."

"I had no idea what I was getting into."

"Carter, I can see that. That's why I'm here. And you say he wants five hundred?"

"He does. These are his richest customers, obviously. Given where he lives, he has a wide base. Something I can only dream about but he will be introducing me to his base. Along the way I have met others when we were on horses together, he for furniture, me for jewelry."

"You have a lot of ladies . . . and men, too, I guess."

"I try to travel to at least two hunts per month. Jewelry tends to be an emotional purchase. If I'm called to another state, a big city, I go. I go because it is so emotional people can change their minds in a heartbeat." He laughed.

"Typeface." Betty got back to business.

"Oh God." Carter's expression nearly curdled.

"Script is always proper for a formal invitation and it should be in black. Traditional script, not brush script or anything with an unnecessary flourish. Script flows as it is. So you pick an ivory card, script, and then a little pizzazz, say with a border, and given that his people for this list know the minutiae of etiquette anyway, I'd not stray far from a deep blue or a burgundy. If it were just for me, I'd use bronze. But that might be too much for the Main Line."

Relief flooded Carter's face. "I could never have done this by myself."

"People don't think through what paper grades, fonts, and colors truly mean. Tells you a great deal about the sender."

"Well, you are right. I have never received a piece of stationery from a man with his name in script at the top or even his initials."

"There you have it." Betty smiled.

"Did you know that Philadelphia was the largest English-speaking city in the middle of the eighteenth century, larger than London?" Carter asked.

"No. I knew the British took it over and our capital had to move to the other side of the Susquehanna. To York, I think. I'll give our public schools credit, when I was there they actually taught us history, and civics, too."

"Mmm," Carter mumbled. "If people don't know their history or the history of the world, at least in broad terms, think how much easier they are to manipulate. All that those who wish to part us from our money, or our freedoms, have to do is twist things, arouse emotions. Done throughout the centuries. Look at Soviet Russia or Nazi Germany. Nothing new about this, I guess. And think of the fabulous jewelry stolen or hocked. Can you think of a grand duchess's fabulous jewelry? Sold or stolen, all of them."

Betty exhaled. "Okay, back to business here. Burgundy, blue, or hunter green?"

"Burgundy, a deep burgundy."

"And script in black?"

He nodded. "Maybe a paper color a touch darker than ivory, a true cream."

She pulled a sample from the pile. "This?"

"Good. Say, have you ever hunted up there? You know, Radnor, Mr. Stewart's Cheshire Hounds, Fair Hills? They can all fly."

"No, but I did hunt once with Green Spring Valley in Carroll County. Beautiful territory, fabulously managed. If I can ever stop working so hard, I'd like to hunt the Midwest and West; you know, Red Rock."

"Ah, I would, too. They'll spend big bucks in Reno and Las Vegas."

Betty slid the papers together then turned them on their side to tap them all into place. "Have you ever seen any Munnings up there? Given the thefts, it occurred to me that there's enough money in Pennsylvania and Maryland for someone to own a Munnings or even an earlier Stubbs."

"I have only ever seen a Stubbs in a corporate office where the president was a passionate foxhunter. But Munnings . . ." He paused. "I think Buddy once mentioned to me that the late Jack Young owned one. Hmm, *Penelope Tree on a Dappled Grey*. The Trees were once powerful in England. The times change. Now if someone makes piles of money they buy a sheep preserved in alcohol. No art but hot wheels. Then again, I wouldn't mind a Maserati."

"Oh, talk to Sister. She goes through cars like popcorn."

"She does," Carter agreed. "She beats them to death."

Betty laughed. "She can't understand how I keep my old Bronco going. Well, five hundred cards it will be, and you've given me the information, date May 2, 2020. That gives us plenty of time. No rush. Let me go over this with Bobby and I'll call you with a preacher's price."

"Thank you." He interlocked his hands, stretched his arms in front of him. "My fingers are stiff. That was a long hunt yesterday."

"Now that we can again hunt on that territory, it's good. Needs work, but good. I dimly remembered it when the Taylors hunted with us and they got into the argument with Harry Dunbar, so that took care of that."

Betty nodded. "Hounds and horses are easy. It's the people you need to be wary of." She stopped. "You know, my English teachers told me never to end a sentence with a preposition."

"Your English teachers lost that one." Carter dropped his hands back into his lap. "Not much hunting left."

"I always get blue when the season's over. Drag around for a week then I bounce back. For one thing, there's so much to do you can't drag your butt forever. By the way, will you be going to Buddy's party?"

"Wouldn't miss it. I like Philadelphia. I never tire of seeing the boathouses on the river or Independence Hall. The other city I love is Charleston, South Carolina. Those girls know jewelry." He beamed. "Southern women have their own flair."

"Charleston and Savannah, two gorgeous cities, you step back in time. I hate that we keep tearing down our past and putting up blocks. Maybe the windows are blue or sort of shiny gold, but still, a block. No adornment, and if you think about it, Carter, what is jewelry but adornment, so buildings ought to have some adornment, too."

"You be sure to tell the American Institute of Architects."

"Well, who would listen to a Virginia printer? While I'm thinking about lost causes, do you know the murdered man in the truck found at Arthur DuCharme's has still not been identified? Bobby and Sister think because of the missing fingers they all have to be ex-cons and no one will really care."

His eyes opened wide. "That's an awful thought."

"But realistic. Hire an ex-con, train him because you can't have a butterfingers throwing around priceless art, pay good money, then kill him. No witnesses, no one to ask for more money. It's brilliant."

A silence followed. "Maybe. Well, let me get on home. You'll be out tomorrow, of course?"

"Saturdays are always a big field unless the weather is bad. Sister keeps them all in line."

"I wouldn't mess with her." He laughed. "Not if she comes up with killing ex-cons."

C H A P T E R   2 7

March 7, 2020   Saturday

Pears, peaches, forsythias pressed the pause button as the temperature dropped again. The changing seasons meant people could not yet surrender to spring cleaning, needed to keep a heavy coat in the car just in case the mercury plunged in an hour and the errands were not yet completed. People who liked predictability ought not to live in Virginia, especially by the mountains.

Then again, people who liked predictability ought not to fox-hunt. Sister changed the fixture to Tattenhall Station, for The Weather Channel forecast a few snow flurries changing to rain. No need to have everyone at the distant fixture she had chosen. In a perfect world hounds would be working Welsh Harp or even Wolverton, but given that Showoff Stables now separated the two, that took care of that.

Cars lined both sides of the Chapel Cross roads, east, west, north, south. As the Jefferson Hunt Club tacked up, people dressed in warm coats of all varieties, wearing scarves and gloves, held signs reading "No Hunting," "Hunting Is Cruel," "Hunting Is Elitist."

There were more but Sister needed to get hounds and horses out of there. Reading wasn't a priority.

The chanting and waving signs unnerved some of the horses. Staff horses noted the noise, the pressing people, but stood still for their riders to mount up.

Sister, on Aztec, tried and true, knew he might avoid a sign but he wouldn't bolt or spook.

"Weevil, let's move off behind the station as soon as you can. Our people will find us. We need to get the hounds out of here. I don't want any hound mistreated."

"Yes, Master."

Gray, also mounting up, put himself between Sister and the anti-hunting crowd, perhaps fifty deep, noisy, and with no regard whatsoever for the animals much less the people.

"Go on, honey. They won't get past me." Gray's example led other riders, mostly the men, to form a barrier.

Thanks to the hounds' attention to the staff, they managed to ride to the rear of the station. The protesters bedeviled slower riders then followed the last of the riders. Thankfully no one felt compelled to smash a complaining face with a crop. Everyone had the sense to know their behavior needed to be perfect.

As they rendezvoused behind the station, Sister cursed. "Goddamn their eyes." She counted heads.

Kasmir, close to her, as were Alida, Freddie Thomas, and Bobby Franklin, watched as the protesters marched behind the train station.

Kasmir, pulling out his phone from his inside pocket, dialed Ben Sidell, on duty today. "Sheriff, my property is overrun by protesters. They've left the road and are now on Tattenhall Station property. I do hope you and your team can take care of this. I will press charges, of course. I will press charges to the fullest." He cut off his phone, slipping it back into his pocket.

Weevil blew a few wake-up notes and trotted off. Those people carrying signs, in shoes not meant for the country, wouldn't be able to follow far.

Three car followers edged away from the Station markers along the roads, Shaker Crown and Skiff Kane; Yvonne, Aunt Daniella, and Kathleen; and surprisingly, Gigi and Elise Sabatini with Ronnie Haslip, the club treasurer, in the car with them, who explained foxhunting. Ronnie, a fellow who looked ahead, realized the Sabatinis were the kind of people who needed attention. He hoped Sabatini wasn't funding the Standish fellow running for office and he hoped the Sabatinis did not blame the hunt club for Parker Bell's death. He practically roped them into following by car. If anyone could smooth potentially troubled waters, it was Ronnie. He was more than happy to do it and Sister loved him for it. She'd known him since childhood, where his perceptiveness was already obvious. Also, Ronnie was one of her late son's best friends.

Seeing the behavior of the anti-hunting crowd underscored the calm of the hunters. The anti-hunters did themselves no favors.

Hounds reached Beveridge Hundred with only a few yips and yaps. The darkening clouds, the light wind carrying the hint of moisture promised a good day, good if you'd dressed for it.

Juno, a first-year entry, began to feather. Unsure of herself, she needed support, she didn't open but her tail picked up speed. Dasher walked over, putting his nose down.

"I don't know what this is." The lovely young hound turned to Dasher.

"Bobcat."

"Can we chase bobcat?" Juno did not want to make a mistake and the field was huge today, people would see.

"We can. Fox is preferable, so let's open but should a foxtrail cross the bobcat we can switch over. The humans won't know the difference."

"Really? Not even the huntsman and the whippers-in?"

"No nose, sugar. No nose at all. They have to be right on top of some-

thing to smell it. Now staff may suspect but they won't really know unless they see the quarry. In time you'll become accustomed to what they lack but you'll appreciate what they do have. An odd species. Okay, you open first, this is your chance to show everyone, then I'll chip in. Sing!"

"Bobcat." She warbled, her voice still a bit high.

"Warm, getting warmer." Dasher seconded the find.

The whole pack rushed over, Pickens inhaled. *"Finally."*

His littermate, Parker, said, *"If you don't hit in the first five minutes, you get bored."*

"Shut up." His brother snapped back, they were off.

Aunt Daniella, window cracked, listened. "I do hope they get a good run. These temperature bounces don't help, but the conditions are about perfect. Good driving, Yvonne, getting us out of there."

Kathleen confessed, "There was a time when I might have had sympathy for anti-hunters. But learning, as I have, thanks to you all, I realize they have no concept of nature. We're losing it, I fear."

"We are," Yvonne affirmed. "Let's hope they're gone when we get back. I don't want to waste another minute on them."

Shaker, now on the edge of his seat, the window all the way down, predicted, "If it's the usual red fox we pick up here, he'll cut over to Old Paradise in about ten minutes, but if not, I say this is a straightaway run."

Skiff drove carefully. "They sound great."

"You know the first thing you can lose when breeding is cry. It's funny what you can add fairly easily and what you can't."

"That's the truth," she agreed. "What I've found is you can't breed a den dog. That hound has to appear. I don't understand it. On, straightaway. You were right."

He loved hearing that, naturally.

Once hounds were cast, the protesters disappeared from their thoughts. You can't let people spoil what you love, and neither huntsman was in danger of that.

Ronnie, in the backseat, put his hand on the headrest of Elise's seat. "Hounds have found. You can see the two whippers-in moving forward and a bit outward. It's easier to come into hounds than move out, because if you're moving out you usually are trying to catch up. Betty has a clear path right now but Tootie is in the right place."

"How can you tell?" Gigi asked.

"If you think of the face of a clock, hounds are at twelve o'clock, the huntsman is the button where both hands join. Your first whipper-in should be at two and your second whipper-in should be at ten. Many hunts use more than two whippers-in but Sister only uses two. She says if hounds need pushing up, she can do it. Best to keep things simple but our territory lends itself to hunting the old way. So many highways for other hunts."

"The face of a clock. I can picture that." Elise watched as horses picked up an easy canter.

"As I said when we drove off, there actually is a lot to it. As I also said, we usually don't have protest drama. Never had people in pursuit before. We'll get one or two at a county meeting but this was a first and I hope a last."

Back on the field, the hounds now moved in a line, for the territory began to close in. Weevil, behind them, saw the coop in the old fence line, which fortunately would put him on a decent path in the small woodlands on the south side of Beveridge Hundred. He was on Gunpowder today and if he had given the Thoroughbred the horn, Gunpowder could have hunted hounds.

The bobcat charged through the trees, turned right toward the road somewhat visible through the trees still denuded. Leaping straight up an old black gum tree, the bark friendly to claws and climbing, he dug in, heading straight up. High in the tree he surveyed the pack from a thick branch.

Dasher reached the black gum first. Immediately behind him

were Thimble, Giorgio, and Aero, now the fastest hounds in the pack. Dasher's brother and sister remained in the kennel today or they, too, would have been right up front. Coming up ran Juno, Trident, and Zane, the rest immediately behind.

The bobcat looked down, baring his considerable fangs.

"Nothing we can do." Zane sat down as Zorro and Audrey stood on their hind legs, hopping.

"If he were down here I'd teach him a lesson," Zorro bragged.

"Idiot," the bobcat growled.

Weevil also looked up. "Come along. Well done."

Freddie Thomas, in First Flight, fished her phone out of her inside pocket to snap a photo. While it was a great way to smash up a phone, hunting with it, she from time to time would take a photo if it didn't interfere with anything else.

Carter, next to her, also stared straight up and now everyone coming up, even Second Flight, did likewise.

Aunt Daniella asked Yvonne, "Can you see anything?"

"No. Everyone is looking up. That's it."

Ronnie Haslip with the Sabatinis got out of the stopped car, walked to the edge of the wood so he could see better. In a moment he returned, with a photo in his phone, which he showed them.

"The bobcat is up a tree. Big boy."

Gigi felt the roll of cold air when Ronnie closed the back door. "Do you often chase a bobcat?"

Ronnie thought a moment. "From time to time. They are very elusive.

"Weevil will cast on the western side of the road. Soil's decent here, holds scent a bit. You never know, especially now. Of course he wants to run a fox."

"Why now?" Elise asked.

"End of mating season. Those foxes, usually young ones, may not have found a mate yet and will need to wait until next year.

Doesn't mean a few aren't still out there looking, but in the main the long, fantastic runs from December to early March are over."

"The females aren't running?" Elise asked.

"Not much. They'll stick close to their dens, forcing the males to find them. They look them over and when they become pregnant they really stick close to the den. The male usually stays with the female until the young disperse, which is, oh, early October here in Virginia. The young males are pushed out by their father. The female cubs might stay an extra year to help with next year's babies. People don't think foxes are social animals but they are. They cooperate."

"That's fascinating." Elise watched as the handsome huntsman now on the other side of the road, having taken an old sagging coop, cast the hounds.

"Mother Nature doesn't make too many mistakes." Ronnie watched hounds. "If you think about it, most of her mistakes are extinct."

As the car followers talked, Sister waited an extra moment before taking the old coop. Jingle, another youngster, a bit confused, stood in front of the jump. The master said nothing, waiting for the huntsman to call hounds or blow them on. She loved the tri-color girl but this was business. Jingle did not need to be listening to the master but rather her huntsman.

Weevil tooted two notes and the relieved first-year entry now knew to go to him. She vaulted the jump, flying to him and then rushing up into the pack, who ignored her frantic tail wagging.

The cars slowly turned around, for the road was narrow. Yvonne, in front, followed the hounds running close to the old fence, which turned into a new fence once they reached the corner of Old Paradise, where she stopped.

The next hour, stop and start, frustrated hounds as they picked up squiggles of scent only to lose it. As there was no wind, soil moist, temperature maybe 41°F, this should have been a stellar day. Wasn't awful but it wasn't stellar.

Sister, watching now as hounds cast again, witnessed a bright beam of golden sunlight seemingly slice through a dark cloud, where it reached the ground. The gold against the charcoal cloud illuminated the pasture around it. Had she been superstitious this would have been a sign of something, maybe hopefulness?

Parker opened. They all chimed in and hounds crossed the road, leaping over the two jumps. The one at Old Paradise was a stone jump with a telephone pole over the top. The jump into Tattenhall Station was a new formidable coop, painted black. A seven-board coop, so best be alert.

Aztec popped over but the seven-board coop deterred some riders, who drifted back to Second Flight. Hounds roared over the back pasture of Tattenhall Station down to the strong running creek before the railroad tracks. Sister noticed in the distance no cars were parked along the road. The protesters had been dispersed.

The fox, a healthy red, turned south and within minutes all were on Beveridge Hundred again, where the sly fellow made straight for the main house then veered off to Yvonne's dependency, executed a confusing circle only to blast straightaway back to the road, where the cheeky devil ran straight down the macadam road for a quarter of a mile. Ruined scent. By the time hounds reached the road, the loathsome smell of oil and gasoline, not very discernible to the humans, fouled the fox scent. Sister, clearing the two jumps to reach the road, pulled up on the side. Weevil stood in the middle of the road, blowing his hounds back while the car followers blocked one end of the road. Tootie quickly stood in the middle of the other end. Fortunately no cars were about.

"Good work," Weevil praised his hounds, gathering them as he trotted back to Beveridge Hundred.

Sister, following, thought they'd done as much as they could on a strange day. She'd let him determine the next move. If at all possible she did not intrude on a huntsman's decisions.

Weevil, sensibly, chose to hunt back toward Tattenhall Station, where all they found were four deer shooting in front of them. Hounds paid them no mind. Twenty minutes later all reached the parking lot.

Once in Tattenhall Station everyone found a place to sit with food and drink, including the car followers. Elise bubbled with excitement and Gigi, less excited, was happy with his wife's enthusiasm. Ronnie made certain to introduce them to others, seating them amidst a lively group.

Along with the day's sport, the protesters provided discussion.

Aunt Daniella, head of the table, listened and laughed. "If people are out here on a brisk Saturday, you know they have nothing else to do. Then again, some people like to be upset, to have a cause that brings them attention."

Sister happily dropped into a chair. Gray brought her Perrier with lime plus a salad. She thought she wasn't hungry but once she ate a bit she discovered she was.

Betty, now next to Sister, devoured her macaroni and cheese, always a favorite on a cold day. "Have you all been keeping up with this virus thing?"

Yvonne replied, "Not too much. The information is conflicting."

"Odd," Carter simply said.

"As far as we know today, anyway, anyone whose health is compromised with a chronic condition or who just had an operation, or who is older, is more in danger."

"I'm not worried," Sister flatly stated. "Old though I may be, I'm in better health than most of the forty-year-olds sitting behind a computer in a corporation. I'm not going to worry until we are given clear information, and even then I have to ask, who does this really benefit?"

"Cynical." Betty lifted one eyebrow, dropped it. "I am, too. It seems to me if there's any way someone can figure out how to profit from a virus, they will."

"Betty." Kathleen looked at her.

"Well, I'm sick of if Democrats say 'apples' then Republicans say 'bananas.' Nothing gets done. Why should this be any different? Party is more important than people."

"You have a point." Gray nodded. "But we can hope the welfare of our people takes precedence even in Washington; that is, if this turns out to be more serious than we are presently being told."

Aunt Daniella listened then added, "My parents were in their prime when the Spanish flu hit. So many people were dying. No one knew what to do but they carried on. That was probably the worst thing apart from wars to happen in the twentieth century. I remember in 1949 when the polio epidemic took over. We'd always had polio but this was a wave. Again people carried on. I don't recall panic. Some people took their children out of schools. Kids did get polio in school but no one knew how. What I predict is no matter what happens, the media will beat it to death and scare the bejesus out of people."

Freddie said, "Let's hope the media puts news ahead of profit. Scaring people makes them money but I think all the media, electronic or newspaper, must live up to their true responsibility, to give us the most accurate information they can."

Carter changed the subject. "We're almost at the end of the season. Hard to believe. I'll miss next week but not Saturday. Have to go to Charleston."

"Lucky you." Kathleen smiled.

"Clients. The shops on King Street could wipe out any profit I make."

"Well, Carter, discipline," Freddie teased him.

"Easier said than done," he replied.

A beep snatched Carter's attention from the people. He took

his cellphone out of his pocket, stood up, and left the table with an apology.

Elise walked over to Sister. "I'm glad Ronnie wouldn't give up until Gigi and I said yes to following the hunt in a car. It was fascinating."

"I look forward to the day when you're riding with us." Sister smiled. "If you can take those jumps I saw at your show ring the day hounds ran over there, this will be a piece of cake."

Sister neglected to say the show ring had flat ground.

"You're a flatterer." The newcomer smiled.

"You have all spring and summer. We have trail rides. We visit other hunts for their trail rides. I'll send you a schedule. Well, Betty will send you a schedule. She's our hunt secretary. You'll meet interesting people. Foxhunters aren't dull."

Betty grinned at Elise. "Bet you already knew that."

As the Sabatinis left, Carter rejoined the table. "Betty, Buddy agrees to the price."

"Good." Betty beamed.

"Then he told me." Carter addressed the people at this end of the table. "We'd better make hay while the sun shines, given the increasing attention this virus is getting."

Once the breakfast broke up Yvonne drove Aunt Daniella and Kathleen to Aunt Daniella's, where Kathleen had left her car.

"Come on in," Aunt Daniella invited them.

"Don't try to feed us," Yvonne suggested.

"I won't, but we can have a drink."

Ribbon investigated everything in the house. The Norfolk terrier had become Yvonne's constant companion. The three women chatted a bit, talked about the hunt, the members, the breakfast, whatever.

"Well, ladies, best I go home and walk Abdul."

"Are you worried about the virus?" Yvonne asked as Kathleen stood up.

"A little. My fear is that no one knows what they are doing."

Aunt Daniella lifted her bourbon as a goodbye gesture. "Kathleen, no one knows what they are doing wherever they are, regardless of profession. It's all bullshit. If we knew what we were doing, do you think we'd go to work forty hours a week and do it for somebody else?"

CHAPTER 28

March 8, 2020 Sunday

Standing in her tack room, Sister inspected the hunting tack. All was in good order. Church that morning, Reverend Taliaferro gave a sermon on the Four Horsemen of the Apocalypse. Usually sermons did not stray into Revelations or literature, as that was a famous novel written by a Spaniard, Vicente Blasco Ibáñez, in 1916.

She stepped out into the center aisle, all cleaned, horses out in their pastures, stepped back in, for it was chilly. Raleigh and Rooster stuck with her. Shutting the door to the tack room, she sat down at the small desk. Lifting up the top, it was an old school desk, she pulled out a notebook and a pencil. She liked No. 1 lead pencils, having good pencil sharpeners in the stable, in the kennels, and at the house.

Raleigh sat next to her, head on her thigh. Rooster sat on the other side.

Looking into those warm eyes she said, "I'm going to list things. You listen. If I read my notes, maybe the lightbulb will click on."

"Okay." Both dogs perked their ears.

"Four Sir Alfred Munnings paintings have been stolen. One from Virginia, two from Kentucky, one from New Jersey. While the locations are not bunched together, they are all reachable by car. Right?"

"Right," the two agreed.

"Three ex-cons have been killed. Although we are not sure that Parker Bell is involved, but he has the same two fingers missing from his right hand that the other two victims had. The painting from Lexington, that owner was murdered. All are murdered in the same way, strangled with a lead shank. Then there's Delores Buckingham, strangled like the others."

"Yes."

"No fingerprints. So far nothing. However, where there were trucks they were all of the same type, a box truck, used for delivering high-end sinks, tubs, stuff like that. Most anyone can drive a box truck. They are so ubiquitous as to not cause anyone to pay too much attention." She looked down again at the dogs. "In each case the thief knew exactly where the painting hung, walked in undetected, and made off with it. And each painting is of a beautiful woman or women riding sidesaddle. So, Raleigh and Rooster, you can see there are similarities, a connecting thread. Who would be no threat? Who deals with wealthy people?"

"Lots of people deal with the rich," Raleigh replied.

As if understanding her intelligent Doberman, she mused, "Who would be trusted? An art dealer? Who had access to ex-cons and could still be trusted? That's what trips me up. Most people who work with prisoners or integrates them back into society after they have served their term are social service types. Good people but not the kind that run with the rich. That's a blank space for me, as is the murder of Delores Buckingham. I can understand why the drivers were murdered, the ex-cons, to shut them up. Surely they knew they were transporting paintings and had no doubt helped steal them. We still don't know the driver found at Arthur's Gulf station but he is missing those two fingers so I am banking on him being an ex-con if and when he gets identified. They knew too much for whoever is behind this or they blackmailed the instigator for more money. This has to be masterminded by someone who can move with ease at the high levels of society." A long, long pause followed this. "Almost any foxhunter would qualify because even if a foxhunter doesn't have money, they are participating in a sport long associated with the rich. It's open to all now, but it still has that patina, if you will, and the old, old foxhunters do have money. Golfers at a country club usually have money. People with yachts, say a yacht salesman, would be a candidate. I keep finding threads but nothing ties together."

"Don't hurry. Don't trouble yourself."

"I usually assume a criminal is male, the stats support that, but this person could be male or female, maybe wellborn or has learned the manners of those who are." She tapped her pencil on her forehead.

"We have good manners," Rooster bragged. *"We could get into rich homes."*

"Maybe," Raleigh corrected him. *"Some people are weird about dogs."*

"I doubt this is someone young. Has to be someone established. Okay. I say this is a man or woman, middle-aged, smooth manners, attractive, can talk to anybody. Actually, we have some men in the club who fit that bill. Gray is handsome, can deal with senators, corporate heads; Kasmir; Crawford, but he's rough around the edges; umm, Walter. Now there's something. A doctor can go anywhere. Hadn't thought of that. Carter, another smoothie, and his friend Buddy Cadwalder. Gigi Sabatini has a big business but he's not really smooth. He's not badly mannered, but the polish isn't there. You guys, now what?"

"Wait for another murder or theft?" Rooster offered.

"Hey, someone's coming." Raleigh stood up and barked.

The motor cut off. Sister rose, went to the outside door. "Good God." She opened the door. "Come in."

Jordan Standish stepped into the tack room, inhaling for the first time the aroma of oiled leather and *eau de cheval*. "Why didn't you tell me who you were at the 1780 House?"

"You didn't ask. Sit down. To what do I owe this pleasure?"

"Will those dogs bite?"

"No, not unless you threaten me. You were lucky no one was hurt yesterday. No horse spooked. No one fell off."

Jordan fiddled with the zipper of his heavy jacket, running it down, for the room was seventy degrees. "Are you going to press charges?"

"No. You weren't trespassing on my land. You trespassed on Kasmir Barbhaiya's land."

His lower jaw jutted out slightly. "Can you ask him not to do that?"

"No."

"We won't disrupt a hunt again."

"Once was enough. You really were lucky no damage was done to people or property." She remained cool.

He heated up a little. "Foxhunting is cruel. All hunting is cruel."

"People kill one another every day. Women and children are raped and beaten. First, I don't think hunting is cruel if responsibly done. Second, why don't you focus on the big issues?"

His face reddened. "It's elitist."

"You haven't answered my question. Are you more concerned about us chasing foxes we don't kill than you are about the violence humans inflict upon one another?"

He sat there mute as maggots . . . finally, "It's so frivolous."

"Beating women or hunting?"

"What purpose does it serve? Hunting, I mean."

"Well, I keep moving, for one thing. I'm, we are all, out in fresh air, we must keep fit, and we see the beauty of nature. There's no such thing as a foxhunter who is not an environmentalist. But Mr. Standish, what do you think of golfers? Skiers? Surfers? What about someone who goes out in the bay with a small sailboat? Have you no hobbies? Are you intent on removing all passions and joys? A modern Oliver Cromwell?"

"I want to improve Virginia."

He knew little about Cromwell.

"Banning foxhunting isn't the way to do it. Try this, Mr. Standish, one out of eleven children in this state has slept on the streets at night; Virginia, the best-managed state in the union. At least that's what those kind of listings say. For years we top that list. So how about addressing that instead of fooling around with foxhunting?"

"New people are pouring into Virginia. They don't believe in foxhunting, shooting, you know, guns."

"And you intend to be their leader? Have you ever shot skeet?"

He shook his head. "Never."

"It's a good hobby. Need hand-eye coordination and you can do it pretty much by yourself, with one person to loosen the target. Or clays; anything, really. It's relaxing. Just you and an inanimate, moving target. But perhaps you can't enjoy anything that doesn't align with your purpose."

"So you will not willingly stop foxhunting?" He evaded her questions.

"No and neither will any other hunt club. Have you any idea how much money horse-related activities pour into this state? Over one billion dollars. One billion. Do you want to be the elected official, say you get elected, who costs the state one billion dollars? And the horse world is a clean world. No pollution discharged into our rivers, no destroying our beautiful land for housing developments. You really ought to think this through."

"I knew you wouldn't listen."

"I have listened. You do as you wish with your campaign but those who agree with you aren't, shall we say, our people. Few will have been born here. Even if you continue to think badly of us, you have to make compromises to lead."

"Our president doesn't."

"Mr. Standish, he makes compromises every day, even if he denies them. So did every prior president."

"Did you vote for Trump?"

"Did you?"

"Never. I'll vote Democratic."

"You think they aren't hypocrites?"

This made him squirm. "The rich are the problem. The corporations are the problem."

"Given your refusal to answer my questions, I will assume women and children are the problem as well as any man who doesn't think like you."

"I never said that." He raised his voice.

"You can't go around attacking people's pleasures. I am sure Mr. Barbhaiya will press charges. He is his own man. If you want to succeed in politics, focus on the big issues. Creating an uproar over less important matters might arouse emotions, gain you followers, but you'll be like every other half-wit who lies his way into office, sits on his fat ass, and does nothing."

"I'll make things better." He paused. "You are not what I expected."

"I'll take that as a compliment." She smiled, an irresistible smile. "Now let me ask you something that has nothing to do with politics. If you masterminded a plan to steal valuable art, million dollars' worth of art, what would you do with it?"

"I would, uh . . ." He paused. "Find a black market." He thought again. "Not in America. How can you hide a million-dollar painting?"

"I agree. When you go home, look up on your computer Sir Alfred Munnings. Four of his paintings have been stolen within a month. Not a trace of them or even a lead as to who has stolen them. Equine art, much of it about foxhunting and racing, I should add. Worth millions, some of his works are over three, four million apiece, the big ones."

"Big as in size?"

"Yes."

He stood up. "I will think on what you've said."

"Ditto. You can come to a hunt anytime you wish. I will have someone drive you around. I bear you no ill will, Mr. Standish, but I will fight if I must."

As he drove away in a fairly new Honda Accord, a nice car, she watched the exhaust curl out of the tailpipe.

"Ah, Raleigh and Rooster, even the politically correct emit carbon dioxide. And you know, there is no way to live out in the country without driving distances. No public transportation. Not much of anything. One has to be self-reliant. Oh well, come on. I've made my list. I know something about our killer. I think of the mastermind as the killer; even if he didn't strangle anyone, he gave the orders. My hunch is, not only does this person understand equine art, he is part of or at the edges of the horse world or the art world. Not a happy thought."

Unbeknownst to her, other unhappy thoughts lurked just around the corner.

C H A P T E R   2 9

March 9, 2020   Monday

Matchplay and Midshipman, two almost five-year-old Thoroughbreds walked along the farm road. Weevil and Tootie worked with them. Both horses had hunted, Midshipman a touch older than Matchplay. Next year they'd be ready for consistent hunting, the big hunts. Following behind rode Sister on Matador and Betty on Outlaw. They'd trotted a half mile, walked, trotted again up hills, and now walked once more.

Sister believed trotting or walking up hills muscled up hindquarters, aided balance. Most any horse can negotiate a flat arena or show ring. Jumping over uneven territory, jumps set where they could be set, called for a bold animal, steady nerves. Those drop jumps could get you.

The four wore turtlenecks, old short jackets over that. Spring nudged forward but the swollen red buds on deciduous trees had yet to open. Daffodils popped up and in some places the forsythia burst open. The temperature rested in the high forties, pleasant, but one needed a jacket and gloves, warm long socks under boots helped.

"Have you been watching the news?" Betty asked Weevil, to her left.

"Not much. What's the latest?"

"Some public officials are predicting we will be hard hit by the coronavirus. Others are saying it'll be like a bad cold, don't worry. But since this subject comes up for every news report, I'd bet things are not good," Betty answered him.

Tootie piped up. "Mom says once the doctors get on the air, especially those who are government appointees, people will take this seriously."

"The only thing I can gather is that the virus transmits easily." Sister looked up at a startling blue sky. "On a day like today it seems that nothing could go wrong."

She had told them about Jordon Standish's visit. They all gave him credit for coming to her face-to-face even if it was to try to avoid charges. His programs seemed far-fetched but possibly not to a suburban person or someone in a city. They exhausted that topic on the way from the stable. The return called for other topics.

"Is your mother going to hunt closing hunt?" Weevil asked Tootie.

"She swears she is. Sam said he will take her to Horse Country Wednesday. She's determined to look perfect."

"That won't be hard." Betty smiled. "Say, Sister, have you heard anything from Crawford?"

"No. Sam mentioned that he is obsessed with finding the painting. Good luck to him." The older woman now rode Matador on the buckle.

"So the high-priced detective hasn't turned up anything?" Weevil wondered.

"Actually he did. They finally identified the driver found in Kentucky. The men killed had all worked in Atlantic City in the casinos. Still don't know about the driver at the Gulf Station."

"Cardsharks," Betty said with satisfaction.

"Yes, but each had been arrested in Virginia for petty theft, stealing from convenience stores, holding them up. Over time, as they served their time, they were sent to Goochland to learn to work with horses. Not all were incarcerated at the same time, but it's possible they knew one another."

"Sister, that's something." Betty dismounted as they'd reached the stables. Once inside each of them untacked their horse, wiped down the animal, no one was really sweaty, threw on a blanket, then repaired to the tack room to clean the tack. The working tack was cleaned as thoroughly as the tack reserved for hunting.

As they worked away Sister told them her conclusions, the thoughts she'd written down yesterday.

"Maybe the mastermind was at the prison facility, too. Maybe that's how he gathered his team," Betty thought.

"Could be." Weevil cleaned the simple D-ring bit with fresh water, then wiped it with a clean rag, paying attention to every detail. "It's fate how people meet both good and bad."

"I believe that," Betty chimed in. "I often think everyone you meet has a message for you."

"My message for you is hand me that girth." Sister poked fun at her.

"Hey, you're lucky I didn't hand you a Fennell's lead shank."

They heard a car engine then it cut off. A knock on the door revealed Carter.

"Come in." Sister motioned for him.

"Well, this is a busy crew." He smiled. "Our hunting season may be over. There's talk of shutting things down."

"So far no one has said or done anything," Sister replied. "We'll hunt from Foxden tomorrow. I don't want to fuel panic and you know how people can get. I'll wait and see."

"I'm driving down to my boat tomorrow," Carter informed them. "If this does fire up, I want to make sure everything is ship-shape."

"How often do you go?" Tootie was curious.

"I check once a month in the winter but when the weather warms up I sometimes stay down there for weeks. Anyway, thought I would check in." He looked at Weevil, winked, then left.

"Weevil, why don't we all walk up to the schoolhouse tomorrow and cast there? Sort of a reverse cast."

"Yes, Madam." He smiled.

"You are so polite." She smiled back.

As they left the barn to go home, Weevil opened his car door, found the small package, nicely wrapped, on the driver's seat, put it in his pocket. Carter had left it for him. Weevil would decide when to give it to Tootie.

They worked well together, liked each other. He knew better than to court her in the conventional sense, but this was a present he had to give her. Maybe after the last hunt of the season.

Sister walked up to the house. Gray's Land Cruiser sat outside. She was glad he was back from yet another short business trip.

She opened the door, heard the dogs barking as she hung up her coat.

"Hey, honey, I'm home," she called out.

He called back, "I'm in the library, watching all hell break loose."

She hurried in, dropped down next to him. "It's kind of like watching the pot call the kettle dirty, isn't it?"

"Well, honey, just in case, we'd better make some preparations."

"Hunt tomorrow."

"I know, but afterward I'll make a run to Harris Teeter. If people get scared they will buy everything."

"We have enough."

"For how long? I mean it. I think people will go crazy."

"Scare tactics?"

He flipped to CNN then to Fox then to CBS. "Thought I'd

check the different flavors. One thing no one can refute is that China has been overwhelmed, Italy's starting to slide, and Angela Merkel is taking no prisoners. It's here that it's murky."

She silently watched. "What do you think?"

"I think after hunting tomorrow we should talk to Walter. Rich people will be buying freezers and buying all the meat in the stores. I mean, if some agreement doesn't soon emerge between our federal government and the medical professionals. In a case like this, best to trust your governor."

"Fortunately, our governor is a physician."

"Yes, he is." Gray put his arm around her. "At this point I'm more wary of other people than the virus."

"Well, let's take it a day at a time."

CHAPTER 30

March 10, 2020   Tuesday

Fog as thin as a veil shrouded the old schoolhouse at Foxglove Farm.

A light mist swirled, barely visible. Hounds waited for Weevil's instructions and the field waited by the clapboard schoolhouse, still inviting and still sturdy although abandoned in the 1960s when bussing became the method, children hauled to large schools, consolidated districts that created rectangular, big, mostly ugly new schoolhouses.

In the distance below, Sister beheld the huge cow and her son, Clytemnestra and Orestes, in a paddock. The Jefferson Hunt always parked by the stables and the cow barn, to Clytemnestra's irritation. Best to be distant from the enormous crab.

This Tuesday the field swelled to thirty-some people. Given the continuing bad news about the coronavirus, many members felt this would be the last hunt despite the season's normal end in mid-March.

Rickyroo, Sister's bay Thoroughbred, waited as patiently as the hounds. He did wonder why every nose had to be accounted for before they took off.

"All right, then, lieu in." Weevil cast downhill from the schoolhouse.

The gray vixen Georgia lived in the schoolhouse in splendor. She rarely gave hounds a run but the hope was another fox may have visited her, sort of like visiting your rich aunt. Georgia had everything, plus Cindy Chandler would open the door, put in a large bowl of dog food sprinkled with treats. If weather turned ugly Georgia need not trouble herself. Sister fussed at Cindy because the fox didn't give them runs, staying right where life was easy. Cindy would laugh, which settled it, as no one could argue with such an inviting laugh.

So down the terrace they would ride once off the flat site, down to the two ponds at lower levels before them. The small waterwheel sending water from the upper pond to the lower via a buried pipe, end sticking out at the lower pond.

Hounds veered toward the woods to the right of this. The moisture intensified scent.

"*Someone.*" Diana kept walking.

Her littermate, the egotistical Dragon, walked beside her. "*Red.*"

"*Yes. We'll see.*" She continued walking but not speaking.

Dragon irritated many of the other hounds but none so much as his own littermates. Diana seemed to be the only one who could work with him, so his hunting days were limited to hunting with her. He was fast, strong, and determined, which was the good part. He thought nothing of pushing another hound off the line, going first, taking credit. The younger hounds would now push back, so Weevil had to keep an eye on him.

Ardent walked fast then trotted. "*Two of them.*"

The scent, having warmed, revealed a double line. The humans had no idea but the hounds, noses down, now trotted. Finally all opened.

Cindy, over the years, opened many paths in her wooded areas helped by the hunt club. Those late spring and summer days brought everyone out with limb loppers, chain saws, even a bush-hog.

Thanks to a wide path, hounds and horses could run without negotiating debris.

Rickyroo, ears forward, listened intently. Sister, leg firm, re-laxed on the fellow, for he was a most sensible horse. His smooth gaits made him a joy to ride.

"Split!" Dragon bellowed before Diana could say the same.

While he cut to the left, she did not. She slowed, nose down, going from one line to the other to determine which was the hot-test. She turned to the right while Dragon could be heard, boom-ing deep voice, on the left.

Weevil, not a moment's hesitation, followed Diana.

Tootie, on the left, per usual, now had the thankless job of pushing Dragon back to the pack. Weevil might thank her but Dragon would make her work for it. He was determined to be right. To hell with the pack, which is a major sin for a foxhound.

"Dragon, leave it." Tootie called his name.

"Screw you," he answered.

As he did not respond to his name, Tootie unleashed her crop, the kangaroo woven crop ending in a tightly woven plait of hay twine. The sound cracked like a rifle shot. His head came up and she rode right for him.

Now beside him, for Iota could easily keep up with Dragon, fast though he was, Tootie turned her right thigh in, pivoting as she leaned over on her left side, and this time aimed her cracker right for Dragon's rear end. Easier said than done, but Tootie, practicing over the years, nailed him.

"Oww!" he yelled.

"Go to him."

Dragon did turn right and hurried to catch up. Hardheaded, he couldn't be taken out with youngsters, as he might lead them astray. He would have today. Dragon was lucky Sister kept him, to use him on days when the veterans were out with only Diana from his litter. His nose and drive were worth it but she was the only person who thought so.

The pack, full cry, raced through the woods, emerging on the far eastern side, a plowed cornfield forcing riders to go along the side. No one should run through plow anyway. Bad enough to risk a crop even if the shoots had not come up, it was also a good way to bow a tendon if the going was deep, which it usually was.

Hounds could go over the plow. Weevil skirted the large pasture. A simple tiger trap in the fence line gave him a way out because hounds were now racing across an old meadow.

Hounds reached the far side of that meadow, once fenced, pieces of the fence standing, the rest fallen down. Scent disappeared.

"Push him. Push him," Weevil encouraged.

Hounds fanned out but their fox, now racing away, had foiled his scent by jumping up, then climbing to the top of the remaining fence, walking that top board then jumping off hundreds of yards away.

The field waited. Hounds tried. Weevil gathered them and hunted back. Two short runs rewarded them but that was the day.

After the hunt, they gathered in Cindy's house, light and sunny. Carter carried a box in, placing it on Cindy's sideboard.

Sister, Kasmir, Alida, and Gray stood at one end of the big hunt board, for Cindy always put on a breakfast.

"After you called, I thought about the protest. There will always be people opposed to foxhunting, any kind of hunting, whether we kill or not. But given that Jordan Standish is running for office he was easy to reach. I spoke to him at length," Kasmir spoke. "I also asked him if Gigi had helped fund his campaign."

"What did you think?" Gray asked.

"I think he was smart enough to make a bargain. And no, Gigi isn't sending money."

Sister smiled. "What's the bargain?"

"No protests at hunt fixtures and he must drop the anti-foxhunting plank from his platform. I expect he will then get around that by speaking against it but not having it written. No anti-foxhunting posters or campaign flyers."

"Even if he shuts up he can always declare his campaign people spoke out without his approval. They all do that and you know perfectly well the candidate is back there stirring the pot." Alida snagged another chestnut wrapped in bacon, a toothpick sticking out from the chestnut.

"I dropped the charges," Kasmir told them. "Confrontation usually doesn't work. It just drives people further apart. Although there are times when confrontation is the only route, having exhausted every other. So we shall see."

"Kasmir, thank you. I do think we are better off." She turned to see Carter handing out face masks. "What the devil?"

"Mandating social distance. Won't be far in the future. Trust me." Alida filled her in.

"What's the distance?"

"Six feet. If we are six feet apart, supposedly the virus droplets won't affix to us," Alida answered. "But other governors are taking more stringent measures."

"Like sending police out to enforce social distancing? How can you enforce this stuff?" Sister was aghast.

"You can't. So the next step will be a lockdown. Businesses will close. Except for crucial ones like a gas station." Gray had watched more news than Sister. "New York is almost draconian, but then again New York has more cases, with people packed together like sardines."

"Do you really think it will come to that? People will be laid off work and the most vulnerable will be laid off first?" Sister, thanks to being a master for decades, worked with everybody, her heart always with the poor.

Kasmir considered this. "It may. We will have to balance profit against life. Now, granted, this seems to be attacking people who have, say, diabetes, and the elderly, but it has swept through China like wildfire, Italy is suffering, too. And if our political leaders don't wake up, ditto here."

"Good Lord." Sister then faced Carter, now standing in front of her.

"Here." He handed each of them a face mask. "If you have to be around people, put this on."

"Carter, we are out here in the boonies." Sister did take the mask.

"Better safe than sorry," Carter announced.

"Aren't there laws against wearing a face mask except if you're going to a party?" Alida asked.

"More bullshit. So if someone marches to protest anything and our authorities, who really have no authority, don't like it, they can identify and arrest the miscreant. It's bloody stupid." Sister was heating up like scent.

"Honey, wait and see. No one is saying you have to wear a face mask to hunt but I expect our season will be over," Gray prudently noted.

She calmed down, surprised that a flash of anger leaked out of her normally tight WASP ways. "You're right. I guess we will have to wait and see. I don't think we are a danger to anyone. We're out here in the country on horseback and we don't need to have breakfasts after our last hunts."

"But if nonessential activities are canceled by the governor, in this case the governors are the front line of defense, will you do it?" Carter asked.

"I will. I think it's a bit much and the thought of all this worries me for the future. How do I know the power won't go to their heads?"

Kasmir smiled. "As an Indian, I think you can trust your Constitution and your people. If those issuing the orders don't return to their prescribed duties after this passes, I expect the people will take care of that." He took a breath. "You do know that India is the largest democracy in the world?"

"I do now." Carter moved on to give out more masks.

"Let me take this one day at a time. If it really does get awful I will cancel the rest of the season. We can all give thanks that we live in the country," Sister glumly said.

"Isn't that the truth," Alida echoed.

On the other side of West Virginia, formerly part of Virginia, rested the magical state of Kentucky. Its governor, Andrew Beshear, dropped the hammer before Virginia.

Catherine Clay-Neal, having finished hunting, rode back to the gallery with Jane Winegardner. Both, fortunately, had grooms today.

"I'll keep the staff on as long as I can. There's always work to be done." Catherine, like everyone, was worried.

Turning down Old Frankfort Pike, the two discussed the abrupt change in everyone's situation.

"One minute. I'll park in front. Come on in. I won't be a moment with the girls."

The two walked in. Not a soul to be found.

Then they heard pounding, voices from a closet in the rear.

Hurrying to the closet, Catherine turned the knob. It was locked.

"We've been locked in."

"Hold on. I'll get the key. You stay here with them. Talk to them." Catherine ran to her desk, opened it, and pulled out museum keys. She ran back and unlocked the door.

Three young assistants blinked, stepped out. Without thinking, the girls hugged Catherine and O.J., who hugged back.

"What happened? Well, first, are you all right?"

Melissa, the oldest, took a deep breath. "We were up front and two men came through the front door wearing those hospital masks. They had guns, herded us back and locked us in. We could hear them. They didn't touch us, really, but then again, they had guns."

"Let's each take a room," Catherine ordered.

Within two minutes a yell came from the big room to the right of the center hall, which also could serve as a gallery. Catherine was checking the strongbox, which was untouched.

She hurried into the room along with O.J. The light, turned on, revealed the divine painting of Catherine and Dude was missing.

"Oh. Oh, how awful," Catherine whispered.

"Sidesaddle," O.J. mentioned. "Awful and bizarre."

"Let me call the police and then I must call Andre." She named the painter.

"Girls," Catherine always called them girls, "we'll all have to wait for the police. Are you sure no one was roughed up when pushed into the closet?"

"Yes."

"I can say whoever they were, they knew what they were looking for, as we heard no talk, no searching about," Melissa said.

"What a beautiful painting. I am so sorry." O.J. then thought a moment. "Delores Buckingham. Thank God no one was killed."

"No one was in the way." Catherine sat down. "Actually, Delores wasn't either, was she?"

"No." O.J. sat down, too, as did the assistants, all felt the wind had been knocked out of them.

"You know what I think?" O.J. sat back. "I think Delores knew what this was about. She figured it out."

"Well, I don't have a clue." Catherine breathed out.

"Be thankful for that," O.J. quietly replied.

CHAPTER 31

March 11, 2020   Wednesday

"I like getting up with the sun." Sister buttered an English muffin with real butter. "But after we shifted to Daylight Savings Time, it's getting up in the dark again."

"The time shifts aren't made with farmers in mind." Gray held a cup of eye-opener coffee. "The real point of it is so people will shop after work is over. If it's dark, people usually go home. That's why in the fall there is now a delay switching back to Eastern Standard." He patted Rooster, head right by his thigh. "Everything that's done regarding time is now commercially driven. Everything."

"That's a depressing thought." Sister pinched off a bit of muffin for Raleigh nudging her thigh.

"Not if you're a businessman. It's all money. Mammon. Nothing new."

"You're smarter than I am, honey. I remember when I was teaching before I married and right up until RayRay was born. I made little . . . I mean, before I married Big Ray . . . but I managed. Sometimes I think I was happier with my little salary than later.

Money gives you choices. I really didn't have many choices, so I was happy. I did okay."

"Your parents wouldn't have let you fall between the cracks."

"No. But I never asked them for a penny. I was too proud." She had to give Raleigh another bite then looked at her diminishing muffin. "Better make another one."

Gray laughed. "You can't help yourself."

"I remember that passage in Arrian, Second Century AD, where he writes that there was one hound he loved so much he let her sleep with him even though he shouldn't have spoiled her. I'd rather spoil those I love than not."

"You do." He nodded. "You spoil me."

"Works both ways." She thought a moment. "Can't say that I look back on my own life much. I'm too busy living today, but I think my parents were proud of me going out on my own. Granted, I took up a female job, teaching, but it was at the college level."

He leaned back, stroked his chin while Rooster tried to work him over, so he dropped his hand on the smooth head. "Beggar."

"I love you." Rooster gave him a soulful look, which elicited a reward.

"You're as bad as I am."

Gray shrugged. "Oh well. But thinking on Mom. Dad died when I was young. I remember him but not all that well. You probably knew him better than I did in ways, but I think Mother was proud of me. Sam broke her heart."

"He did. I regret that Graziella did not live to see him sober up thanks to you."

"Thanks to him. He had to do it himself. I paid for it. Drinking runs in the family. I'm careful but I want that scotch every night. I think we're born not only with talents but predilections. I know Sam carries a lot of sorrow about the pain he caused Mom."

"He's a good man. I'll never forget the day Sam received his acceptance into Harvard. Aunt Daniella had to tie ankle weights on

Graziella. It was a great day. I mean, how many black kids got into Harvard?"

"Few. My brother is brilliant. He's a lot smarter than I am."

"He is not. You can do anything. Apart from your profession, you can fix things, you're welcoming to people. You put yourself together."

"Mercer showed me that." He got up and fixed her another muffin. "Let's split it. I've been a little too generous myself."

"No. You've been perfect," Rooster mumbled.

"How can you two eat muffins? Boring." Golly, prancing on the kitchen counter, criticized them.

The two dogs ignored her but Gray scratched her ears. She was a beautiful cat and persistent.

The phone rang. Sister rose to answer it as Gray buttered another muffin then reached for the orange marmalade jar. She nodded that she would love some orange marmalade.

"Hello."

"Sister. I don't know if you saw the news, but the governor is reinforcing six feet apart, and closing nonessential business. The state liquor stores are considered essential, by the way," Carter's voice informed her.

"What?"

"The virus really exploded in New York . . . New Jersey, too. So this is a preemptive strike. I know we are to hunt Heron's Plume tomorrow, but it might be unwise."

"I'd call the Ingrams to see how they feel about it. Apart from wearing a mask, a new fashion accessory," she paused, "this might be the right thing to do but it will cause panic.

"I'll give the Ingrams another hour. Late risers. And I'll have Betty send out an email once Walter and I figure out what to do."

"I'm thinking about going to the boat and living there until this passes. Have to think it through."

"You should be far enough away from everyone."

He agreed. "Unless the Covid-19 knows how to swim. I've got two bedrooms, a big kitchen, a living room. It's quite nice, really."

"Sounds sumptuous."

"You only go round once. My goal is not to leave anything behind." He laughed. "You might want to consider how this looks to people who don't hunt. If you're out there, you look arrogant and disobedient. I know and you know we're in the open and far apart. And we could stay apart at the trailers. Non-hunting people don't know that."

"Carter, you have thought about this."

"I have. I'm not in an endangered group, people with preexisting conditions or over sixty, but I like my life right now and have no desire to upend it."

"Yes."

"Bet the art thefts stop." He added, "One less thing to worry about, I suppose. Not that I was worried, just curious. Has been a bit of time since the last one. No, I'm wrong. A sidesaddle painting was stolen from the Headley-Whitney Museum in Lexington. Not a Munnings, though, so that's a new wrinkle. By the way, their governor has put out restrictions, too." He heard a beep on his other line. "Have to take this call. I'll look for the email. Take care."

"You, too." She hung up the phone then repeated the news to Gray.

"Better call Walter."

She ate her muffin then did just that.

"It is that serious. We should end the season. We'll lose two weeks, but we really must."

"How long will this rage?"

"No one knows. We can't trust the numbers we get from China. Italy is getting hit hard. Then again, it has an aging population, but the virus is also in Germany. We are woefully unprepared. My suspicion is, unless real leadership appears, it will run rampant."

"The president did halt flights from China, as I recall."

"Too late, plus he was roundly criticized for it. His denial of the seriousness looks suspicious," Walter replied. "I'm a doctor. I look at something like this as a doctor. A politician will look at it otherwise. When Congress wakes up, the administration wakes up, we'll be far behind. All they think about is their job security."

"Well, Walter, how long does the bug last?"

"If you show symptoms, and many people don't, so whether you show or not you should be quarantined for two weeks. A month is better until we know how long this bug actually lives, plus what it can live on, say shoes."

"All right. I'll have Betty send out an email canceling the rest of the season. Signed by both of us."

"Difficult as that is, we must do it. The other thing is, we'll have to cancel our fundraisers until this is over, or at least until people are safer."

Sister sat down, worried. "I guess everyone will be canceling their season. Even out west."

Gray placed his fork across his plate. "If this lockdown eventually gets worse, small businesses will go under. Very few businesses have enough cash to shut down for even a month."

"Well, we don't know that yet."

"Honey, if this gets worse, no one will be able to go to a lecture, a restaurant, get a haircut. This is only the beginning. Our governor will have to be clear about essential and nonessential and that will change. This really is only the beginning."

"I hope you're wrong."

"So do I," he agreed.

"Oh, forgot, Carter said another painting was stolen in Lexington but it wasn't a Munnings."

"Ah. Bet it is still worth a lot." He rose, took his dish to the sink and hers as well. "What was that James Cagney movie? *Never Steal Anything Small?*"

"Anything James Cagney was in was terrific. Did you know he started as a dancer?"

"Didn't. He did move with a kind of grace, though, didn't he? Well, honey, you'd better call Betty. The sooner this goes out, the better."

"You're right." Sister walked to the library, as it was easier to use the landline in there.

Betty, who had heard the governor's address, agreed this was the right thing to do and she'd get on it.

No sooner had Sister hung up the phone than it rang again.

"Mrs. Arnold."

"Yes."

"This is Jordan Standish. I didn't have a cell number for you so I called this number. I hope that's okay."

"It is. I'm not much for using my cell. It's a surprise to hear your voice."

"Uh, well, I called to thank you for talking to Mr. Barbhaiya. He has dropped the charges and he said you suggested that."

"He gives me too much credit, but I do hope this works out. I am happy to show you hunting, but as it turns out we've all been grounded."

"Yes. Me, too. I've dropped my campaign until this is over. Well, I haven't dropped it, but no rallies or meetings. The other reason I called you is you asked me about those crimes."

"I did."

"I don't have an answer but I had a thought. Now that people will be wearing masks, at least some of them, it will be easier to steal, I think."

"I would never have thought of that. Thank you for considering my question. I hope we meet in better circumstances when this ends."

"Yes, Ma'am. A lot will change."

"You're right. Keep well."

"You, too. Goodbye."

She hung up the phone and thought, "Will wonders never cease?"

"Done?" Gray called from the kitchen.

"Yes. You'll never guess who I just spoke with." She walked back into the kitchen to tell him about Jordan Standish.

"He's right. Our state law forbids wearing a mask at a rally, gatherings. They can't enforce it now, can they?"

"I guess not. This is all overwhelming."

"It is. Will there be an increase in crime?" Gray breathed out. "Well, if we have to keep away from one another, if businesses are closed, I doubt it, but a well-thought-out crime, maybe."

"What about mass violence?"

"Whenever people are frightened or angry or both, that is always a possibility."

"Animals are smarter than people that way." Sister believed that.

"Of course." Golly preened.

CHAPTER 32

March 11, 2020   Wednesday

Late afternoon.

How quickly the day flew by. After Carter's call then her calling Walter and the unexpected call from Jordan Standish, Sister walked down to the kennels to give Weevil and Tootie the news. Although young, neither one protested. For one thing, no one knew enough about the virus itself and the media had to stir the pot. Never pass up the opportunity to make money off a crisis. The political version of that was never let a crisis go to waste. The finger-pointing was in full swing.

She turned to the *Richmond Times-Dispatch* for sobriety, where she found it. No screaming, no predications of mass death, simply what the governor's speech meant for Virginia and what was known about the virus. After reading, feeling more clear, she picked up the phone and began calling Betty, Aunt Daniella . . . another surprise, for she took it all in stride . . . Yvonne, Sam, Kasmir and Alida, Freddie Thomas. That took her to noon. Betty sent out the email but Sister felt next she needed to speak to every landowner and those calls carried her to tea time.

Golly, in her special bed on the counter, a place much resented by the dogs, lifted her head as Sister boiled water.

"Golly, it's one thing after another."

"It would be easier if you didn't have two dogs."

"Golly, shut up," Rooster grumbled from his three-hundred-dollar bed with sides and a removable fleece interior.

Sister spoiled them in every respect, except they had to learn manners when puppies.

Raleigh, not bothering to lift his head, remarked to Rooster, *"Rooster, no one could take a cat seriously. Pay her no mind."*

The water boiled while Golly did, too. As Sister poured the water over a Yorkshire Gold teabag, Golly vaulted from her luxurious bed, raced over to Rooster, smacked the harrier on the nose, immediately leaping back up to her bed.

"I'll get you," Rooster threatened.

Golly did not deign to reply but purred loudly, so Sister rubbed her head.

Sitting down at the kitchen table, Sister drank the strong English tea, which snapped her right back. "All right you all, I'm back at it."

Once in the library she pulled out the last volume of Sir Alfred Munnings three-volume autobiography. No sooner had she opened the book than she shut it.

Walking over to the graceful desk in the corner she picked up the phone, dialed the 859 area code followed by O.J.'s number.

"Sugar, I meant to call you this morning after I heard the news, but all this coronavirus stuff has taken up the day," Sister said as she heard O.J.'s distinctive voice.

"Actually, O.J., I meant to call you because I heard the Andre Pater painting of Catherine Clay-Neal had been stolen."

"You have good connections. Will be on the six o'clock news."

"Oh." A silence followed this. "Carter Nicewonder told me."

"Well, there you have it. Good connections. Is there a woman with some means to whom he hasn't tried to sell jewelry?"

"Probably not." Sister laughed. "Some of it is beautiful."

"Is."

"Is everyone at the museum okay?"

"Yes. Catherine and I were coming back from a hunt. She wanted to stop for a moment, we walked in, no girls. They must have heard our voices because they started screaming from the closet. Locked in. Two men with face masks. Guns. No one was hurt. Once released we all walked through the museum, which is when we found Catherine's painting gone. She's distressed. Who wouldn't be?"

"Sidesaddle." Sister had seen photographs of the large, stunning painting. "Well, O.J., this is the first painting that isn't a Munnings. Are you all right?"

"I'm upset for her and for the museum. They have a fine security system but this happened in the broad daylight. All those two had to do was walk inside."

"You would think this would stop. The longer it goes on, the more vulnerable the thieves are, or the mastermind."

"You would think. So far no dead driver has been found. Of course, the girls never saw the vehicle, but they made off. Zip. Just like that."

"Well, let's keep in touch. We can still walk out hounds, we'll be six feet from one another and in the open. I think this is extreme but Walter says, given our lack of preparation and it's such a different type of bug, we have to do this. I guess six feet apart is better than six feet under."

"For how long? People will lose their shirts."

Sister thought a moment. "Yes. We've lived through flu epidemics before. I mean recently, not 1919, which was mass death worldwide. But all those recent flus that have names like SARS. I bet I have that wrong, but you know what I mean."

"I do. Vaccines developed pretty quickly, so we can hope this does, too."

"If this were up to the medical profession, I would agree. But the politicians are in it and both parties will try to use this to advance themselves. They don't give a damn about the American people." Sister revealed bitterness.

O.J. sighed. "I remember reading *The Gilded Age* in college. This is the second gilded age."

"Yes."

"Maybe it's also the gelded age. So many men aren't men."

"Now, there's a savage thought but funny," Sister responded.

The two chatted a bit more then Sister hung up, returning to the sofa. Raleigh and Rooster laid on each side of her, their heads on her lap. Golly rested on the back of the sofa, her tail occasionally flicking over the human's nose.

Sister stopped, brushed the tail back, then referred to the index in the back of the Munnings book. She rose, disturbing the dogs, looked in the index of volume one and volume two. Then she sat back down, looked into those warm brown doggy eyes.

"He never mentions Florence. Why didn't I notice that?"

"Who's Florence?" Golly asked.

Sister rose again, went over to Gray's far too expensive computer and looked for Florence Carter-Wood. Photographs showed up of a beautiful woman then paintings of her. Paintings by Alfred Munnings.

"I wonder," she muttered under her breath.

Florence was Sir Alfred's first wife. They married in 1912. She committed suicide in 1914. She had tried to kill herself on her honeymoon but somehow pulled it together. She herself painted and was part of a group of painters before World War I known as the Lamorna Group. Others painted her as well, for she was so beautiful. She could ride. Sidesaddle, of course.

Sister thought about that. Today Florence might be considered depressive. Then she seemed to have a streak of melancholy but nothing so severe as to cause comment until her suicide attempt on her honeymoon.

Sitting there, surrounded by the best love, Sister considered what little she knew.

She said, "He never mentioned her. Not once in his three volumes, and according to this brief biography, not once after she died. Not once."

Rooster replied. *"I like it when you talk to me."*

"Ha. She's not talking to you, she's talking to herself. Humans do that." The cat tossed her head in what she considered a fetching manner.

"She talks to us." Raleigh couldn't bear criticism of Sister. *"When she talks out loud even if it isn't to us we can learn something."*

Once again, the tall woman whispered. "Not once."

CHAPTER 33

March 12, 2020 Thursday

Brilliant sunshine flooded pastures, trees almost blooming. Sister, Betty, Weevil, and Tootie walked hounds across the large field between her farm and the Bancroft's After All. The temperature, in the low fifties, promised spring.

Hounds knew they were not hunting, as no one was on horseback. But the humans, far apart from one another, walked briskly. A human brisk pace was a hound's fast walk sneaking into a slow trot.

Sister and Betty, in their hound-walking shoes, began to trot. Weevil and Tootie, up front, kept pace with the hounds. Sister and Betty brought up the rear.

"I'm going to have to work up to this." Betty slowed.

"Me, too." Sister smiled, watching the two young people and the hounds move away.

"I never was much of a runner." Betty looked down at her breasts. "No support bras in my youth."

Sister laughed. "Those protuberances can get in the way. I used to wrap mine with the tape used to wrap ankles. You know, that stretchy fabric. At least it was soft, but then again I am not as generously endowed as yourself."

"You're a C. That's enough to hurt when you run or take a big jump."

"Well, when you're young, or at least for me, I noticed, but it wasn't awful. Tell you what, when those first support bras came out for athletes, I bought one. Helps. Originally the material didn't breathe, so you sweated like a horse. Then things improved."

"Has. Look at the knee braces we can wear that don't interfere with riding. Those are made out of elastic cloth. My left knee has gotten to the point where I hate to climb the stairs."

"Operation?"

Betty groaned. "I guess. Maybe this summer. I lack enthusiasm but I hate losing mobility."

"Honey, sooner or later age humbles you."

Betty rejoined, "I was born humble."

"I'd better duck before one hits me."

As Tootie and Weevil turned to come back across the meadow, a few shoots peeking up, they beheld two women laughing at each other; they couldn't hear what was being said, but more laughter.

"They never stop," Tootie remarked.

"Good to have a friend like that. Do you think women make friends easier than men? Deeper friendships?"

"I don't know. Maybe the way we go about it is different. Men like to do things together. Women sit around and talk. I'm not much of a talker."

"I've noticed."

She dropped her head and smiled. "But when Val and some of my classmates from Custis Hall and I get together, usually over their college vacations, I'll talk. 'Course, no one can outtalk Val. I hope she runs for public office someday. She has that gift, you know?"

"I've never met her."

"If Princeton lets people out early maybe she'll stop by. She's as tall as Sister. Maybe a little taller, a terrific athlete, blonde, blue-eyed, the American dream. She really is beautiful."

"Tootie, she couldn't be more beautiful than you." He worked up his courage and it wasn't a false compliment.

"I, well, thank you. I've always been in Mom's shadow. I'm happiest in hunt clothes, that's my idea of getting dressed up. The rest of the time, you can see."

"A turtleneck sweater, jeans, and cowboy boots. Very sensible." He smiled.

She laughed. "From the rear people will call me 'Sir.'"

"Tootie, all you have to do is turn around. I bet they're speechless."

She laughed again. "They're embarrassed."

"I love you, Tootie." Trident slid his head under her hand and the pack moved up a tiny bit to be close to the humans they all loved.

"I feel better with animals."

"I do, too," Weevil replied. "They're honest and they try so hard for you. And I thank you because you try so hard as a whipper-in. You can ride like the devil." He grinned a lopsided grin.

"You think?"

"I do. I don't say much when we're out there because my focus is on the quarry and the hound. I do try to thank you all after a hunt. That's only proper for a huntsman. And Sister thanks us."

"Sister's hunting manners are impeccable. No matter what, even something right out of the blue, she's calm, cool, collected, and diplomatic. I have to bite my tongue," Tootie confessed.

"Me, too. Can you believe some of the dumb stuff people do and say, and this is a pretty wonderful hunt club? Still, every now and then I'll look back or someone will yell out and I just want to paste them."

They reached the two friends.

"Paste who? Wait, I mean whom. I'm standing next to a grammar queen." Betty gave Sister a look.

"I am not."

"You always correct me with *lie* and *lay*."

"I never argue when you say you got laid." Sister burst out laughing, as did everyone, most of all Betty.

"There are children present." Betty blushed.

"Betty, they know more than we do. Think what Weevil and Tootie have been exposed to? I mean stuff we didn't even know existed until our forties, and my forties precede yours."

"It's the Internet." Weevil stopped and hounds stopped, sitting down, loving being out and being with staff.

"Our idea of racy was to smoke a cigarette." Sister reached down to pet Diana.

"Not anymore. Everyone would jump down your throat," Tootie said.

"Isn't it amazing how many people want to live your life for you?" Sister's voice lifted up. "As we walk back let me ask you two a favor. I've been rereading Munnings's autobiography. Nearing the end of the last volume, the third. Will you do me a favor, since you can do anything with a computer, and research Captain Gilbert Evans? He was a friend of Munnings. They became estranged over the woman that was Munnings's first wife and she, unfortunately, killed herself in 1914. But root out anything you can, including descendants."

"Okay."

"She's on a mission," Betty filled them in.

"I am. What I'll be doing as you all are doing that is digging up great art thefts in the last century. The theft of the Munnings and now the Pater are bad, bold. It's not the *Mona Lisa* but it's, well, it seems to me, well coordinated."

"Was the *Mona Lisa* stolen?"

"In 1911," Sister informed them.

"What a memory you have," Betty teased her.

"Betty, I am not the Ancient of Days. Granted, I'm no longer young, but anyway, I've been researching. The *Mona Lisa* was stolen from the Louvre in 1911. Took a full day for anyone to notice."

"That's impossible." Betty couldn't believe it.

"It doesn't say much for the staff at the Louvre at the time, but those were different times. Anyway, Pablo Picasso was a suspect."

Weevil looked over his shoulder. "Picasso?"

"He was living in poverty at the time and he was suspect because he had unwittingly purchased sculpture stolen from the museum. Obviously, this was prior to this major theft. He had no idea and he handed them over. Picasso had some major flaws as a human being but thievery wasn't one of them." Sister had indeed been doing research.

"Well, what happened?" Tootie's curiosity rose up.

"The painting was missing for two years. The fellow who stole it was an Italian carpenter, Vincenzo Peruggia. He wore his work coveralls and walked in on August 21, stole the painting, and hid in a broom closet until late. He wrapped his coveralls around the painting, which he removed from its case. He walked right out. Actually, he thought the *Mona Lisa* belonged to Italy. After all, Leonardo da Vinci was Italian. He believed the painting was stolen by Napoleon and his troops. So it should be returned to Italy."

"Incredible." Tootie opened the draw pen and the hounds walked inside, as did the people.

"How did they catch him?" Weevil knelt down to check feet.

"He sold the painting to an Italian museum. The Italians celebrated for two weeks then returned the painting to the Louvre. Da Vinci had painted it for King Francis I so it was always French."

"Did he go to jail?" Weevil wondered.

"He was given a one year and fifteen day sentence but released after seven months. Peruggia returned to France and worked as a house painter. The war broke out, he enlisted in the Italian army. Lived, married, had a daughter, and seems to have troubled no one." Sister opened the door to the girls' pen.

"That's incredible," Tootie exclaimed, again.

"Well, the truth is stranger than fiction." Betty watched the girls prance into their quarters.

"There was another theory, which couldn't really happen today. Some people thought this was a theft masterminded by Eduardo de Valfiermo, a crook. He was a well-known thief who had hired an art forger, Yves Chaudron, to make copies so he could sell them as the missing original," Sister told them. "Today our media is relatively insistent, so if anyone wanted to see pictures of the stolen Munnings's paintings, they would have that and if approached to buy the stolen painting, unless they, too, were a crook on some level, they'd know."

"But how would they know what they were buying was a fake?" Tootie shrewdly asked.

"They wouldn't. The longer the originals are not found, the easier it would be to sell a fake. But again, the nonstop media makes these things more difficult than in 1911. Still, it could be done."

"But the originals would need to be stored somewhere." Weevil then said, "It would really be crazy to destroy them, because in time they either could be discovered and the discoverer considered a hero or they could be sold back to the people who owned them."

"Have to be pretty slick. To deliver the painting and get the money without being caught." Betty thought it a clever plan.

"If whoever did this is smart enough to walk out of people's houses with fabulous art, I'm sure he or she, but I think it's a he, would have that figured out."

"The drivers were killed," Betty interjected. "Those were the original thieves."

"Yes, I think so, too. And now they are safely out of the way. Although there is one not yet caught or found."

"Sister, maybe two men have been killed . . . possibly Sabatini's man, too, I mean, there is the forefinger and middle finger thing . . . I doubt our mastermind would take that chance." Sister opened the door for the boys.

"Well, whoever this is will make a lot of money." Weevil counted hounds even though all were there; it was a huntsman habit. "All on." He smiled.

"How about we walk out tomorrow, ride Saturday, then take Sunday off. It's good for them. Good for us," Sister said.

"Sure. Nine? Seven?" Weevil gave her an impish look.

"Okay." All agreed. "Nine."

After hound walk, Sister returned to the library to research art thefts. Thefts differ not just in time but in countries. What they had in common that she could discern was some were only about money. Others seemed to be the work of unbalanced people.

She wasn't sure which camp the Munnings and Pater fell into.

As Golly peeped around Gray's big computer, Gray let Sister take over while he studied the pictures of Munnings's paintings. It didn't occur to Sister that finding out which camp these thefts fell into could be dangerous.

C H A P T E R 3 4

March 13, 2020 Friday

S ister rubbed her watering eyes. "Blurred. Well, pollen is starting."

"It's all that reading." Gray sat at the kitchen table, where she
had moved her books and her inexpensive computer, which she
rarely used. Her research project took over the room.

Golly, at that moment, jumped up on the table, pushing newspaper articles onto the floor. *"Whee."*

"Golly, you're insufferable." Sister got up to fetch the papers
before the dogs walked over them or before Golly, in a moment of
wickedness, jumped off and tore the paper to shreds. She lived to
tear paper. Good thing she didn't live with the Franklins.

"There." Sister placed the cut-out newspaper articles in a pile.

"With all this material you must have reached some conclu-
sion." Gray had helped her find some items.

"I have." She looked at him. "Last night I realized art thefts
fall into two categories. One is pure profit, well thought out. Im-
pulse thefts, on the other hand, seem to be by people who are un-

balanced or think they are righting a wrong, like the theft of the *Mona Lisa*."

"And?"

"These thefts fall between both camps." She held up her hand. "Sounds odd but here's what I think. Of course, money is the primary motive. Shadowing that is the suicide of Florence Carter-Wood, Munnings's first beautiful wife. The second was beautiful, too, but made of sterner stuff. All of the thefts involve sidesaddle. There's a luscious painting, *The Morning Ride*, painted in 1913, showing Florence sidesaddle on Merrilegs, an elegant bay. She's elegant, too, in a white jacket and a straw broad-brimmed hat. The marriage was not a success. Munnings was not a particularly sensitive man and she may have suffered from a bit of depression. Hard to say, given the times and the fact that these things were not medically considered. Anyway, she tried to kill herself on her wedding night."

"Good Lord. What happened next?"

"He continued to paint her, seems to have bumped along, but he said the marriage was never consummated. Anyway, one of Munnings's best friends, a tall, handsome gentlemanly fellow, Captain Gilbert Evans, liked her, fell for her and loved her. She in turn loved him. Evans left the country in 1914 for Nigeria, the colonial service, feeling this could not go on. He later joined the army, saw action in World War I in West Africa. Retired as a major, returned to Nigeria. She killed herself a few months after Gilbert left. So here's the thing. The paintings of his second wife are easy to identify. The paintings commissioned for the main subject, usually a wife, are easy to identify. Men love to show off their wives. But other paintings where there are a few women or someone in the background, even racing crowds, it appears to me they resemble Florence."

"Her image was burned in his brain." Gray touched his military moustache.

"I think so. As he never mentioned her again the wound cut to the bone. I expect he felt some guilt. For all we know he may have smacked her around, but I truly believe he felt guilt."

"Did Gilbert and Munnings meet again?"

"Years later Gilbert returned to England with his wife, Joan, twenty-two years his junior, whom he had met in Nigeria. Some event, I forget which. I'm trying to cram all this in. It was pleasant enough. And Munnings did see that Gilbert was given a painting of Florence. But the friendship wasn't rekindled. The painting gift, that's a deep gesture. Munnings had to have known that Gilbert was the better man."

Gray took a deep breath, thought about that. "Two men of different temperaments. Gilbert seems to be the more giving man, able to respond to emotions. I don't know. The ideas of how men and women behave were different then." He paused. "But not as different as we would like."

"True," Sister agreed.

"Yes. What a sad story. What became of Gilbert's wife?"

"She outlived him by many years. He died in 1966. She seemed not to have been troubled by Florence. That was long before her time. A wise woman, I think, and a respected and loved one. They had three children. In the end he returned to Cornwall, retired there, and the family was happy. It's quite a story. There are even descendants, none of whom capitalized on the past." Sister changed subjects. "There will be only four of us. If you want to ride out tomorrow, do."

"Think I will," he replied. "If you've been researching art thefts—"

She interrupted. "With your help."

"A little. I became fascinated by the Isabella Stewart Gardner theft. Saw the museum long before the theft. In my youth. Mrs. Gardner must have been quite a girl. I discovered that on her birthday, April 14, soon to be here, a requiem is still conducted for the repose of her soul. Kind of like royals in Europe."

"I consider a requiem mass an insurance policy." Sister laughed. "In college I visited the museum. Loved it. She must have known everybody."

"The very wealthy often do. For one thing, most of the people who inherit great wealth are given superb educations. I wonder if our thief is well-educated?"

"Could be. But I would think any successful thief, of big stuff, be it art, jewelry, or even in the old days racehorses, possessed a certain ingratiating charm. Like men who marry heiresses."

"If a man marries a woman with more money than himself, I think, fine. If he marries her for her money I think he's a bottom-feeder. A man can't help it if he loves a rich woman but to marry her to live off of her, the worst. Like Rubirosa." He named a famous gigolo. "Barbara Hutton, Doris Duke, plus a regiment of women for lovers, all beautiful. And the funny thing is, if we'd met him, we'd probably like him."

Sister grinned. "Apparently he could charm women into a coma. But it was for the most part a superficial set. I'd die of boredom."

Gray grunted a bit. "You know, back to research. Why don't you ask Carter about jewel heists? I think people who do things like that may have common personality traits. Just a thought."

"A good one."

She got up, walked over to the landline, dialed Carter's number after checking the hunt club directory.

"Carter."

"Sister. Sorry to learn the rest of the season was canceled, but it was wise."

"You're not yet at your boat."

"Thought I'd wait a few days to see how all this plays out. Will more restrictions be put into place?"

"I have a question. Can you think of great jewel heists?"

"Hmm. The Hope Diamond was stolen a couple of times. Originally it was the third eye of a Hindu god and pried out. Never a good idea to assault a god. Are you interested in historic jewel cons or thefts or recent ones?"

"Whatever comes to mind."

"Well, one of the most famous was the theft of the English crown jewels by an Irishman, Thomas Blood, 1671. Couldn't keep his mouth shut, of course, plus how did he come into money? Anyway, he was caught but the funny thing is, King Charles II was amused by his cheek. Pardoned him, gave him an estate in Ireland and a title. Originally, Blood had passed himself off as an aristocrat to the Keeper of the Tower of London and promised to marry his daughter. Once accepted by the family he was curious, he said, about the crown jewels. The poor Keeper showed him, got bashed over the head. Blood ran with the jewels, stuffed under his clothing I think."

"That's a good one. Even better for what it says about Charles II. Clearly not a boring man."

"Of course, no one can match the thefts of the Nazis during the war. They even dismantled the Amber Room in Russia, a room made entirely of amber for Peter the Great. Catherine the Great loved it so much she had it moved to her palace in St. Petersburg. It's never been found. The Nazis looted everybody and everything, among their other achievements."

"So some of these were thought out, others maybe more of a daring adventure?"

"I think that applies to any form of major theft."

"Like the Munnings's paintings?"

"Perhaps. Profit is always a big motive."

"Carter, don't you think, like with the crown jewels, someone will have to show off?"

"Maybe. There was another jewel thief, closer to our time,

Murf the Surf, a partier. He eventually threw one party too many, bragged."

"Would you divide major thefts into purely business or a huge adrenaline rush? Then throwing the cash around?"

He laughed. "Well, maybe some thieves put their gain into a brokerage account. I guess the smart ones."

"Think Buddy would know about furniture thefts?"

"Yes, but due to the size of the furniture there aren't as many . . . unless, of course, you have an army like the Germans. Well, any conquering army. And furniture doesn't seem to inflame people the same way as jewelry. The great blue diamond is still missing. A Thai gardener stole it from his employer, a Saudi prince. There was murder, diplomatic relations strained between Saudi Arabia and Thailand. Jewelry causes huge problems."

"Well, someone stole Uncle Ray's Louis XV desk. Still hasn't been found."

"True. But furniture theft is more rare. Then again, maybe you should rummage through Buddy's storage unit." He laughed. "Oh, movement is more curtailed in Pennsylvania right now and you'll never guess what Buddy is doing?"

"You're right. I won't."

"Baking. He wants to bring Kathleen something he bakes when he can next visit."

"How thoughtful."

"Buddy's not much of a talker. He's a doer and he hopes if he gives her croissants or really fluffy biscuits he might win favor," Carter declaimed with relish.

"I think he will. You've been helpful."

"You do know a Munnings was stolen from Belle Baruch on July 31, 2003."

"I don't know enough. I know she was Bernard Baruch's daughter, sort of an original, especially for her time."

"Seventeen art works were stolen. The Munnings was *Belle on*

Souriant III, thirty-nine inches by thirty-six. In 2003 it was worth one million. Belle was a fantastic rider. She commissioned the painting in 1932."

"I take 'an original' meant she was gay?" Sister wryly mentioned.

"Well, I suppose," Carter replied.

"But wasn't Belle dead?"

"In 1964. But her sixteen thousand acre estate on the coast, near Georgetown, South Carolina, was left intact as a fundraiser. The art was there. Eleven of the paintings, including the Munnings, were recovered in 2016. Thirteen years later. Quite a story."

"You tell it well," she complimented him.

"What are you thinking about the thefts?"

"Money, of course. But I keep circling back to Florence Carter-Wood. I can't quite tell you why, but I think her shadow is over this. And I think Delores Buckingham figured it out."

"Ah." Carter drew out the "ah." "Who is to say, but it's an intriguing thought."

"We're taking hounds out here tomorrow. Only five of us, plus we'll be far away from one another. But I want to take hounds out one more time and put all the first-year entry in. It will be the first time they hunt all together."

"Hope it's a good hunt. Stay safe."

"You, too."

C H A P T E R   3 5

March 14, 2020   Saturday

Acold front blew through last night and early this morning,
leaving behind a definite drop in temperature and clouds,
which did not promise to disperse.

Aztec, although clipped, had begun to grow out a bit, so the
temperature was fine with him. Sister sat outside the kennel as Tootie opened the draw pen and eager hounds, all who were fit, trotted
out to gather at Weevil's feet.

Betty stood on one side of him while Sister stood on the other
until Tootie could mount up. Gray, on Cardinal Wolsey, was next to
Sister.

"Just don't get in front of me," Aztec ordered.

Cardinal Wolsey looked at the dark chestnut, so full of himself,
saying nothing. Let the vain thing go first. Also Cardinal Wolsey was
a flaming chestnut so he knew everyone would be looking at him
despite the fact there was no field today. He'd still outshine the staff
horses.

"I called the Bancrofts and Cindy Chandler, too, in case we
wind up over there. All are fine with it."

"How's Edward?"

"Better. All this virus talk had Tedi worried that he might have the Covid-19 virus but he had the standard flu. They wish us luck."

Turning to his two whippers-in, Weevil said, "We'll start in the big pasture, head for the hog's back. If we don't pick up scent I'll let the hounds tell me.

"Come along," he called to the hounds.

Riding side by side, Gray observed the sky. "Anybody's guess."

Looking up, Sister said, "Well, it is, but the temperature is in our favor."

"You were wise to take the pack out today. Who is to say what further measures will be ordered. And we are all at least six feet away, with less than ten people."

"No one knows what they are doing. That's how it looks to me. Then again, it is a newer kind of virus. But every TV channel or app one looks at gives confusing information. I'm shutting it out. I believe the social distancing will help, but all these predictions, how can you predict something you've never experienced?"

"Depends on how much the network is paying you." Gray felt Cardinal Wolsey play with his bit. "Ready?"

"Of course." She popped over the jump in the fence line near Tootie's cottage.

Thimble, glistening today, her coat shining, walked with determination. Her littermates, all out today, followed her, as did the youngsters of the "B" line and the "J" line. The "T" line wasn't that many years older than the first-year hounds.

Trooper shifted to the north slightly. He paused. Walked a bit faster, then his tail flipped.

Sister noticed his stern as she watched to see if any other hounds drifted his way. They can see a stern as easily as a human. All moved fairly close together.

"*Aunt Netty.*" Trooper identified the old line.

Bachelor hurried over. He took one big whiff, his eyes bright. *"A red fox."*

"A nasty vixen," Thimble informed him. *"All right, you two. Let me sing first."*

Thimble let out a lovely deep baying note, followed by Trooper and Bachelor, so excited it sounded like a squawk.

"Calm down, boy. You sound like a mouse," Trooper teased him. *"Take a deep breath. Do it again."*

"Fox." Bachelor lowered his voice as the pack hurried over to the three hounds, trotting now.

"Aunt Netty," Zane called.

Everyone was on the line now but it wasn't yet so hot that they were screaming.

Weevil rode behind, gave an encouraging shout as his whippers-in moved slightly in front of him on their respective sides. One of the good things about starting the cast in the big meadow was one could see.

Hounds picked up speed, as did the humans. Horses' ears flicked forward, spirits rose.

Weevil, first over the hog's back jump, a jump he quite liked . . . one can grow weary of coops . . . surged into the woods. The sound grew louder. Hounds ran faster.

Sure enough, Aunt Netty headed toward her den. She was far ahead but as hounds closed, her scent intensified. The old girl, irritated at hearing the hounds, put on the turbocharger, zipped to Pattypan Forge. The terrain favored her. Within minutes she slid into her den. Of course, the hounds would come to her door. Bother.

As the clouds lowered the light grew fainter inside Pattypan Forge. Hounds roared in, surrounded one of Aunt Netty's den entrances.

"Go away," Aunt Netty growled.

"That wasn't a long run," Aero complained.

"It's not my job to entertain you," she called back.

Weevil dismounted, walked to the den. He noticed hounds weren't digging. Well, Aunt Netty pulled the same tricks over and over again.

"Come along." He turned to walk back outside, noticed an old wrench on the floor.

Odds and ends, not many, for the space was vast and its abandonment occurred decades ago. Some bits of wheel, nuts and bolts were scattered but not much. Once this space housed a large forge plus a smaller one with coal dumped in a huge pile by the coal chute. The forge teamed with activity.

Hounds turned as Dreamboat gave a passing shot. *"One of these days."*

"Dream on," she barked from her den.

Once outside, Weevil mounted, Showboat being held by Tootie.

He looked at his beautiful whipper-in and asked, "What about casting to the Old Lorillard place? We can take the long way back if we don't find."

"Sure."

He headed in that direction. Betty was already on the road. Sister and Gray brought up the rear.

Noses down, hounds worked. The trail, narrow, meant ducking every now and then to spare yourself a whack from a low-hanging branch.

Cardinal Wolsey warned Aztec, *"Someone's behind us."*

As horses have almost three-sixty-degree vision, Aztec replied, *"I don't see anything but I can hear a crunch now."*

Weevil tooted the horn up ahead. As he did so a black-clad figure, lumberjack cap pulled down and a black virus mask over his face, even over his nose, stepped behind Gray, ran alongside, and pulled him off Cardinal Wolsey.

"*Aztec.*"

Aztec slowed but Sister tried to urge him on.

The black-clad man pulled a gun, pointing it at Gray's head.

Sister turned to say something to Gray. He wasn't there. He always kept up. She knew he didn't fall off or she would have heard.

Stopping, she listened then turned just in case there was a strange accident and he was knocked out. She soon saw Gray, gun to his head, standing on the ground with Cardinal Wolsey at his side.

Curious, Aunt Netty emerged from her den to peep out of one of the long windows. She crept out of the forge and hid in the bushes so she could watch. She knew who Sister was. The human put food out once every two weeks for her. Aunt Netty didn't much mind that Sister hunted her on horseback. After all, humans are inept.

The old red vixen also knew what a gun was. Lifting her head back she yodeled as loud as she could. "*Hounds, come back. Come back now.*"

Trident, bringing up the rear, heard this, as did Aero. "*Diana, Diana, turn back.*"

Diana stopped, as did the pack. They could just hear Aunt Netty calling. "*Come back. Come back.*"

"*She's crazy.*" Giorgio moved forward.

"*No, she's not. Let's go. Something's not right.*" Diana turned.

Running now, the pack moved back toward the forge. Weevil had no choice but to turn with them. Tootie and Betty also turned. No one knew what was going on but hounds were now in full cry.

"Goddammit, I'll shoot those worthless curs," a familiar voice cursed.

"Carter." Sister was aghast.

"The same." He executed a mock bow, never taking the gun off Gray.

Aunt Netty showed herself as she moved back toward the

forge. Sister saw her, as did Gray. Carter did not, but hounds were closing.

Hounds jumped into the forge. Weevil quickly rode up behind. Carter took a shot at him through the closest window, which creased his left coat arm. Weevil flung himself on the ground.

"Tootie, Betty, keep away. Someone's got a gun on Gray and Sister!"

Weevil next dove through a window as Carter fired again. The bullet ricocheted off the stone walls.

Betty, hearing the shot, dismounted, started creeping toward the forge. Tootie, on the other side, did the same. Neither woman had a .38 but each had a pistol with rat shot and each carried her pistol, not knowing the other woman was doing likewise. Tootie also carried her crop. The shots heightened their senses.

Weevil, back flat against the inside wall, slowly moved toward a faraway window. His idea was to climb out and then go around the forge to see if there was a way to disarm whoever that was.

Carter knew he couldn't walk Sister and Gray out now that Weevil was there with the pack. He'd have to shoot them all.

Betty could now see Sister and Gray held at gunpoint. She knew the pack was in the forge. Tootie, on the far side of the forge, could make out through the windows that Sister and Gray were standing still. She saw Weevil inside. She stepped through a window. He put his finger to his lips.

He jerked his thumb toward a window behind him, then made a gun out of his forefinger and thumb. She understood.

Betty slowly made her way through the bushes. She knew if she made noise or the black-clad figure saw bushes moving, he'd shoot in that direction.

She reached the edge of the thicket. "I'm over here. You won't get away with it."

Carter fired a shot in her direction.

That fast, Tootie, now on the other side of the forge, stood in the open window, fired her rat shot right at the black-clad figure. She hit him. He yelled and whirled around. Gray, tall and strong, pushed him to the ground as he whirled. Tootie leapt out the window, as did Weevil.

The two men subdued him as Betty appeared, her gun held level. Rat shot it might be, but if she shot his face, he'd be blind.

Weevil grabbed Carter's wrist, his knee in the man's back as Gray took the edge of his hand and smashed it on Carter's throat. As Carter started to cough and double over a bit, Gray pulled him back up; Weevil took both balled-up fists and crashed them on the back of his head. Tootie, next to him now, hit him with all her might with the back of the gun. He crumpled.

Weevil reached down to tear off his mask.

"Good God," Betty exclaimed then went to Sister and Gray. "Are you all right?"

Gray put his arms around Sister. She rested her head on his shoulder for a second then looked into his eyes. "I was scared to death he'd shoot you."

"Betty, call Ben Sidell," Weevil ordered, a huntsman used to commanding his whipper-in.

Tootie was kneeling down tying up Carter's hands behind him with her crop thong. "What's this about?"

"I made a foolish mistake." Sister reached for Aztec to give him a pat while the hounds, having had a full discussion with Aunt Netty, came out to sit down by Weevil.

"What could you have done? I mean, he must be crazy." Betty wanted to kick his teeth in.

Instead she reached into her pocket, pulled out a large handkerchief, stuffed it in his mouth. "I don't want to hear what he says when he comes to." She pulled her cellphone from her inside pocket, dialed the sheriff's cell number.

"Are all the horses okay?" Sister asked.

Weevil whistled as Betty and Tootie called out. Their good four-footed friends came to them.

Cardinal Wolsey said to Iota and Outlaw, *"You won't believe what happened. I knew someone was following us."*

A spirited equine discussion followed.

Betty clicked off her phone. "What was foolish?"

Sister, leaning on Gray now, knew she was more shocked than she had at first realized. "I didn't think of it until I heard his voice. We were talking on the phone about the new restrictions over this virus. Then he told me the painting of Catherine Clay-Neal had been stolen from the museum."

"It had," Betty replied.

"Yes, but it wasn't made public until the next day and when I talked to O.J., she told me it was not yet in the news and how did I know? I replied that Carter told me. She said he had good connections in Lexington. I never put two and two together. He could only have known that early if he was in on it."

Tootie, heel on Carter's tied hands, said, "But Carter didn't know you realized he told you before anyone else."

Weevil, brushing his coat where the bullet had creased the arm, said, "He slipped."

"But so did I. I called him last night to ask about famous art thefts. He knew some and we had a good talk. Then I told him what I thought about Munnings's first wife, Florence Carter-Wood. I was getting too close."

They heard a siren in the distance, then closer, then turned off. Ben knew exactly where they were and that the last part would be on foot. He had two young officers with him.

"Sister. Gray. Is everyone all right?" Ben reached them, looked down at Carter. "See if you two can drag him out." He looked at the crop, knelt down to untie it, handing it back to Tootie, who'd held her hand out. "Can someone tell me what happened?"

They spoke at once as they heard Carter's feet being dragged through the narrow path. Eventually everyone got their story out except for Cardinal Wolsey and Aztec.

"Bear down on him regarding Florence Carter-Wood," Sister told Ben.

"I will. Then again, don't expect anyone in custody to tell the truth. We'll see." He looked at the hounds. "Quite a day."

"Yes, it was." The hunt staff spoke over one another with the same reply in a sense.

"Does anyone need a ride back?"

"Ben, we'll ride back. Hounds need to go," Sister said. "Thank you."

"Thank you. If we can pin this on him it will be quite a sensation." Before everyone mounted up, Sister hugged each one. "Sorry, I can't obey the six feet. Thank you. Thank you so much."

Gray shook Weevil's hand, kissed Betty then Tootie on the cheek. "I have no doubt he would have shot me or used Sister and me as hostages. Your placing yourselves in danger saved us. I don't know how to thank you."

Betty stepped into Weevil's cupped hand and mounted Outlaw. "You know, the strange thing is, I didn't think about the danger."

"Me, neither," Weevil echoed her.

"Me, neither." Tootie swung up. "You just act. You know? If you think about something too much you're paralyzed. All I wanted was a clear shot. I knew Betty was out there. Weevil was next to me, of course. We had to subdue Carter before he pulled the trigger."

"I owe you my life, Gray's life. It's a gratitude that can't really be expressed."

"Sister, who knows what you'll do for us someday?" Weevil replied. "All right, children, let's walk home."

CHAPTER 36

March 14, 2020   Saturday 4:00 PM

Shaken or not, when hounds returned to Roughneck Farm at one in the afternoon, chores needed to be done. Each hunting hound had paws inspected before being sent to their kennels with a full stomach. Given the rain, no temperature drop but rawness, Weevil warmed up the food. The kennels, efficient, had a small stove off the large feed room for such occasions as well as for helping anyone in sick bay. Despite all, this had been a lucky year in terms of health. Not one hound came down with Lyme disease, bad sniffles, or deep cuts.

Once hounds were curled up in their bunks and the condos, Weevil and Tootie walked over the herringbone brick walkway to the stables. Laid decades ago, too expensive to do now, the brick had gained the patina of age. Rain or not, Weevil was glad for changing his boots into workboots, a rubber tread. Tootie had done likewise. The adrenaline of foiling Carter's murderous plans had vanished. They were tired.

Walking into the center aisle, their Barbour coats dripping

rain, they arrived to help put blankets on the horses, all of whom had been wiped down then left to dry off totally, which they did.

Those outside were brought in as well, although Keepsake didn't want to leave his run-in shed. He'd hunt in the rain but he didn't want to stand in it or walk through it. Finally, Weevil wooed him in.

Sister, surprisingly calm for a woman who had a Glock 30 pointed at her, finished up with Aztec. Betty finished, too.

"Well, let's do the tack. It only gets more onerous if we wait." Betty walked into the warm tack room.

The others followed, each carrying their hunt bridle over their shoulder. Then they walked back to the center aisle to fetch their saddles.

Sister advised, "Hang your saddle pads over the railing there. They're all wet."

Back in the tack room, bridles on bridle hooks, they worked, feeling the supple leather between their fingertips.

As they were too far apart to talk while bringing hounds back, now they did.

Betty, of course, started. "I had no idea. Not even a hint."

"No one did, Betty. You'd think seeing all his new purchases year after year we would have figured out he had a sideline apart from antique jewelry." Sister wrung out a sponge.

"So you think he's been stealing for years? Art?" Tootie asked.

"Stealing, but I don't know what. I doubt he stole jewelry, because clients would have sooner or later figured that out. Someone might recognize old pieces. You know, like the Erté ring Yvonne bought last Christmas. It wasn't stolen, of course, but many fox-hunters would recognize it because the deceased owner wore it to hunt balls. That sort of thing," Sister said.

"He could have pried out the jewels, replacing them with fakes. That would bring a lot of money," Weevil suggested. "It would, but the people he sold to, like Delores Buckingham, would have everything appraised by a local jeweler. He couldn't afford it."

"His jewelry ran to the thousands. Thirty thousand and more for those pieces with big jewels. True old pearls. Think of Antique Hunt jewelry, the stuff E. B. Stutts has. Horns, lovely gold stock pins, lots of crops. Some of it can be a thousand or more but most of it is affordable."

Betty, using a clean cloth now, wiped down the cleaned bridle. "E.B. can find Jasperware. Do you know how much I want a teapot and creamer, sugar boat? Oh, I love that stuff."

"Carter's competition would have been Marion at Horse Country but he wisely left the hunting stuff, the expensive jewelry, to her. Although once he offered a pin owned by the late Mrs. Markey, of her racing colors, all in precious stones. But in the main he did not go for that. And shocking as all this is, he did have a great eye." Sister gave him credit.

"What were her colors?" Tootie asked.

"Devil's red and blue. But those were sold to a Brazilian investment group," Sister replied.

"You can do that? Sell your colors?" Tootie was aghast.

"Yes." Sister shrugged. "Remember Citation raced under that devil's red and blue. He's my hero, Citation." Sister smiled. "Back to Carter. How did you all know Gray and I were trapped at Pattypan Forge?"

Weevil wiped his hands. "We didn't. Betty, Tootie, and I had hounds marching toward the Old Lorillard place and they stopped. Just stopped. I could see how intently they listened and then they turned and ran back. I thought maybe they picked up another line. Once I got near I could see Cardinal Wolsey and Aztec, but I couldn't see you all clearly. Knew something was wrong, then hounds blasted into the forge and he took a potshot at me."

"For me, I saw Weevil's horse ground-tied."

"Same here. Saw Iota and Aztec. Something wasn't right. All I had was rat shot but it would help." Betty added, "Of course, we didn't know who it was because of the black breathing mask, he was all in black with a black lumberjack cap. Hadn't a clue. But once I jumped into the forge, he heard me and, well, you were there. So I knew he had a gun."

"You all were incredibly brave," Sister again praised them, overwhelmed.

Betty laughed. "It's odd, Sister, but I have been more frightened taking a four-foot drop into a hard-running creek. Anyway, I had a gun."

"Me, too." Tootie smiled. "When the mask came off I couldn't believe it."

"Evil often wears a friendly face." Sister sighed.

"That's the truth." Betty lifted her saddle onto a sawhorse to start cleaning it. "Think of those people who foster children or take in the elderly then steal from them or the government. The funds for medications alone are enough to motivate someone with no ethics."

"They'll cheat on food, too." Tootie had read of such low behavior.

"Well, 'Thou Shalt Not Steal' is one of the Ten Commandments. We've been doing it for thousands of years." Weevil took a toothbrush to the bit.

"Funny. I thought of that commandment days ago after a painting theft. I guess Sunday School was good for both of us."

Weevil smiled. "Sure didn't like it at the time but now I'm glad my mother made me go. You've got to learn ethics somewhere."

"One hopes." Betty sat down to clean the underside of her saddle. "You know, I'm exhausted."

"Emotion does that to you." Sister looked out the window. "Is this spring ever going to really be spring?"

"It's only mid-March." Betty reminded her. "Some years the forsythias have bloomed by now. Other years we've been buried under two feet of snow. The changing seasons, well, they're changing."

"Gray and I truly owe you." Sister again returned to gratitude. "I hope I can find a way to let you know how much I care, how much I trust you, and . . ." She teared up. ". . . how much I love you."

Betty put her arms around her best friend. "You'd have done it for any of us." She kissed her on the cheek. "The hell with social distance. We're all together, anyway."

Weevil laughed. "You two could be a sitcom."

Sister wiped her eyes. "Weevil, you could be a movie star. Tootie, too. I'll spare you hugs and kisses, but when this is over, watch out."

They all laughed.

By six everything was in its proper place, cleaned up, hounds checked again. Betty crawled into her unbeatable old Bronco and drove home to her husband, to whom she told everything.

Running through the rain, Tootie said, "Weevil, come on with me. No point in driving in this."

"I'll be there in a minute." He ducked his head in his truck, a three-quarter ton, two years old, to fetch the box that Carter had put there a few days ago before all this.

Once inside her delightful cabin with a clapboard addition, she threw him a towel. He wiped his face.

"I've got a Crock-Pot Mom brought over. I'll turn it on. I need to call Mom before Betty does."

"Why would Betty call your mother?"

"She won't be able to resist." Tootie smiled.

Before she could call, Sister rang up. "Tootie, Gray made dinner if you'd like some. And Ben Sidell will be here tomorrow at two. He'd like to see us."

"Okay." Then, after declining dinner, Tootie called Yvonne.

Twenty minutes later she walked into her kitchen, where Weevil was stirring the pot. "Smells wonderful."

"That took longer than I anticipated. Mom had a fit. I told her I was fine. I told her you were here, which made her feel better even though Carter is in custody. And I'm hungry."

"Me, too."

They ate the beef stew brimming with carrots, potatoes, peas, and parsley. Neither talked much about Carter. Done is done. Sooner or later the truth would be known. They talked about the hounds, about Tootie's studies, about Weevil's mother, who lived outside of Hamilton, Canada.

Finished, Weevil made a fire in the stone fireplace; laid in the mid-eighteenth century, it had warmed many people.

"Mom brought wine. I don't drink, as you know, but she said you have to have wine, scotch, bourbon, gin, and vodka, as well as mixers. I actually have those drinks."

"No thanks. If I take a drink I'll fall to sleep. Apart from the rain and cold, it's been quite a day. To make it more interesting, I have a little present for you that Carter found for me."

"Carter."

"He found exactly what I asked for, so crook that he is, I hope you like it." He walked to his hanging Barbour, reached into the pocket, and retrieved a small box wrapped in silver paper, the ribbon being navy blue.

She took it. "Weevil, you don't have to give me presents."

"You've been a terrific whipper-in."

She slyly smiled. "Does that mean you've bought something for Betty?"

He laughed. "Actually, I did, but it's not the same at all."

She unwrapped the box, lifted the lid. Two white pearl studs greeted her. "What?"

"Those are fake. You need them for hunting, as a lady wears

pearl studs. But if you lift that little cardboard up, the real present is underneath."

She flicked up the cardboard onto which the fake studs were affixed, placing it on the coffee table. "Oh. Oh, those are beautiful. Exquisite." She beheld two pink pearl earrings, perfect pink pearls in size and luster, 8.5 millimeter. "Weevil, these are beautiful."

"Hold them up to your skin."

She did, couldn't stand it, so walked to the mirror. "This is too much. Really."

"You have helped me so much. It's my first full year hunting the hounds. I couldn't have done it without you and they will look beautiful on you."

She put the pearls in her ears. Indeed, they did look beautiful on her, but then anything would. Tootie had all of her mother's beauty with none of her mother's vanity.

"Weevil, I like working with you. I like your gentleness and how you watch the hounds. You know what everyone needs and you're kind to them, kind to people, and way too generous to me."

The rain pounded on the standing seam roof. He pulled his chair closer to hers when she sat down because they had difficulty hearing.

"I ask you to give me a chance." Weevil folded his hands together so he wouldn't show how nervous he was. "You don't date. You have your girlfriends from Custis Hall. I don't know if you don't like men or maybe you would rather spend time with a woman, but I ask you to spend time with me, and the pearls aren't a bribe, that really is for whipping-in."

An agonizing silence followed his declaration.

"My parents' marriage was poisonous. And I saw the way men behaved around my mother. I . . . I don't want that and I feel like I'd be a failure. The only good relationships I've seen are since I've been here, Sister and Gray and Betty and Bobby. It's not that I don't like men, but I have this fear, I guess fear and mistrust."

He took a deep breath. "You're honest. So I'll be honest back. I know that. You hang back even in groups. That's okay but not all men are pigs, and I take it your father was and is a real pig." She nodded so he continued. "He cut you out of the will."

"Mom will make up for it but he was awful, especially since she moved here."

"I am not your father. Most men are pretty decent. Maybe sex-obsessed." He laughed. "But decent. Do I want to go to bed with you? Of course I do. I'm not dead. What I really want is to hear you sing when you're happy, to maybe breed and make horses down the road when you're out of vet school. And I want to work with you with hounds. I know women say they can take care of themselves and I believe it, but I still want to take care of you. Don't worry about sex. I can wait, but I hope you get around to it."

She laughed. "I have no idea what to do."

"Well, I can help you there."

They both laughed.

She brightened. "What do you have for Betty?"

"Crystal fox-head earrings. I've been on an earring kick. Women like earrings. Marion found them for me. She's been terrific, as has Betty."

"The pearls are better." She smiled, got up, and kissed him. Then she kissed him again.

He blurted out, trying to contain his body. "Tootie, I love you. You must know I love you."

"I'm not worth it."

"You are worth every breath I take. What is that line from the Bible, a virtuous woman is more precious than rubies? Change it to pearls." Then he really kissed her.

That was all it took.

C H A P T E R   3 7

March 15, 2020   Sunday

Gray, Sister, Betty, Tootie, Weevil, Walter, and Ben sat spread out in Sister's living room. The rain continued to pour outside. A fire warmed the room. Even though it was two in the afternoon, it was dark, the clouds hung low outside.

Walter and Ben sat farthest away, praticing the social distancing. As both men had to see people they kept their distance. No reliable tests were available yet in the area. However, both felt fine.

Sister and Gray sat close, as did Tootie and Weevil. Betty sat on Sister's other side on the sofa.

Aunt Daniella, given her advanced age, stayed home and Tootie told her mother to stay home. Gray told his brother he would call him, and Aunt Daniella wanted Gray to call her immediately then she would call Kathleen. Everyone, while irritated at not being allowed to be there, did understand.

"The Ides of March," Sister simply said.

Walter replied, "This is only the beginning."

"That, too," she replied. "Ben, you've taken our statements, those of us in the middle of this. Did you get anything out of him?"

"His first concern was reducing his sentencing. He swears he didn't kill anyone, which I believe, but I also believe he ordered the killings. He would have killed you two but he says he just wanted to scare you."

"Including Delores Buckingham?" Sister asked. "Did he order her death?"

"Most especially Delores. She figured out, to a point, the scam, which involved drivers with prison records. Ex-cons have trouble finding work. Some can be lured back into crime, fortunately many can't. The ones Carter recruited had all wracked up gambling debts. Cards, as you might suspect from the removed forefinger and middle finger on the right hand. Even with that advantage, they lost money. Drugs didn't help."

"So they were destitute and desperate?" Gray inquired.

"Add lax morals. Since the dead don't talk, I can't say whether they cared one way or another what they were doing. Carter refused to identify the driver found in the Gulf station. He's vague about how he recruited these men, which means, to me, he knows a lot more about illegal gambling than he admits."

"His problems are bigger than that. How did he get the idea to steal Munnings's paintings?" Betty, having seen Carter at his worst, wanted to know particularly, since she'd thought she knew him.

"Carter visited many rich peoples' homes, especially those who are older. He knew where good art hung. Over the years he might walk off, having someone else do the dirty work, with a small painting by a good artist. Not the biggest and not always highly expensive, but good. For a time he would lift street scenes from Paris by very good painters during the last half of the nineteenth century. The thefts were reported but he never got caught. Whatever happened to the men, and I'm not sure his minions were always men, he won't say. I believe that he used women from time to time, those employed as housekeepers or even nannies."

"He made money. Right?" Tootie asked.

"Enough to live well, buy a new car or truck every two years, and he blew a lot of money on his small yacht, which he calls a big boat. It's a small yacht." Ben leaned forward. "Foxhunting proved another entrée into an upper-class world."

"Ben, most foxhunters are not all that rich," Sister quickly said.

"No, but enough are to make learning to ride and ride well useful. Essex, Piedmont, Orange, Middleburg, Green Spring Valley, Radnor, to name a few, contain wealthy people. At one time or another he hunted at those hunts and made friends. He hunted at the hunt outside Franklin, Tennessee, hoping some country music money might be there. He was nothing if not thorough."

"I guess. Did he hunt in Great Britain?" Weevil wondered.

"He did, but he would need a real network there among former or practicing criminals and there wasn't time. Plus how to manage it? Also, his American accent wouldn't help him."

"Ah. I never think of that," Betty murmured.

"How did he come up with the Munnings's idea?" Sister echoed Betty's question.

"He had visited The Munnings Art Museum in England. Learning about Florence Carter-Wood gave him the idea that a painting featuring her would be worth quite a lot. There were fewer of them. Then he also realized that the sidesaddle paintings existed in small number compared to the rest of Munnings's work. Hence the idea to steal what showed Florence or a figure that could be Florence as well as other beautiful women. The key was the rarity."

"It must have worked." Weevil wanted to hold Tootie's hand but, of course, did not.

"Yes, it did. He had an oil prince with God knows how many skyscrapers in Dubai."

"One person?" Sister's voice rose.

"A prince, a leader, they all must have money beyond imagining. Yes, it was one person. One person with billions. He sent his personal jet to pick up the paintings here and in Kentucky."

"How do we get them back?" Betty wondered. "And why don't you say his name?"

"Because I spoke to our State Department in Washington as well as a few of my buddies in the C.I.A. To openly shame someone with whom our country does critical business would be foolish, and dangerous in a different way."

"How do we get the paintings back?" Tootie had little patience for high-level politics, perhaps a feature of her generation.

"I believe our government will, and I think much of the money is still in Carter's possession."

"Why?" Gray wondered.

"Because he tried to buy me off." Ben smiled. "Which will be another charge against him."

"Who murdered the drivers and was Parker Bell part of it?" Weevil could still feel the force of that kick.

"Parker had gotten wind of the driving. He knew some of those men from his time in the pen. Others were imprisoned elsewhere but they knew one another. Parker wanted in on the take. He would have been killed ultimately but he didn't know that. He saw money. So Carter realized he had to go. He also realized, thanks to Parker, that he would have to kill the drivers, save one, one that he trusted or perhaps was his partner. That man that escaped in Shelbyville. Carter killed Parker himself. He doesn't admit it, but it falls into place."

"Why won't Carter identify the Gulf corpse?" Walter asked.

"We don't know enough. He's told us some truths, some half-truths, and some outright lies. Once he hires a good lawyer, and with his money he will, the lawyer will try to bargain first. We might be able to pull some stuff out. But it was a network. It was well-organized and it was to be Carter's grand accomplishment. He would make so much money, which he did, he wouldn't need to worry about money again." Ben stared at the fire for a moment. "I don't think he would have stopped. There's a high to getting away with this, plus the money." Then he smiled. "He had Fennell's lead shanks used because they are so supple yet sturdy. Idiot bragged no one was killed with shoddy goods. The murders were like dominoes. One driver killed another then he was in turn killed until only the Shelbyville man was left. Possibly the drivers from the Headley-Whitney Museum's heist, too. We'll get to the bottom of that."

"Was Buddy Cadwalder part of this?" Sister wondered.

"No. Carter said Buddy was a straight arrow plus he wasn't smart enough to pull off something of this size."

"If Carter were so smart, he wouldn't have gotten caught," Tootie quite rightly said.

"Sister scared him," Ben informed her. "And he knew she was closing in because she figured out the Florence Carter-Wood link." Ben looked out the window a moment at the downpour. "Having seen photos of the famous *Florence at Sunset* painting plus those of Florence herself, she was quite beautiful, as was Munnings's second wife. But Florence really was a sorrowful figure, not of her own doing, I think." Ben smiled a sad smile.

"He didn't think out how to kill me?" Sister mused.

"He said you were always smart. Plus he didn't know who you would tell. He told me he bore you no personal animus, it was strictly business, and he felt he had to get rid of you fast."

"Lucky for me, Gray rode in the back with me and the hounds turned back. If it weren't for Betty, Tootie, and Weevil, he would have succeeded."

"Sister, the odds were against you, but who is to say?" Ben smiled at her. "Over time the details of names, perhaps hidden contacts, will leach out, but you have the big picture. And of course, Carter believed the rarity of sidesaddle and Florence's image would drive up the prices for those special paintings, which it did. Which isn't to say the value of the works featuring other women were low. Far from it."

"You know, Ben, Munnings never spoke of Florence but I think he was haunted by her." Sister then changed the subject. "Would anyone like tea or coffee or something stronger? I should have asked before we sat down."

All demurred.

Walter shook his head slightly. "Sister, we both lose our bet. Both wrong. You thought the thieves would be part of the show world and I thought they'd be part of the art world, dealers, museums. Well, we saved money."

She laughed. "That's one way to look at it."

CHAPTER 38

March 16, 2020   Monday

S till cool, the rain had stopped, clouds scattered. Golly reposed in her bed as did the two dogs, while Sister cracked eggs into a mixing bowl. This morning, rain free, called for her famous omelet as well as bacon. As she was whisking eggs with a little milk in the bowl, Gray walked in.

"Coffee this morning or tea?" he asked.

"Tea, Irish Breakfast. It's in the green tin."

They focused on their respective chores, then Gray said, "St. Patrick's Day parade canceled. Happened days ago but no time to take notice and now St. Patrick's Day is almost upon us."

"We can wear green tomorrow."

"Yes, we can." He smiled then trotted upstairs to the bedroom to his closet, where he pulled out a long thin box, beautifully wrapped in hunt-club colors, dark green with a gold ribbon.

He came back down, placed the box on the table.

"That's pretty."

"How about you open it after breakfast."

"Aha. The wrapping is green. Is it an early St. Patrick's Day gift?"

"You'll have to wait and see."

They ate those fluffy omelets, biscuits with Irish butter.

While the dogs would prefer meat to omelets, that didn't mean they wouldn't beg. Golly, on the other hand, waited for bacon. She knew she'd get a piece and each dog also got a piece of bacon, for Sister had made a lot of it.

After polishing off the last piece of bacon . . . Gray nabbed it . . . Sister carried the plates to the sink.

"I'll do the dishes," Gray volunteered.

"We can share. I'll scrape and you wash."

"Come here and open your present," he urged her.

She sat down and, per usual, painstakingly opened the paper, folding it for future use, as well as saving the lovely gauze ribbon. She lifted up the box top.

"How fabulous." She took out a leather-wrapped crop, a stag handle exactly the right size, a thong and cracker. "The collars are gold. Oh, initials."

He read them out loud. "N. L. A."

She looked over at him. "And?"

"Nancy Langhorne Astor."

"Gray. It's sensational. However did you find this?"

"My secret, but she was a neighbor, almost, over there at Mirador. Born in 1879. We missed her by a few years." He smiled.

Sister ran her hands over the crop. "What a thoughtful gift."

"It's a bribe." He reached for her hand. "I can't wait for the next Sadie Hawkins Day to be married to you, so I am asking you now. Will you marry me?"

She held his hand, leaned over to kiss him. "You are the kindest, smartest, handsomest of men. I will marry you and hope I make it to one hundred."

He stood up, walked behind her to wrap his arms around her. "Thank God we weren't killed. Made me think how much I love you. I don't know why I didn't ask before. It seemed unnecessary, but after almost being murdered, I want you as my wife."

"At least you know what you're getting into." She laughed then quietly said, "We were lucky Saturday. Very lucky."

"Given this virus, I have no idea when we can have a ceremony but I would like something small, something so Aunt Daniella can come as well as our best friends, celebrate with people we love. We've both been around long enough to know, well, a lot."

She stood up, faced him, hugged him, and put her cheek next to his. "The until-death-do-us-part part is closer."

He hugged her more tightly. "One can die at any age. But now we truly know it, so I say let's make the most of every minute. Oh, I have one more present."

"You're spoiling me."

"Men are supposed to spoil women. Once the weather permits, the drive out to the paved road will be lined with pink and white alternating dogwoods. One pink. One white. You love color. So there."

"I'll have to think of something for you. Those are two extraordinary presents."

"You're my present." He kissed her again, then said, "Strange, isn't it, that we need death to teach us about life."

"I've never felt so alive or so young." She kissed him again, marveling at how things change in the blinking of an eye.

You never know.

AFTERWORD

The paintings herein stolen are not owned by my fictional characters. I claimed a fiction writer's liberty.

Perhaps you'll be motivated to seek the works out or look at as many Munnings's paintings as you can. He was one of England's greatest painters.

We are currently in the midst of a flowering of equine art in the United States. Art, like hemlines, goes in and out of fashion. Equine art and the requisite good draftsmanship are out of fashion. A regiment of gifted artists can barely scrape out a living, with few exceptions. My prayer is this changes and my fellow country people will soon appreciate these remarkable artists.

This novel was written in real time. I thought, fool that I am, well, this will be fun, as I'll be perfect on the weather, which is important for the Sister Janes. Halfway through, clear about plot, bam, the coronavirus knocked me sideways, as such a global phenomenon will affect my characters. How could I ignore it? So I did the only thing possible. I took it day by day, changed things, and implored the gods for help for all.

May you be well.

We'll get through this.

Up and over,
RITA MAE

Dear Reader,

I wish for you incendiary passion, whatever it may be. Otherwise you will slide into the abyss of middle-class tedium. Even if you are poor as a church mouse, and I have been, you live a life of inner richness.

Allow me to acknowledge your life. As to your passions, your laughter, your loves: Do it now. You'll be dead a long time.

ACKNOWLEDGMENTS

As always, Marion Maggiolo gives me ideas. Every time I visit Horse Country I walk out with a new thought as well as something beautiful. This time she suggested I investigate Belle Baruch. As Munnings had painted her in 1932, I began to focus on his lady subjects.

The Virginia Museum of Fine Arts has a spectacular Munnings, which set me off on seeing as many as I could.

For many years I have been indebted to the National Sporting Library & Museum, established in Middleburg, Virginia, in 1954. I've learned so much over the decades and can never see it or the Museum of Hounds & Hunting enough. I'm tempted to bring a sleeping bag and hide out.

The South overflows with a wealth of art galleries offering outdoor sporting art. The problem there is, you'll want everything for sale. Again, you can learn a great deal. The proprietors usually forgive you and happily talk about the art, even knowing you'll leave empty-handed. It's a passion and therefore not subject to hag-ridden reason.

If I have neglected to thank anyone who helped, forgive me. Having to re-think the last quarter of the book due to the crisis prevented me from keeping good notes regarding research.

PHOTO: © MARY MOTLEY KALERGIS

RITA MAE BROWN is the bestselling author of the Sneaky Pie Brown series; the Sister Jane series; the Runnymede novels, including *Six of One* and *Cakewalk; A Nose for Justice* and *Murder Unleashed; Rubyfruit Jungle; In Her Day;* and many other books. An Emmy-nominated screenwriter and poet, Brown lives in Afton, Virginia, and is a Master of Foxhounds.

ritamaebrownbooks.com

To inquire about booking Rita Mae Brown for a speaking engagement, please contact the Penguin Random House Speakers Bureau at speakers@penguinrandom house.com.

ABOUT THE TYPE

This book was set in Baskerville, a typeface designed by John Baskerville (1706–75), an amateur printer and typefounder, and cut for him by John Handy in 1750. The type became popular again when the Lanston Monotype Corporation of London revived the classic roman face in 1923. The Mergenthaler Linotype Company in England and the United States cut a version of Baskerville in 1931, making it one of the most widely used typefaces today.